THE OFFICIALLY UNOFFICIAL FILES
OF
DR. GORDON B. GRAY

DARCY FRAY

NERDMOB|USA

ISBN: 0991253213
ISBN-13: 978-0-9912532-1-0

FOR STEPHEN.

CHAPTER ONE

Dr. Gordon B. Gray

A LONE BOY shuffled along the desolate dirt road, fueling the billowing dust cloud that nipped at his heels. His thousand-yard stare and gaunt, disheveled frame amplified the word he repeatedly mumbled to none but himself, "Gone...gone...gone..."

Nearby, a rusted sign protruded from the overgrown roadside -- "Dust, City Limit, Population 23." Buried deep within West Virginia's Appalachian backwoods, Dust was the kind of place that went unnoticed for decades at a time.

•••

Lieutenant General John Wilkinson's sagacious nose preceded him as he entered the darkened corridors of Caltech University's Bridge Building.

Sweet English roses. Errant chalk dust. Cherrywood pipe tobacco. The must of old books. The distinct aromatic blend of academia offered only a moment's distraction. The Dust incident weighed heavily upon his mind and there was little time to be wasted on the whims of the senses.

His burdened footfalls resonated through the eerily lifeless hallway, standing the hair at the back of his neck on end. It was true that he had weathered battles on five of the seven continents, but he was not immune to the disquiet of a deserted corridor.

Eagle-eyed, Wilkinson scanned the names and titles affixed to each door: *Physics Lab - Dr. Sophia Holtzman, CMS Advanced Particle Theory Lab - Dr. Harsimran Gupta, Applied Mathematics, High Energy Physics* and so on. Finally, the very last one at the end of the hall read: *Dr. Gordon B. Gray.* The title beneath his name sounded impressive: *Deputy Chair of the Division of Physics, Mathematics and Astronomy.*

Wilkinson's unanswered knock reverberated along the corridor as the worn brass door knob surrendered to his iron grasp.

A photo perched on the edge of Gordon's desk caught his eye. The fixed gazes of the late Thomas B. Gray, a peerless U.S. Army General, and his beloved wife Margaret stared out at him. How long had it been since the funeral? Three years? Four?

Wilkinson suddenly felt guilty for falling out of touch. *The kid has no one.*

Gordon had just completed his first semester of grad school when he got the call. His parents, both presumed dead in a freak car accident that left the military community shocked and bewildered. Their bodies were never found, which naturally sparked lively debate among the conspiratorially inclined. How does a man who commandeered Humvees and tanks through ambushes and impossibly difficult terrain accidentally drive off a bridge he's traversed hundreds of times? No snow, no ice and no telltale skid marks. Made no sense at all.

The Lieutenant General's attention shifted to Gordon's recently awarded Nobel Prize in Physics, consisting of a gold medal and diploma mounted on the wall behind his modest desk. Wilkinson seemed to recall Gordon had been the youngest physics Nobel laureate of all time, and in fact, at the tender age of twenty-three, the youngest laureate in any Nobel prize area. *Not bad for an Army brat.*

The rest of the room was in apple-pie order. Not a paperclip or pen out of place. *He will be perfect for the job ahead.*

•••

Splat. Splat. Splat. Splat. Splat. Splat. A barrage of liquid nitrogen frozen pumpkins shattered upon impacting the plastic tarp-covered ground ten stories below the roof of the Millikan Library, nestled in the heart of Caltech's Southern California campus.

A hundred or so students looked on, clustered behind the yellow caution tape that demarcated the safe viewing zone. It was Halloween and close to midnight; half the crowd was under the influence and the other half were merely present because their second home, the library, was closed in recognition of the event.

Gordon peered over the edge of the roof, observing the spectacle below. It had been a few years since his first pumpkin drop and although he'd never seen the elusive triboluminescent spark himself, he had heard tales of past sightings. Nonetheless, it was always good fun, and something to do on an evening when one was, after all, expected to do something.

Gordon had recently celebrated his twenty-third birthday over a burger and a pint of beer with a few colleagues. Even so, with his bright complexion and schoolboy looks, visiting parents often mistook him for an eager young undergrad, albeit a sartorially inclined one. Gordon's athletic six-foot frame was always garbed in a Scottish-made Taransay Harris Tweed jacket, gray flannel trousers, suede saddle oxfords, a white shirt and maroon tie. It didn't matter if it was midsummer, winter, a wedding or funeral, he had one outfit and he stuck with it. And though unimaginative, his fashion sense did little to deter his popularity among the opposite sex. With a full head of perfectly tousled chestnut brown hair, light green piercing eyes and a smile that weakened women's knees, he was forever destined to be the center of attention of every woman on campus, an admittedly thin, yet eager populace.

Splat. The last of the pumpkins hit the ground. No triboluminescent spark this year, although a few of the more inebriated students were convinced they saw something.

"Bro, the blue light. Bro, I like saw it on the second-to-last pumpkin," a freshman proclaimed, belying his command of a far more ambitious vocabulary and near-perfect SAT score. His costume, consisting of a cardboard box with an original Macintosh 128K computer drawn in Sharpie, bobbed around on his head as he spoke. It did little to bolster his credibility.

"Dude, me too," echoed his roommate, who was disguised as a "data pirate." He had updated a standard seafaring pirate costume with flash drives hanging from his hooped earrings and belt. Earlier that evening, he had jumpstarted his buzz by beer bonging a six pack and was well under the influence.

The growing rumble of the crowd led Wilkinson directly over to the two young men.

"Hey, man, swag costume," the Macintosh 128K computer remarked, as he snapped a salute, knocking the box on his head slightly askew.

"That's Lieutenant General John Wilkinson to you, and this is a uniform, not a costume. Do either of you know where I might find Dr. Gray?" The combination of Wilkinson's decorated uniform, his chiseled chin, razor-sharp silver flattop, husky baritone and six-foot-something frame was more sobering to the inebriate than a cold shower and a triple espresso.

"Yes, Lieutenant Master Chief…errr…Wilkinson. He's ten stories that way," the data pirate said, doing his best to hold back a smirk as he pointed skyward.

"Am I amusing you?" Wilkinson's furrowed brow snapped to attention, accenting his soldierly bark.

"No, sir. On the roof, for the pumpkin toss, sir," the pirate's friend interjected, pointing to the smashed-pumpkin-covered plastic tarp.

"I see. Dismissed."

The two students left so quickly, they seemed to disappear into the ether.

The Lieutenant General marched over to the entrance of the Millikan Library, a 1967 modern industrial style mass of concrete and glass. Ten stories high, it was the tallest building on campus. Rumor had it that the neighbors found the library to be such an architectural eyesore that the City of Pasadena forbade Caltech from building anything over three stories ever again.

Wilkinson rattled the first set of doors he came upon. Locked. He spied an open fire escape on the side of the building. Head down, he bounded up the staircase, each step reverberating through the lively chamber of concrete and steel. Most men of sixty-eight would have been winded after the first floor, but years of strict military conditioning and diet had left him with the body and stamina of a forty-five-year-old man. He reached the roof with a barely elevated pulse.

Gordon sat alone on a corner of the building, precariously dangling his legs over the edge. The view was spectacular. The majestic San Gabriel Mountains rose before him, basking in the glow of the waxing October moon, providing a much needed stolen moment with nature.

The sound of rapidly approaching footsteps startled him.

"Gordon?" Wilkinson inquired tentatively, not wanting to alarm the yet-unidentified parlously perched man.

Gordon spun around to find an imposing silhouetted figure standing directly behind him. His eyes took a moment to adjust before revealing a familiar old face. Grinning from ear to ear, Gordon leapt up to greet the man he had once considered a second father.

"John!" Gordon enthusiastically embraced Wilkinson, leaving all military protocol behind. "What on earth are you doing up here on the Caltech library roof on Halloween night?"

"I could ask you the same thing."

"Annual pumpkin drop."

"So I heard." Wilkinson concluded their embrace with a hearty slap on Gordon's back. "We need to talk."

CHAPTER TWO

Dust

THE LAST TIME a stranger had set foot in Dust was fifteen years earlier, at the turn of the millennium.

Betty Lovell, of nearby Crum, West Virginia, had accepted the 2000 Census Bureau job after the Crum Post Office was forced to close, leaving both her and her husband unemployed. It would be easy cash, or so she thought. She tucked the census documents into her husband's pleather briefcase, hopped in their rust-riddled '83 Ford Escort, and made the five-mile journey up to Dust.

The first residence she came upon was a ramshackle single-wide propped up on cinderblocks in the center of a weedy lot with a few engineless old trucks, two claw-foot bathtubs and one disemboweled toilet.

Some might think twice about approaching such a dwelling, but Betty was born and bred in West Virginia; heck, she and her husband Bob Lovell lived in a single-wide too.

She adjusted her freshly permed hair and brassy makeup in the rearview mirror, before grabbing her briefcase and exiting the vehicle.

Just three short steps from the car, a crazed bloodhound came bounding around the side of the trailer, heading straight for her. The dog's neck violently snapped back just six inches shy of her pounding carotid artery as she stood there, helplessly frozen with fear. She whispered a quick "thank you" to her savior -- the heavy steel chain lassoed around the bloodhound's neck -- and hurriedly retraced those three doomed steps back to her car.

As her fingertips grazed the door handle, Caleb Crimm threw open the trailer's front door. Wearing nothing but a pair of filthy briefs and a bedraggled beard, he pointed a 12-gauge shotgun in the air and fired off a warning shot.

"Hold up der." Caleb's lack of teeth further muddled his already incomprehensible hillbilly accent. "You guv'mint?"

"'Scuse me sir?" Betty responded, seriously beginning to regret her decision to take the job.

"I said, you from guv'mint?" Caleb repeated, as he scratched at his nether regions with the tip of the 12-gauge.

Sporting her sunniest bureaucratic smile, Betty replied, "Oh, yes sir, I'm a federal government employee here to take the 2000 cen--."

A booming gunshot rang out and that was the end of Betty Lovell. The West Virginia State Police never found a body or her car. Rumor had it, Betty had been planning on leaving her husband for years and had finally found the gumption to pick up and move down to the Florida Everglades where her secret penpal lover awaited her. Poor Bob went to his early grave, three years later, swearing up and down that it was the Crimms of Dust who had "done her in."

Needless to say, the 2010 Census taker erred on the side of caution and skipped over Dust all together, which brings us back to the road sign. "Dust, City Limit, Population 23" should have read more accurately, "Dust, City Limit, Population 1." That's right, two days before, every Crimm brother, sister, son, daughter, uncle, aunt, niece, nephew, grandpa, grandma, mother and father disappeared into thin air... except for one, young Caden Crimm, who was slowly making his way down the dusty road.

•••

"I'm gonna be frank with you, Gordon. I'm up shit's creek without a paddle and you're the last guy to call on my 'Save the World' Rolodex."

"Rolodex?" Gordon smiled. In his high tech world, finding a Rolodex atop a desk was akin to spotting a dodo in the wild.

"I've outlived fifteen different computers, but I can assure you that I will not outlive my Rolodex." Wilkinson's firm tone and rigid gaze suggested that the debate had ended and the winner had been decided. "So, I've had every government expert and scientist from here to East Poughkeepsie looking at this thing and all we're getting are shoulder shrugs and head scratches. Not to mention, the UFO nut jobs are all over it since a couple of kids uploaded a damn cell phone video of the blue light in the sky...which just about every news outlet has picked up. We've got the area quarantined under the guise of a possible anthrax outbreak, but that's not gonna hold much longer." Wilkinson took a final swig of coffee. He set down the empty "World's Greatest Physics Teacher" mug on the corner of the desk. Gordon discreetly slid a cork drink coaster under it. The kid was thorough.

Gordon began to rock back and forth in his chair. Motion was his mantra and he found comfort in it.

"Gordon?"

"Sorry." Gordon stilled as he focused on the Lieutenant General's pleading stare. "I'm not really sure what to say. It just seems so...well, crazy. I know I'm young, but I've worked super hard to get to this point and from what it sounds like, you're not just asking for a weekend commitment. I've got some major work in the pipeline -- theories, seminars, books--"

"I get it, wunderkind, believe me, but this is different. There's a lot at stake. Your country -- hell -- maybe even the world. Anything you request is yours, and that's coming straight from the top. The president would have come himself, but I thought a familiar face might help seal the deal."

"I hope you know I'm thrilled to see you and flattered that you thought of me, but you really should have sent the president," Gordon stated flatly.

An awkward pause extended between the two men, before the Wilkinson's widening smile broke the tension.

"Ha, got ya," Gordon continued. "It's just that, well...I don't know what to make of all this. Can I have some time to think about it?"

Wilkinson rose from his chair and glanced down at his self-winding 1971 Hamilton Khaki Field watch. "Certainly. You've got exactly one hour and thirty-seven minutes to make up your mind. I need to get back to camp A-double-SAP, but there will be a car waiting right outside, should you decide to accept my offer."

Wilkinson took a few steps toward the door, before abruptly turning back. "Gordon?"

"Yes?"

"I know your father would be very proud," he said, before making a hasty retreat.

Gordon slumped back in his chair, exhaling deeply. He had always felt the need to please his parents. Even after their deaths, he still weighed their approval in every decision he made. This one was already made for him and Wilkinson knew it.

•••

Gordon packed a few shirts, an extra pair of gray flannel trousers, some freshly laundered cotton boxers, assorted argyle socks and his laptop into his suede carry-on bag.

After a mere moment's consideration, he opted to leave his Nobel Prize in the care of Caltech. It would be of more use to the university, and would leave the door open for his triumphant return to professorship one day.

He stole one last look around the faculty apartment he'd been living in for the past few years. Bare white walls, minimal furnishings and not a personal touch in sight...well, except for a vanilla scented pillar candle given to him as a housewarming gift by a female colleague; its virgin white wick standing as pristinely as it had the day he removed it from the gift bag. *What kind of man can pack up his entire life in five minutes?*

Two sharp beeps from a car horn alerted Gordon to the rigid timeline now governing him. He picked up his bag and left his apartment for the last time.

•••

Caden Crimm continued his shambling gait down the dirt road. His vacant stare and dust-coated gaunt frame gave him the appearance of a survivor from some unknown apocalyptic disaster, which perhaps was not so different from growing up a Crimm.

He was tall for his eleven years, despite being malnourished since birth. Caden had made do with so little food that he sometimes chewed old pieces of shoe leather to fight off the hunger pangs. Grandma Boo Crimm often wondered if it was that "ol' shoe that turned Caden blind." He had lost his vision less than a year ago, and unbeknownst to him and his family, he was suffering from a plum-sized tumor crowding his optic nerve.

But he had bigger problems at the moment. Two nights ago, every other Crimm in Dust had vanished into thin air.

At first, he thought it was all a big joke orchestrated by Uncle Caleb or Cousin Colton. Uncle Caleb always got the biggest kick out of laying obstacles in Caden's path and then watching him stumble over them. Rusty bikes, firewood, cinder blocks, old toilets -- you name it and he'd tripped over it.

And Cousin Colton had his own unique game for Caleb that he called "blind and seek." Basically, Cousin Colton would walk Caden out into the middle of the woods, leave him, and then wait and see how long it would take Caden to find his way home. What Cousin Colton didn't realize was that when Caden lost his sight, his sense of spatial hearing became far more acute, and finding a Crimm trailer just meant listening for jawin', shoutin' and Grandpa C's fiddle playin'. Caden would sit in the woods for hours absorbing the sounds of nature, before wandering back to the trailer. It was a chance for him to escape the chaos of being a Crimm.

But this night was different. It started with him sitting on the couch listening to his *Braille for Beginners* cassette on his small portable player and following along in the accompanying book, both gifts from a social worker who never returned after an uncomfortable encounter with Uncle Caleb. He had picked up braille quickly. As Grandma Boo always said, "he be the only Crimm wit' a lick a sense. The rest of y'all dumber than coal buckets." He handily mastered the *Braille for Beginners* cassette and accompanying book and longed for more reading material, which sadly had about as much of a chance of arriving on his doorstep as a scholarship to Harvard. So, he sat on the couch every night and listened to and read the *Braille for Beginners* book and cassette over and over again.

The night of the disappearance started with a special birthday dinner for fifty-sumthin'-year-old Cousin Cole, featuring Grandma Boo's famous chitlins. After the meal, the Crimm men migrated to the overgrown backyard where they continued to drink their homemade white dog moonshine well into oblivion. They liked to play a modified version of horseshoes using an old rusty claw-footed tub as the target. Occasionally, a Crimm would end up in the tub trying to catch the horseshoes as they flew in, a game that typically ended in fisticuffs and bloodshed.

With the men out of the trailer and the women busy stacking the dirty dishes on top of the dirty dishes from the previous evening, Caden had the opportunity to escape to the couch. He was right in the middle of his favorite chapter, *Five: Whole-Word Contractions Part II*, when a sound unlike anything he had ever heard thundered down from the heavens above. When asked to describe it later, he would say, "It done sounded like TV static turned full up, with a licka tornado on top." The sound persisted for about a minute, and then everything fell silent, dead silent.

He rose tentatively from the couch, imagining that the entire Crimm family was in on the joke. What would they trip him up with this time? One step, nothing; a second step, still nothing. Ah, they were probably all outside waiting to trip him up as he exited the trailer. He walked toward the door, taking comically high knee-steps in order to avoid any obstacles. He opened the front door, distrustfully continuing the high stepping as he descended the two cinderblock steps to the ground below.

"Grandma?" Nothing.

CHAPTER THREE

Departure

Van Nuys, CA - Airport

THE BLACK ESCALADE came to a stop outside a private hangar on the outer perimeter of Van Nuys Airport. A night owl by nature, Gordon was fully alert and primed for action.

"Here we are, sir. You'll find a jet waiting for you inside the hangar," the driver said as he opened Gordon's door.

Dozens of high-powered T5 fluorescent lights snapped to life as Gordon entered the expansive fifty-six thousand square foot hangar, revealing an impossibly clean and polished white floor. Hanging from the rafters above was one of the largest American flags he had ever seen. Just the sight of it struck a patriotic chord within. He wished his father could see him now.

The far back corner of the hangar housed a lone jet, a U.S. Air Force Gulfstream C-37A. The words *The United States of America* were proudly embossed in large black letters above the six circular windows that lined the polished white exterior of the one-hundred-foot-long, high speed twin-engine turbofan aircraft. An image of the American flag adorned the tail.

Materializing from thin air, two handsome young pilots approached him, both dressed in khaki U.S. Air Force flight suits.

"Dr. Gray?" one of the pilots asked with a puzzled expression.

"The one and only."

"Sorry, sir, I was expecting someone a little older."

"Me too. You guys ever land one of these?" Gordon quipped, gesturing toward the jet.

"Yes, sir." The pilot smiled as he handed Gordon a manila envelope. "Lieutenant General Wilkinson requested that I pass this on to you, sir. Flight time is about two hours and forty minutes. After you, sir." The pilot stepped aside, allowing for Gordon to board the aircraft first.

The interior of the main cabin looked almost regal, with oversized royal blue leather seats complimented by the crisp white cabin upholstery and mahogany paneling. Gordon chose a seat, threw his things down next to him and pulled the single sheet of paper from the manila envelope; a handwritten note on official Department of the Army letterhead. It simply read: "I knew I could count on you. Your father would be proud. Welcome aboard. Get some sleep. See you at 0700. John"

● ● ●

Dust, WV - Base Camp

Six forty-five a.m. Gordon followed Pvt. Wilder Short through a maze of large dark green Army-issued TEMPER tents stationed in an expansive grassy field. A brief conversation revealed Wilder was nineteen, from Old Forge, Pennsylvania, and he had absolutely no clue what either he or the military was doing in Dust, West Virginia.

"Far as I know, a bunch of rednecks were making anthrax and infected themselves, but then on CNN I saw a cell phone video of a blue light coming from this place, so I can't really say for sure. That's Lieutenant General Wilkinson's tent there. He's expecting you," Wilder said, pointing to a nearby tent.

Gordon proceeded on alone, oblivious to the fact that in just six small steps, his life was about to change. He paused inches from the entrance to the Lieutenant General's tent, taking a moment to second-guess the decision that, by his own standards, had certainly been rash. *Too late now.* He pushed the tent flap aside to find Wilkinson at a large communal table, diligently typing away on his ballistic armored laptop. Spread out in front of him were carefully arranged and labeled papers and photos.

"Lieutenant General."

Wilkinson looked up from his laptop and rose to greet Gordon.

"It's John to you. How was your flight?"

"No excess baggage fees, no TSA pat-downs, can't complain."

Gordon's expectant smile was met by Wilkinson's resolute stare. No room for humor in this tent.

"Let's get straight to it, shall we? Have a seat."

Gordon pulled up a chair next to the General, who was busy shuffling around photos atop the table. "On October thirtieth at approximately 1900 hours, twenty-two of the twenty-three Crimm family members of Dust, West Virginia, disappeared from their residences." The General handed a photo of Caleb Crimm's trailer to Gordon. "Our sole witness, eleven-year-old Caden Crimm, was sitting on the family couch listening to a cassette through his headphones, when he heard a loud sound he described as a cross between a tornado and TV static. The sound lasted for approximately one minute and by the time it ended, his entire family had disappeared. He waited at the house for them to return until the next afternoon, and when they didn't, he made the decision to walk the six miles to the nearest town, which is Crum, West Virginia. He ended up in the hands of the West Virginia state police, which is where we retrieved him, before bringing him back to camp. As far as the rest of the surrounding community and media are concerned, the Crimms were planning an anthrax attack which went horribly wrong and the entire town of Dust has been quarantined. We've got men in hazmats suits and decon tents set up around the perimeter to keep the press and UFO lookie-loos at bay."

Gordon picked up a photo of a boy he presumed to be Caden Crimm. He was tall for his age and his searching, bright blue eyes seemed to penetrate the camera's lens. "What did the boy see?"

"Well, here's the kicker...he's blind." The General handed Gordon Caden's medical file.

"You're kidding." Gordon perused his charts, focusing on a brain MRI report, which detailed a large frontal lobe mass.

"Wish I was. Docs found an optic glioma impacting his optic nerve in his medical work-up. Most likely operable, but the kid has never set foot in a hospital in his life. He was terrified during the exam; he thought the doctors wanted to kill him. Apparently, his uncle Caleb is a renowned militia-type wingnut. Hates the government, doctors, dentists, teachers, you name it."

"And that's all you have?"

"Not quite. A couple of teenagers, approximately six miles away in Crum, shot a cell phone video of a pulsing bright blue light, which corresponds to the exact coordinates of the Crimm trailer, as well as the exact time of the incident. Unfortunately for us, all of the national networks have been running the hell outta the thing. You put that out there with the anthrax cover story and it's a damn media circus down in Crum. The good news is that every Crimm on the planet lives right here in Dust. In fact, they are the *only* inhabitants of Dust, so at least we don't have any other family members to deal with. The poor kid's going to be in isolation indefinitely."

"Can I see the video?"

"Sorry, I assumed you were one of the three hundred and eight million who'd seen it already."

"I don't own a TV." Gordon felt embarrassed uttering that sentence. Certain types seemed to wear the self-righteous proclamation like a badge of honor, but he didn't own a TV simply because he was never home to watch one.

Wilkinson navigated to the video on YouTube. The camera work was predictably shaky, accented by a drug-fueled commentary from its less than scholarly videographers:

"Dude, that is freakin' me right outta my mind." A perfectly geometric series of concentric rings radiated from within a pulsing blue light that rose in the sky above Dust.

"That was some bangin' O.G. Kush, bro. Are my feet touchin' the ground?"

"Maybe aliens are abductin' the Crimms."

"ET phone home."

"Man, I wish I had me some Reese's Pieces."

"Me too. Let's hit up the Double Kwik."

The video came to an abrupt end.

"Any thoughts?" Wilkinson asked.

"Not really. I mean, I have a few ideas floating around, but every one of them would make me sound about as idiotic as those kids. I'm assuming you've checked the area for radiation, bio-agents, that sort of thing?"

"Done it all. We've checked the soil, air, the well water, the moonshine, even the potatoes in the field behind the trailer. We've got nothing." Wilkinson's confident tone and perfect posture belied his true feelings of fatigue and disappointment.

"Any other similar reports?"

"You're one step ahead of me. Two weeks ago an entire village went missing in the Qinling Mountains in the Shaanxi province. A rather vague AP story came out of China, but the reporter has since gone missing and China's denying the whole thing. They're claiming there was a small explosion at a nearby nuclear plant that caused the villagers to flee. I gotta tell you, Gordon, there's a serious concern extending all the way to the top, that the Chinese are behind both incidents. It's not news that they're running low on resources and real estate, and that they'd love to acquire an additional continent or two."

"Wow. This is a lot to process, and I haven't slept in almost twenty-four hours. My head feels like it's stuffed with cotton and marbles. Any chance I can grab some shuteye before I really dive in?"

"Soldier up" was the first response that popped into Wilkinson's head. After all, he had fought entire wars on less sleep and often made do with three or four hours a night, but instead he simply replied, "By all means. I'll show you to your tent." *Choose your battles wisely.*

•••

Dust, WV - Base Camp

Gordon lay awake on his GI cot staring up at the roof of his spacious tent. At 16' by 16', it could easily sleep another nine or ten men, but this one had been set aside just for him. His name had been stenciled on the tent's outer flap and his bag had been waiting for him atop a quick deployment footlocker at the base of his cot. A fully equipped spacious desk sat in the far back corner of the tent. It was homey, by Gordon's standards.

His mind was swimming with the information he had just been delivered. A wave of anxiety washed over him. Was he really their last hope? The thought overwhelmed him. Sleep seemed an impossibility.

The feeling was not new to him. As a child burdened with a boundless brain, this level of stress would have thrown him into an incommunicative state. It was his way of coping. Shut out the world. He had his mother to thank for patiently teaching him self-awareness and for giving him the tools to not only survive the day, but to actively participate and positively influence the course of it. Her voice rose above the anxious din in his head, "One thing at a time, Gordon. One thing at a time."

Gordon pulled out one of his notebooks from his bag and jotted down some notes.

Possibilities for dematerialization:
1) Family left town - kid is lying - hoax a la balloon boy.
2) Kid is a mass murderer. Buried all the bodies.
3) Focused biological extinction event - where are the ashes, bodies, etc.?
4) Dimensional fold/wormhole - powered by what?
5) Experimental Particle Beam Weapon
6) Aliens? Why choose atypical uneducated specimens? Why leave the boy?
7) Biologically focused antimatter weapon. China?
8) Dr. Dmitry Zolkin - Dusha studies. Energy experiments. Find him.

Gordon set his pen down, and the weight immediately seemed to lift from his shoulders. He laid his head back down on the cot and succumbed to his heavy eyelids.

One thing at a time.

•••

Dust, WV - Combat Support Hospital

Caden Crimm could not have been any happier. He had hot showers, warm meals, his own bed (with sheets!), clean clothes, an indoor toilet, dozens of braille books and his first pair of socks...ever. If he had known about all of this stuff earlier he would have prayed for the disappearance of his family years ago... Well, maybe everyone except Grandma Boo.

His uncle Caleb had been so wrong about nurses and doctors and hospitals. At first he felt sure they all wanted to kill him like Uncle Caleb said, but in real life, they were the nicest people he had ever met. Nurse Wilson had just introduced him to his first fresh pineapple for dessert, and he simply couldn't believe anything could ever taste that good coming from such a weird spiky thing like that (she had let him feel the outside of the pineapple before cutting it up on his tray). And Dr. Bennett had told him the greatest news ever this morning...he might be able to see again soon.

Caden rose from his bed and walked over to the bathroom, unassisted. *Easy. Five steps toward the door and four to the left.* Dr. Bennett said he had an excellent sense of space. It was easy to get around when there weren't any cinder blocks and old toilets being thrown in his way all the time. Dr. Bennett said that wasn't a normal way to treat someone with a visual impairment and that he wouldn't have to worry about that anymore. So that was good.

Caden ran his hands under the hot water in the bathroom sink. He could spend hours at a time doing this. It just felt so good. The Crimms never had any hot water, but six times a year Grandma Boo boiled a dozen pots of well water and made a bath out in the old claw-foot tub in the yard. By the time it was Caden's turn to bathe, the water had always gone lukewarm and smelled kind of weird from all the previous Crimms' filth. And real soap!

The smell was like a field of wildflowers, but even better. He felt sure he had died and gone to heaven, just like the good book preached.

•••

Dust, WV - Base Camp

Wilkinson sat on the edge of his cot and slowly removed his boots. It had been a long day with disappointing results. Gordon had not re-emerged from his tent since their initial meeting. The kid was certainly lacking his father's fortitude. *All brains, no gumption.*

A vinyl purist, he walked over to his portable VV-50 Victor Victrola phonograph, lifted the tone arm and gently set it down on his favorite recording of Tchaikovsky's final symphony, No.6 "Pathetique." He poured himself two fingers of Macallan's eighteen-year-old scotch and disappeared into the somber melodies.

•••

Crum, WV - Ynot Lounge

Crum, West Virginia, sat right off Highway 52 less than a mile from the Kentucky border. Once a thriving coal town, Crum now begrudgingly accommodated a meager population of one hundred eighty-two souls, all of whom subsisted well below the poverty level. There was one gas station, the Double Kwik; one part-time police officer, Rocky Carter; one drinking establishment, the Ynot Lounge; and one motel, the Dewdrop Inn. When the cell phone video hit CNN and every other major news outlet around the world, the population of Crum suddenly exploded. The early-bird newshounds and UFO aficionados snagged all thirteen rooms at the Dewdrop for the bargain price of $27.35 each per night. Contrary to the standard economic model of supply and demand, Cooter Boone, the owner of the Dewdrop, decided that it would be a great time to run a sale; at the same time, some of the more business-minded town folk were charging up to $250 per night just to pitch a tent in their backyards.

The Ynot Lounge quickly became the town's social hub. The dirt parking lot was full of news vans from ten a.m. to two a.m., and the lone beer on tap, Budweiser, flowed like the Mississippi. Americans love a good homegrown bio-terror story, and the Crimm anthrax coverage certainly fit the bill.

The bar was abuzz with gossip surrounding the morning's briefing on the cell phone video. The Army had cleverly explained it away by suggesting it was a combination of a blown power transformer and the lens distortion of the teen's cell phone camera.

One bar patron, Fletcher Crisp, didn't buy the story...at all.

Fletcher, ex-British Army Special Air Service (SAS) and current member of the underground investigative truth movement, Veritas Bellum, had been one of the first people to arrive on the scene. He had keenly observed the establishment of the Dust perimeter by the U.S. Army, and he'd noticed an odd timeline discrepancy. Why would the Army come in and set up base camp a good eight hours before they created the much wider anthrax quarantine zone? Common sense dictated the entire base camp population would have risked exposure long before the hazmat suits and decon tents arrived. The story was full of holes, but he had come to the realization long ago that people believe whatever they're fed.

Fletcher sat belly-to-bar, working his way through a pint of Budweiser. He'd grown accustomed to drinking American beer, but it didn't mean he had to like it. He pulled a bag of jumbo sunflower seeds from his cargo pants pocket. He kept a bag with him at all times. In-shell and salted. He relished the process of separating each seed from its salty shell and then expelling the shell as if it were tobacco spittle. This evening's target was a coffee mug emblazoned with the "West Virginia is For Lovers" logo that sat right next to his pint of beer.

"I keep seeing you in here," a perky blonde South Carolinian Fox News correspondent offered as she slid into the empty seat beside Fletcher.

"Not many other options in town, love, are there?" Women of all ages swooned over his gravelly British accent, permeative masculinity and rugged good looks, which turned grown women into nervous little girls.

"Ohhh," the blonde giggled coquettishly, "You have an accent. Whereabouts you from?"

"Old Blighty, my dear." Having had this conversation before, Fletcher knew how it most often ended -- a less than satisfying midnight liaise and a bad case of regret in the morning.

She watched him spit the sunflower seeds into the mug. "Is that chewing tobacco?"

"Gave that filthy habit up many years ago, dear. Sunflower seeds."

"Oh, I didn't know they had shells." She giggled.

"Amazing, the things you can learn, belly to the bar," Fletcher smiled. "I'm sorry to say this is my final pint of the evening," he said as he emptied his glass. He waved over the bartender, Bobby Boone. "Bobby, bring this pretty lady -- what's your name, love?"

"Suzy." Still giggling.

"Please bring Suzy a pint of your finest ale."

Bobby obediently pulled a tall glass of Budweiser and set it down before her.

Fletcher pulled a twenty dollar bill from his wallet and slapped it down on the bar top. With an unstinting tip of $5.25, he singlehandedly hoped to disprove the myth that all Englishmen were bad tippers.

"Hope I see you again," Suzy said batting her mascara-laden false eyelashes.

"I shall look forward to the moment. Enjoy the rest of your evening." Fletcher could feel her eyes on the back of his head as he made his way to the exit. He knew the type all too well.

He walked back to the Dewdrop Inn, a mere five-minute jaunt from the Ynot Lounge. He entered his room, number thirteen, changed into black fatigues and checked the contents of his unmarked waterproof backpack: AN/PVS7-3A night vision goggles, Bell and Howell S7-R night vision digital camera, portable handheld radiation detector, black wool ski mask, first aid kit, water, emergency rations and lead-lined storage bag. *All there.*

He exited his room, walked briskly across the pothole-ridden parking lot, and unlocked a black mountain bike that he'd acquired from an enterprising local teen for the ridiculous sum of $500. He swung his leg over the cross-bar and pedaled off.

After passing by the Ynot Lounge, the last sign of civilization for miles, the untouched night sky quickly enveloped him in darkness. His eyes took a moment to adjust to the ambient light of the star-crowded canopy. He couldn't recall the last time he had seen so many stars. It was oddly humbling.

His destination, the Tug River, lay at the end of a ten-mile-long old unmarked hunting trail, which passed through heavily forested rolling terrain. The river bisected the Army's quarantine zone on the outskirts of Dust and would serve as his point of entry. Fletcher's rigorous fitness regime allowed him to easily maintain an accelerated pace, and he reached his checkpoint on the south side of the river at approximately 0100 hours.

Fletcher dismounted the bike, laying it down quietly in the soft underbrush. He pulled the black ski mask over his head and equipped his night vision goggles, before going prone.

Two Army sentries were posted half a klick apart on either side of the Tug River, about two klicks east from his position. Neither guard wore a biochem suit or M40 field protective mask. His instincts had been correct: the hazmat and decon tents setup in direct view of the media, on the southern tip of Dust, were a ruse.

He waited patiently.

CHAPTER FOUR

Discoveries

Dust, WV - Base Camp

GORDON AWOKE FROM a deep dreamless slumber. The digital clock resting on the trunk next to his cot read 1:17 a.m. He had slept straight through the entire day. Not exactly the initial impression he had hoped to make.

He walked over to the desk parked in the far back corner of the tent, grabbed his notebook and reviewed the list he had made earlier that morning. Ideas number one and number two could be ruled out, which left six legitimate concerns.

> *Possibilities for dematerialization:*
> *1) Family left town - kid is lying - hoax a la balloon boy.*
> *2) Kid is a mass murderer. Buried all the bodies.*
> *3) Focused biological extinction event - where are the ashes, bodies, etc.?*
> *4) Dimensional fold/wormhole - powered by what?*
> *5) Experimental Particle Beam Weapon*
> *6) Aliens? Why would they choose atypical specimens? Why leave the boy?*
> *7) Biologically focused antimatter weapon. China?*
> *8) Dr. Dmitry Zolkin - Dusha studies. Energy experiments. Find him.*

Dr. Dmitry Zolkin. Gordon picked up a highlighter and ran it over the name. He took his cell phone from his blazer pocket, navigated to his contacts and paged through them until he came to rest upon the name Dr. Pyotr Sidorov.

Dr. Sidorov was the Department Chair of Molecular and Biological Physics at the prestigious Moscow Institute of Physics and Technology, or more colloquially, "the Russian MIT." He and Gordon enjoyed an unspoken academic rivalry that had begun when they were both child prodigies representing their respective countries at international science and engineering fairs. They traded off first and second place awards yearly, but Gordon was up one, with the Nobel under his belt.

Gordon initiated the call. At four hundred twenty-five Hz, the Russian ringback tone was pitched fifteen Hz lower than the U.S. tone. It rang for eight-tenths of a second and then paused for three and two-tenths seconds, as opposed to the U.S. tone which rang for two seconds and paused for four. It was just one of many trivial facts stored in the depths of Gordon's capacious brain.

Pyotr recognized the number instantly. "Hello, Gordon, how are you?" Pyotr's command of the English language was impeccable, and leaps and bounds beyond Gordon's elementary grasp of Russian.

"I'm well, Pyotr. How was the Emergent Quantum Mechanics Convention in Vienna?"

"Fine, just fine, but it would have been far better with you present, my friend. To what do I owe this great pleasure?"

"Dr. Dmitry Zolkin," Gordon stated succinctly.

"Zolkin?" Pyotr's voice cracked as he posed the question. "Why?"

"I have a student who is incorporating some of Zolkin's early, more experimental particle physics work into his thesis, and I was hoping to track him down. Maybe fly him over for a lecture or two." Try as he might, Gordon was a lousy liar. His throat tightened, voice cracked and he tended to over-explain. Fortunately, Pyotr was buried just far enough inside his own mega-brain that he didn't notice such things.

"Zolkin disappeared seven months ago."

"Disappeared?"

"Yes, I'm surprised you hadn't heard. He was teaching at Saint Petersburg State University. Apparently, he was drinking heavily and arriving late to lectures. One day he just never showed up. Nobody has heard anything from him since."

"Has there been any sort of formal investigation?"

"Of course. When a man with a mind like Dmitry's goes missing, there are national security implications."

"What was he working on? Do you know?" Gordon inquired, doing his best to bury his excitement.

"Oh, you know Dmitry -- less than forthcoming when it comes to his experimental indulgences."

"What about his Dusha research? Was he still pursuing it?"

"I should hope not, it was complete nonsense and highly unethical. Soul energy," Pyotr dismissed scornfully. "What forces are holding this alleged soul together and how does it interact with common matter? I fear that what started as an interesting dinner conversation turned into a destructive obsession."

"I'm sure you're right. Well, I'm afraid I have a stack of exams I must return to."

"Will I be seeing you a few days from now? Are you attending the QuantumCon in Saint Petersburg?" Pyotr asked.

"I hope to. Don't you still owe me a kvass?"

"You'll get your kvass, my friend. Goodbye, Gordon."

Gordon set his phone down on the side table and smiled. His hunch was correct. He had to stop himself from running to tell John the news, as he was fairly certain that waking a Lieutenant General at two a.m. for anything short of a declaration of war was verboten. Instead, he settled back into his cot for a few more hours of sleep. A little voice in the back of his mind told him he wouldn't be getting much pillow time in the near future.

•••

Dust, WV - Tug River

Fletcher had been observing the two Army sentries for more than thirty minutes. The soldier stationed on the south bank, his side of the Tug River, was clearly new to the job; he had an unfocused, meandering gaze and a proclivity for fidgeting. However, the sentry on the north bank appeared rigid and alert, without any lapses in focus.

A railroad trestle spanned the river halfway between Fletcher's position and the sentries, about one klick due east. Fletcher removed his night vision goggles and carefully placed them in his watertight backpack, double-checking the seal was without compromise. His footfalls barely disturbed the silence as he deftly maneuvered down the steep dirt embankment and slipped into the river. The depth dropped off drastically just three feet from the shore. Submerged to eye level, he allowed the brisk river current to carry him along.

The water was seasonably cold. He hated cold water. It immediately brought him back to the Falklands. On May nineteenth, 1982, Fletcher and thirty other SAS D and G squadron members departed in a Royal Air Force Sea King Helicopter from the deck of the HMS Hermes en route to the nearby HMS Intrepid. On approach to the Intrepid, a booming thump was felt and heard, and the Sea King dipped and plummeted into the sea. Fletcher and eight other survivors managed to jump from the helicopter before impact. The other twenty-two were not so lucky. Fletcher awaited rescue, treading water with a shattered femur in the thirty-five-degree water for nearly twenty-five minutes. When they finally pulled him from the grasp of the frigid sea, he was semiconscious and suffering from hypothermia.

He hated cold water.

Fletcher drifted under the railroad trestle as he approached the two sentries. At half a klick out, he fully submerged and didn't resurface until three minutes and thirteen seconds later, well within the Army's Dust perimeter. His toned arms seamlessly cut through the advancing current as he swam to the north bank, where he emerged from the river and scrambled nimbly up the hillside. According to his calculations, he was less than two klicks south of the Crimm trailer.

Fletcher unzipped his backpack, equipped his night vision goggles and surveyed his surroundings. Nothing. Not a soul. He calculated a concealed route and moved forward stealthily through the forested terrain.

A glowing sky blossomed above a nearing hilltop. *The trailer.* He flipped up his goggles, dropped to his knees and fell prone into a low crawl. The Crimm trailer slowly came into view below him as he inched forward atop the crest. High-powered utility lights flooded the immediate area. Even at this early hour, there was activity around the residence. Soldiers walked in and out of the trailer carrying boxes full of the Crimms' belongings to a covered M35A2 Army truck. No one wore any biochem or protective breathing apparatuses. Fletcher removed the camera from his backpack and photographed the scene, followed by a quick check of radiation levels with his portable detector. Well within the norms.

He had what he needed.

Fletcher gathered his equipment and reoriented back in the direction of the river. Just as he was about to take his first step, he froze. Less than fifteen feet from where he stood were two young privates indulging in a smoke break. His heart skipped a beat. With the unobstructed full moon beaming down from above, there was no way he would go unnoticed if either soldier turned even slightly in his direction. He crouched low, breathing shallowly, acutely aware of the tinder-dry leaves and branches just itching to crackle underfoot.

The burlier of the two soldiers took a deep pull from his cigarette. "How does an entire town disappear, anyway?"

"Beats the hell outta me," his partner replied. He flicked his spent cigarette butt to the ground and stomped it out.

"I just wanna finish packing this hillbilly shit up and get back home. This place gives me the creeps."

"Hell yeah, did you see the monster dog chain tied to the trailer down there? Frickin' ET even took Cujo."

"Heard EOD is coming in to blow this thing tomorrow." The thick-chested soldier pulled one last drag, before carelessly tossing his glowing cigarette butt to the ground. "Tick tick boom. Duty calls."

The two soldiers walked back down the hillside toward the trailer, oblivious of the pair of eyes that followed their every move.

Fletcher inhaled deeply, allowing his rigid musculature to relax. The glowing tip of the cigarette butt caught his eye. One of the soldiers had failed to extinguish it and the dry forest bed was already beginning to smolder. *Bad time for a fire.* Fletcher stealthily maneuvered to the location and patted out the glowing embers with his bare hands. As he scooped up a handful of surface soil to sprinkle over the smoking debris, a sharp object slashed his palm. *Damn.* The pain was momentary, but the cut was deep and his hand was already slick with blood.

A cursory examination of the soil revealed a protruding dark pyramid-shaped object with a razor sharp point. Fletcher sunk his fingers into the rich soil and extracted the pyramid. It was matte black, about three inches high, and unusually heavy. A gut instinct told him the object was important to his mission, and his gut was rarely mistaken. He gingerly placed it inside the lead-lined bag from his backpack.

He couldn't believe his luck.

CHAPTER FIVE

A Fresh Start

Dust, WV - Base Camp

THE TEMPERATURE HAD dropped significantly overnight and when Gordon first stepped outside his tent that morning, it almost felt like a slap in the face. The chilled air, combined with a strong cup of coffee and a hot breakfast, helped to clear his jet-lagged mind.

Gordon and Wilkinson walked side by side up the dirt road leading to the Crimm trailer. The last leaves of fall lingered, the forested rolling hills around them colored in fiery oranges and reds. Morning dew still saturated the air.

"You wanna get out of that monkey suit? I'm sure we've got something in your size," Wilkinson remarked, appraising Gordon's restrictive wardrobe -- white shirt, maroon tie, gray flannel trousers, tweed blazer.

"I'm good, thanks," Gordon replied dryly.

"You're a better man than me. I haven't willingly worn a hangman's rope around my neck in years," Wilkinson said as he grabbed his neck reflexively. "The last time I had--"

"I have something," Gordon interjected. He despised small talk. He had learned the script through the years, but had little patience for adhering to it.

"Go on." Wilkinson paused, allowing Gordon his undivided attention.

"Yesterday I made a list of possible theories for the dematerialization of the Crimms and an inquiry regarding one of the theories early this morning."

"Dematerialization? You make it sound like they evaporated into thin air."

Gordon responded with a shoulder shrug as he pulled the crumpled notebook page from his pocket and handed it to the Lieutenant General, who eagerly absorbed every word.

"Well," Wilkinson thought aloud, "we've already considered and ruled out one and two...combed the entire county and state, and the kid has been subjected to some heavy psychological analysis and profiling. His story checks out. I gotta be honest with you, the rest of the list is a little outside my wheelhouse. Start with the inquiry you made." He handed Gordon back the list and they continued walking up the road.

"I phoned an associate of mine in Moscow to discuss a Russian physicist named Dr. Dmitry Zolkin. A brilliant man, but his research is -- let's just say, *interesting*."

"And?"

"And apparently Zolkin went missing seven months ago."

"Missing?" Wilkinson's curiosity was piqued.

"He stopped showing up to his lectures at Saint Petersburg State University and no one has seen him since."

"Why is he of interest?"

"Early in his career he did some highly theoretical and experimental work related to the human soul, commonly referred to as the Dusha Theory."

"I thought you science types don't believe in souls."

"Well, Zolkin does. He believes that the energy of the human soul, Dusha, is immeasurably powerful. According to his theory, the only way to capture that energy is upon its departure from a dying body, making the research itself morally questionable."

"I'll say. And how does this relate to the Crimms?"

"If you look at the list, every one of those theories -- wormholes, particle beam weapons, anything -- would involve a source of power far beyond anything within our current inventory. Anti-matter could be the only other feasible possibility, if it didn't cost over twenty-five billion dollars a gram to make. Beyond that, it's almost impossible to store since it reacts with any matter it comes into contact with, annihilating both itself and the container. We're years if not decades away from fully understanding it."

"What makes you think this Dusha energy is any different?"

"There were rumors."

"What kind of rumors?"

"Well, Zolkin left academia for a number of years. Some believe he was conducting his Dusha experiments on prisoners in remote Siberian jails...at the request of the Russian government."

"Christ, if the Russians have this in their hands, we're all screwed. In your opinion, is this Dusha stuff even possible?"

"Zolkin is a brilliant physicist."

"Then we'll have to find him, won't we?"

•••

Crum, WV - Dewdrop Inn

Fletcher Crisp was fast asleep in room number thirteen at the Dewdrop Inn. The motel hadn't seen a decor change since the late seventies, and was awash in mustards, dull greens and cheap wood paneling. The owl patterned bedspread, matched cream colored sheets and pillows were all laid in a heap at the foot of the bed. After all, an Englishman need look no further than Lord Jeffrey Amherst and the smallpox blankets to learn of the dangers of communal bedding. Fletcher slumbered atop the bare queen-sized mattress cocooned in a high-altitude mummy sleeping bag.

Five hours earlier, he had returned from his expedition damp, tired and chilled to the bone. He hurriedly shed his wet clothing before examining the wound on the palm of his right hand, a two-inch clean, straight laceration. The blood had clotted, but it would require stitches.

He rustled through a bathroom vanity drawer, unearthing a complimentary sewing kit, which he set down on the nightstand next to an empty glass. He poured and downed three fingers of vodka from his silver hip flask that was proudly engraved with the SAS emblem of a downward-pointing Excalibur wreathed by flames and bearing the motto "Who Dares, Wins." He poured another and immersed both the needle and thread in the glass of vodka, allowing them to disinfect while he scrubbed his wound clean in the bathroom. After thoroughly drying his hands, he removed the needle and thread from the glass and casually closed the laceration with ten easy stitches. Didn't flinch once.

Fletcher reached for his backpack and removed the enigmatic pyramid from the lead-lined storage bag. It was far heavier than it appeared. He ran his handheld radiation detector over it. *Nothing out of the norm.* He slowly rotated the pyramid on the palm of his good hand, examining it from all angles. The unusual matte finish absorbed light like a deep-space black hole. He set it down on the nightstand, fired up his laptop and proceeded to upload the photos from his camera to a private Veritas Bellum server. Not one to watch progress bars, he jumped in the shower. Unfortunately, the Dewdrop Inn's lone water heater had already exhausted itself for the day, so he resigned himself to the lukewarm shower, toweled off, crawled into his mummy bag and fell into a deep sleep.

The phone rang. And rang again. "Hello," Fletcher said, fighting off a yawn.

"Mornin', Mr. Crisp, this is yer wake-up call," Cooter Boone said in his thick Appalachian drawl. He had one hand on the red rotary phone handset and one on the remote for the nineteen-inch TV mounted in the corner of the reception area. He couldn't decide whether he wanted to watch a rerun of *Kate Plus 8* or *The Real Housewives of Miami*.

"Morning," Fletcher replied.

"You have a good one now."

"You too, Cooter."

"Lord willin' and the creek don't rise."

"I can assure you the creek levels are just fine, a little cold, but fine," Fletcher remarked as he hung up the phone, amusing only himself. He deftly maneuvered out of the sleeping bag and walked over to his laptop. The email he was anticipating was sitting in his inbox.

From: veritas 213 <veritas213@veritasbellum.com>
Subject: Dust Photos
Date: November 2, 2015 4:22:13 AM EST
To: veritas103@veritasbellum.com

Photos are amazing. Too explosive and incriminating for both you and Veritas to leak on our site first. Have already distributed via the alternate channel. Over 50,000 hits on WorldOrderUnderground.com in 4 hrs. This is big. Great work, see you this evening. Your flight details are as follows:

Charleston (CRW) to Denver (DEN), Friday, November 2, 2015 - Flight F9 371

Departs	Arrives	Check-in
06:15 PM	07:50PM	FRONTIER (F9), Terminal Unknown

Denver (DEN) to Burbank (BUR), Friday, November 2, 2015 - Flight F9 417

Departs	Arrives	Check-in
08:40 PM	10:03 PM	FRONTIER (F9), Terminal Unknown

Fletcher powered up his laptop, directing the browser to WorldOrderUnderground.com, one of the most popular conspiracy-oriented sites on the net. He had visited the site on dozens of occasions, but each time he opened the homepage, it never failed to crash his eyeballs. *No wonder people don't take this stuff seriously,* he thought as he attempted to navigate through the impossibly meandering, cheap, garish website. It took him a minute, but he finally found his story. It looked like the view count had already bettered one hundred thousand.

Update On Dust, WV "Anthrax" Story
By Jerry Goodspeed
11-2-15
You've all seen the video out of Dust, WV of the crazy pulsing blue light by now. And you've all heard the story the Army's putting out that it has something to do with

the Anthrax-making Crimm family and a blown power transformer. But what you haven't heard is that it's all a ruse...and we have the proof. One of our sources has just sent us the following images of the Anthrax trailer which is where the entire Crimm family were allegedly infected with their own bio-weapon, before succumbing last week. As you can see, those are U.S. Army soldiers walking in and out of the trailer and not a single one of them is wearing a biochem suit or gas mask, while at the South entrance to Dust (where the mainstream media are still camped out), the troops are running around in hazmat suits getting showered off in Decon Tents. Something doesn't add up.

Our insider also reports that not only is the Anthrax story a cover, but the real story is that the entire population of Dust disappeared into thin air on the night of October 30, 2015. Can anyone say Qinling Mountains? More to come...

It will do. He'd rather that CNN were running the story, or even his friend Suzy from the bar, but you take what you can get. He wanted the truth out there, whatever it might be.

•••

Dust, WV - Crimm Trailer

Gordon stood alone in the middle of the Crimm trailer, arms hanging at his sides, like a young schoolboy awaiting either direction or discipline. Wilkinson had dismissed all of the military personnel in the area so Gordon could proceed unhindered, but the silence itself was proving to be the distraction. Everything was just a little too still.

The trailer was scheduled for demolition later that day, unless Gordon found a reason to delay that schedule. The media was to be informed that an explosive device had been discovered in the trailer and EOD would be brought in to safely handle the detonation. The last thing the Army wanted was for the Crimm trailer to become some sort of mecca for conspiracy theorists after the inevitable pullout.

Gordon had already studied the scientific data pulled from the trailer and the surrounding area and felt confident that his untrained investigative eye would be of little help. He felt ill-equipped for the task at hand. Top physicist, yes, but he was no Sherlock. Was he really their best option? Gordon knew such questions led one down treacherous unlit paths, and quickly turned his thoughts back to the trailer.

The living conditions were eye-opening.

By Dust standards, Gordon had been raised in opulence in Fort Huachuca, Arizona, home of the U.S. Army and NSA intelligence complex. His mother, Margaret, had created a handsome home out of the less than inspiring on-base military housing. She was there to greet him every day after school and he never wanted for a home-cooked meal or freshly baked treat.

This was different, so different that it was difficult for Gordon to process. He had seen low-income housing before, but this was different – this was truly no-income housing.

The filth was what really shocked him. Soiled clothing, tattered furniture, grease-smeared walls...garbage everywhere. It looked as though someone had recently thrown a plate of spaghetti against the paneled trailer wall and decided to let it dry there. In certain circles it may have passed as a modern art piece, but in Dust, it was a way of life.

Gordon rummaged through some of the Crimms' remaining belongings, but it was clear to Gordon that whatever happened to the Crimms had come as a complete surprise to them.

As Gordon exited the trailer, he noticed something strange. The area was heavily forested, yet there was no sign of a single bird, squirrel or living creature to be seen or heard, anywhere.

•••

Dust, WV - CSH

Gordon and Wilkinson entered the elaborate combat support hospital that had been established on the outer perimeter of Base Camp. The interior's white arched mylar walls, stainless steel medical equipment and tubular fluorescent lighting, brought to mind the set of a futuristic sci-fi film.

With the initial confusion and complexity surrounding the case, the Army opted for subscribing to the "more is more" principle; the CSH could easily accommodate upwards of fifty patients at any given time. The overkill looked better for the press and helped to support the "official" story, that all twenty-three residents of Dust had succumbed to anthrax. At this point, as far as the media was concerned, the hospital was functioning as a morgue, and young Caden Crimm's body was among those corpses.

In reality, Caden sat in an armchair adjacent to his regulation hospital bed. He was engrossed in a braille version of the *The Hunger Games*, having all but devoured the book in two days. He imagined himself hunting and foraging in District 12. He too, knew what it was like to go hungry.

"Good afternoon, Caden. My name is John and this is my friend Dr. Gray." Wilkinson gently laid his hand atop the boy's shoulder.

"Hi." Caden looked up from his book in their general direction. The only clue to his blindness was his sincere gaze that never quite seemed to hit its target.

"Would it be alright if we ask you some questions?"

Caden shifted uncomfortably in his chair. "I reckon. I might not know too many answers, cause I ain't done no schoolin' in a spell."

"I'm sure you'll do just fine. Dr. Bennett says you've picked up braille very well." Wilkinson's spirited tone sounded about as natural as a tuba in a string quartet.

"Yes sir. Y'all read thisn'?" Caden proudly held up his copy of *The Hunger Games*.

"I'm afraid I haven't."

"It's a goodin'. I clean forgot summa tha words, but I love it anyways," Caden said, with a big smile on his face.

Gordon cleared his throat. Enough with the chit-chat. "Caden, can you tell me if you felt anything strange in the air on the night your family disappeared?"

"If you mean did it feel like a bug zapper, yes, it did."

"Can you explain that to me a little more?"

"Like 'bzzzt' -- dead bug." Caden made a hand gesture of a bug flying into a bug zapper and dropping dead.

"The air felt electric?"

"Dunno, cause we ain't got nary none."

"Bug zappers?"

"No 'lectricity."

"Okay, well do you remember anyone saying anything when you heard the loud sound?"

"I could only hear Grandma Boo sayin', 'the light, the light, the light' and then just nothin'."

"One last thing, Caden. Are there normally a lot of birds and animals in the trees around your house, or is it generally pretty quiet?"

"No sir, it's real loud. All kinds of birds and critters, and I can always hear them 'coons chuckin' in the stump behind the trailer."

Was his hunch correct? The weapon had dematerialized everything with a pulse within a given radius...except for the kid. The thought brought to mind the old English proverb, "The eyes are the windows to the soul." *Perhaps the weapon was able to detect optic nerve transmission?* It seemed an odd parameter to target, but "odd" seemed to be the norm in Dust.

CHAPTER SIX

Zolkin

7 Months Earlier - Undisclosed Location

Dust particles danced in the shaft of light streaming through a slit in the solid steel door. The ambient pocket provided just enough illumination to reveal a man curled up in his own filth at the back corner of the 4'x4' cell. He mumbled to himself incoherently as he picked imaginary nits from his bedraggled beard.

Suddenly, the cell door swung open. A high-intensity work light flooded the room, blinding the prisoner and revealing the cell's grimy, inhuman conditions. A cockroach scurried up the mildewed cement wall. The prisoner nervously twitched.

Silhouetted by the light, an imposing figure stepped into the doorway, dragging a high-volume fire hose behind him.

"Such filth. Look at you. You filthy pig," the thick-chested man spat out in a heavy foreign accent. "Time for a bath." The man turned on the hose and pointed it directly at the prisoner who assumed a defensive posture, bowing his head and lifting his arms to protect his face. The contortions did little to mitigate the onslaught. Within seconds, the water was forcefully entering both his mouth and nasal cavity. He gasped for air, inhaling large quantities of water in the process. He was drowning.

The silhouetted man paused momentarily. "Are you ready to cooperate? Or do you want more?" The brief respite allowed the prisoner to cough up a lungful of water. Even if he had wanted to, he was physically incapable of responding.

The man entered the cell and drop-kicked the prisoner in the jaw, violently snapping his head back against the wall. The prisoner fell to the ground, lifeless. The heavy door slammed shut, returning the cell to darkness.

•••

Dust, WV - Base Camp

Gordon sat at his desk, deep in thought, reflexively spinning a pencil on the palm of his hand. Immediately following his discussion with Wilkinson, Gordon's assigned team had compiled and acquired an exhaustive collection of anything and everything pertaining to Dusha and Zolkin. The entire set of books, journals and printed web matter rested before him, including one of the impossibly rare original copies of Zolkin's Oxford graduate thesis, which was where the theory had first appeared. Gordon picked up the document and perused the cover.

High Energy Physics and the Human Soul
The Dusha Theory

A thesis presented by
Dmitry A. Zolkin
To The Department of Physics in partial fulfillment of the requirements for the degree of Doctor of Philosophy in the subject of Physics

Oxford University
Oxford, England
May 1978

The thesis was legendary in the physics world. The title alone set it apart, sounding more like a bestselling crossover science/self-help book than a serious scientific paper. It certainly hinted at the complexity of its author's psyche. Interestingly, Zolkin possessed not only a brilliant physics mind, but also an expertise in the the Age of Romanticism in Russian literature. He had written two highly regarded books on the work and life of Alexander Sergeyevich Pushkin, and was fond of peppering his scientific papers and books with his poetic phrases. It was Pushkin's seminal poem "I Loved You Once..." that first inspired him to pursue the soul as an energy source.

I Loved You Once...
Alexander Sergeyevich Pushkin

I loved you once: perhaps that love has yet
To die down thoroughly within my soul;
But let it not dismay you any longer;
I have no wish to cause you any sorrow.
I loved you wordlessly, without a hope,
By shyness tortured, or by jealousy.
I loved you with such tenderness and candor
And pray God grants you to be loved that way again.

Zolkin first read the poem as a doctoral candidate in Oxford's prestigious physics program. As a young man he had never paid much attention to literature or poetry. His aptitude in science had been discovered at an early age, and from that point on he was groomed for a life in physics. Art, music and literature fell by the wayside...until he met Sarah Appleton, a classic English rose, with a creamy white complexion, wavy chestnut brown hair, moon-sized hazel eyes and a disarming smile. She was an undergraduate student in the English department at Oxford when their destinies first entwined.

One typically English overcast morning on his way to lecture, Zolkin passed a sidewalk cafe. Sitting by herself, enjoying a cup of tea in the midst of a light mist, was the most beautiful girl he had ever gazed upon. Seemingly oblivious to the current weather situation, she daintily sipped her Earl Grey as if it were the first sunny day of spring after an arduous winter. Zolkin was instantly enamored. He looked down at his clothing with trepidation. Khaki trousers, two inches too short, a stained, yellowing white shirt, and a threadbare corduroy blazer. It was quite possibly the first time he had ever truly acknowledged his challenged wardrobe.

Unflinchingly, he approached her table, by which time the rain had evolved into a nagging drizzle.

"Excuse me, Miss?" Zolkin asked with a hopeful tone.

"Yes." Her enchanting voice melted his very being.

"Is that tea cup taken?" Zolkin inquired, pointing to an extra cup next to the teapot. His voice cracked twice during the question, but Sarah didn't notice. She was too busy staring into his sleepy, gunmetal-blue Russian eyes. Sarah looked beyond Zolkin's careless fashion, and saw the man she was destined to share her teapot with all along.

"It is now. Please," Sarah responded as she gestured to the empty chair next to her. Her welcoming smile was all he needed. "Do you take cream and sugar?"

"No, thank you. I prefer my tea black with a touch of English rain," he replied. It was the perfect thing to say to a literature major, and led to an effortless conversation that carried on far too long, given the inclement weather.

After that fateful cup of tea, their romance quickly blossomed. Sarah introduced him to poetry, opening doors in his mind that he had not even known to exist. She often read aloud to him the poems of Goethe, Rilke, Rumi, and his personal favorite, Pushkin.

Zolkin grew to love Pushkin not only because he was a great Russian poet and the founder of Russian modern literature, but because he was also a man of civil courage and moral integrity. Zolkin's first book about the writer, *The Twenty-Nine Faces of Death*, detailed each of Pushkin's twenty-nine duels, with the final one resulting in his early death. On that fateful day, Pushkin fought Georges-Charles de Heeckeren d'Anthes, a French officer who had attempted to seduce Pushkin's beautiful young wife, Natalia. Pushkin died defending his love, surely the most powerful feeling a human can experience. It made Zolkin wonder...when Georges-Charles de Heeckeren d'Anthes fired that fatal bullet into Pushkin's stomach and Pushkin took his last breath, *where did all that energy go?*

Gordon looked up from the thesis paper and checked the time. An hour and a half had flown by unnoticed. He picked up the AN/PRC-148 Multiband InterTeam Radio resting on his desk and pressed the push-to-talk switch.

"John?" Remarkably, he had never before used a two-way radio and was ignorant of the proper jargon and etiquette. As a child, he had resented the military for stealing his father for months at a time, and thus shunned all military-esque boyhood institutions. He was no Eagle Scout.

"Go for John, over." Wilkinson stood outside the Crimm trailer, overseeing members of the Army bomb disposal team who were preparing the detonation.

"This is Gordon."

"Roger that, this is a private secure channel between just you and me, over."

"Oh, okay, sorry, didn't realize. I need to talk to you about something before you demolish the trailer," Gordon said as he tapped his pencil on the desk.

"Roger, what's your twenty, over?"

"At my desk in base camp. I think we missed something."

A large truck pulled up next to Wilkinson, completely overpowering the handheld speaker. "Say again, over," Wilkinson said, stepping away from the commotion surrounding the trailer.

"I said, I think we missed something."

"Go on, over."

"In my opinion, a targeted attack like this needs a...well, a vessel or a conduit, if you will. I've been mulling over the possibilities and I think there must be some sort of an object that acted as such. I have no idea what that object is or even if it's still anywhere near the site, but we will know it when we see it."

"Roger. That's not much to go on, Gordon. We've completely emptied out the trailer. We have everything boxed in storage, but I can assure you we've uncovered nothing out of the norm, over."

"I need your men to conduct a search of the surrounding area."

"Roger. How wide?"

"The perimeter should be defined by the presence of wildlife. Tell your men to walk out from the trailer until they see birds, squirrels and deer. That will mark the outer boundary for the search. You need to look everywhere within that perimeter."

•••

Dust, WV - Forest

The grid search covered one square mile, with the trailer serving as a midpoint. Ninety-six soldiers, each spaced ten feet apart, slowly walked in straight lines through the densely forested area, carefully scrutinizing the ground below. With this manpower, the search would take approximately three and a half hours per pass, with the possibility of up to three passes.

The key to conducting a successful grid search involved maintaining both spacing and pace, while simultaneously keeping one's attention tuned to the smallest of details. The hilly, dense terrain made for a complicated search, but the soldiers' rigorous training and keen eyes left them well-equipped for the task.

The first pass revealed three menacing vintage china doll heads, one hundred seventy-eight cigarette butts, four toilet seats, fourteen condom wrappers, parts of three pairs of unhinged eyeglasses, three hundred twenty assorted beer and soda cans, one hundred thirty-four miscellaneous food wrappers, one 12-gauge shotgun, an assortment of filthy old clothing and one...human skull.

Pvt. Ben Golden of Little Rock, Arkansas, unearthed the cranium of census taker Betty Lovell, putting to rest a fifteen-year mystery and confirming the suspicions that her husband, Bob Lovell, had held all the way to his grave. A forensic team later exhumed and assembled the remainder of Betty's skeleton which had been hacked into about thirty different pieces, all buried within a six-foot radius. The search continued.

Pvt. Ron Evans of Scranton, Pennsylvania, twenty years old, was midway through his second pass. It was his first grid search and he found it odd that nobody seemed to know exactly what they were looking for...but then again, the whole mission had been obscured by conflicting directives and wild rumors. On his first pass he had uncovered a multitude of food wrappers and cans, and one toilet seat. As he descended toward the trailer from the crest above, he came across a patch of ground which appeared to have been recently disturbed. He stopped to take a closer look. There were two cigarette butts, some charred leaves, and an oddly shaped hole in the ground, about six inches in depth. He lifted the AN/PRC-148 Multiband InterTeam Radio to his lips and pressed the push-to-talk button.

"Break-break, Private Ron Evans for Lieutenant General Wilkinson, over." It seemed odd to Pvt. Evans that the Lieutenant General was manning the search radio; surely it was a job better suited for a subordinate.

"Go for Wilkinson, over."

"Sir, I've come upon an unusual disturbance in the soil. I think you should come take a look, over."

"Roger. What's your twenty, over?" Wilkinson had already been called out three times to look at unusual disturbances, including a human skull.

"Sir, I'm a quarter klick due north of the trailer on the crest of the hill, over."

"Roger, en route, out."

Wilkinson and Gordon walked the short distance up the hill from the trailer to Pvt. Ron Evans' position. They both crouched down to examine his discovery.

"Looks like we almost had a four-alarm smoke break," Wilkinson said as he examined the charred leaves next to the cigarette butts.

"Sir?"

"Yes, Private."

"Take a look at these boot prints. There are two sets that look the same...standard Army issue, but this set over here looks like a civilian trail shoe of some sort."

Wilkinson examined all three sets of prints and nodded in agreement. "Nice find, Private."

"Sir, thank you, sir, err...Lieutenant General Wilkinson," Pvt. Evans stuttered, flustered by the compliment.

"One 'sir' is quite enough, Private."

"John, take a look at this." Gordon pointed to the unusually shaped hole in the ground. "Someone has obviously dug something up here and judging by the footprints, it wasn't one of your guys." Gordon extracted a sample of the soil using a stainless steel soil probe and bucket handed to him by a prudent young private.

The General took a closer look. Nothing particularly revelatory, except for the distinct hard-pressed pyramid shape at its base.

"Captain Dillon, I need you up here stat," Wilkinson barked into his radio.

Captain Keith Dillon bounded up the hill like a dog to its master. "Sir?"

"I want to know which of your men were up here with their thumbs stuck up their asses, when they should've been watching the perimeter...and I want them questioned and held accountable for their actions or lack thereof," Wilkinson demanded, making no attempt to disguise his anger.

"Yes, sir. Right away. Is that all, sir?"

"No. I need a bulletin sent out to all law enforcement and airports in the area. They need to be on the lookout for a pyramid-shaped object with a three-inch base. Understood?"

"Yes sir, right away, sir!" Captain Dillon nodded before making a hasty retreat.

Wilkinson kicked the ground in disgust, sending up a swirling curtain of dry leaves.

•••

Charleston, WV - Yeager Airport

Fletcher Crisp pulled his rental car into the Hertz express drop at Yeager Airport in Kanawha County, West Virginia, which sat upon a bucolic hilltop overlooking the valleys of the Elk and Kanawha Rivers. Yeager's unique setting also afforded passengers a scenic view of the city of Charleston, West Virginia, framed by rolling forested hills. But Fletcher was far too distracted to admire views.

He had disposed of his surveillance gear in a truck-stop dumpster minutes earlier. Though a little known fact, it was technically illegal for non-U.S. citizens to even look through U.S. Generation 3 night vision goggles on U.S. soil, let alone try to get them through TSA. Fletcher's mission was simply to return home with the pyramid, and he would do nothing to jeopardize that.

Fletcher had surmised that the size and shape of the pyramid itself would render it innocuous to TSA personnel, especially at a small airport like Yeager. If anyone asked, he was a visiting artist and the pyramid was his latest modern sculpture. His many years of experience in dealing with Americans had led him to the conclusion that they believed almost anything delivered in a British accent.

However, unbeknownst to Fletcher, just moments before, every airport in West Virginia, Maryland, Virginia, Pennsylvania, Kentucky and Ohio had been put on high alert. The bulletin from the Department of Homeland Security stated that a terrorist was attempting to transport a bio-terror weapon housed in the shell of a small pyramid-shaped object with a three-inch base. There was no accompanying physical description of the alleged terrorist, and because hand searches of every bag would result in unacceptable travel delays, TSA employees were asked to focus on males between the ages of eighteen and sixty-five, hardly a narrow cross section.

As Fletcher approached the TSA desk, an unexpected wave of anxiety passed over him, hitting him squarely in the gut.

"Sir?" A pretty young TSA employee gazed up at him with a cheery smile. It was too late now.

"How very embarrassing, I'm afraid you caught me right in the middle of a midday dream," he replied in his most alluring British accent.

"Happens to me all the time. Your accent is so lovely. Whereabouts are you from?"

"I have England to thank for my accent, as well as for my penchant for fine tea and rose gardens," he remarked foxily, easily winning over his more than willing victim.

"May I see your boarding pass and passport, please?"

"I'm afraid you're going to need to settle for a green card. I'm one of yours now," he responded, pouring on the charm as he handed her his U.S. identification and boarding pass.

The TSA employee looked over the documents, before returning them to Fletcher. "Thank you, sir. Have a nice day."

He proceeded to the x-ray machine and laid his bag on the conveyor belt. His stomach churned and beads of cold sweat sprouted on his brow.

On the other side of the belt sat TSA employee Luke Johnson. He was on the tail end of an eight-hour shift and all he could think about was the date he had scheduled for later with fellow TSA employee Mindy Jacobs. They had tickets to see Blake Shelton at the Charleston Civic Center, followed by a late-night dinner reservation at Bridge Road Bistro, and hopefully a nightcap at his place. He was looking at the x-ray monitor in front of him, but his mind was elsewhere.

Fletcher's bag passed through the x-ray without raising a single red flag, but even if TSA employee Luke Johnson had given the monitor his full attention, it would not have altered the outcome of the screening. The pyramid shaped object did not show up on the x-ray...*at all.*

CHAPTER SEVEN

The Church of the Savior on Spilled Blood

Seven Months Earlier - Saint Petersburg, Russia - The Church of the Savior on Spilled Blood

DR. DMITRY ZOLKIN was late...again. He furiously pedaled his painstakingly refurbished WWII-era Russian military folding bike down Nevsky Prospect, Saint Petersburg's main avenue. He crossed the bridge over the Griboyedov Canal. The view never ceased to take his breath away. The macabrely-name Church of the Savior on Spilled Blood had been built in memory of Tsar Alexander II on the exact site of his assassination. Featuring a medieval Russian style of architecture, distinguished by brightly colored mosaics and multiple onion domes, it was a marvelous sight to behold and always brought Dmitry back to that day in 1979.

In the spring of 1979, Dmitry and his beloved English rose, Sarah Appleton, made their first trip together to Russia, then part of the Soviet Union. Born and raised in Saint Petersburg, Dmitry wished to share his love for the city that his revered Pushkin described as "the grace and wonder of the northern lands." Located in the delta of the Neva River and spanning many islands, Saint Petersburg's waterways and magnificent architecture completely enraptured Sarah, who felt as though she had stepped into a postcard sent from the distant past.

On May 7, 1979, Dmitry awoke at the early hour of 7:34 a.m., left a note instructing Sarah where and when she should meet him, and made his way to the Church of the Savior on Spilled Blood. Earlier that winter, he had arranged for his cousin, a jewelry artisan, to craft an engagement ring for Sarah. Dmitry had spent many hours in his physics lab at Oxford drawing and tearing up designs, before deciding upon the unlikely combination of a river anchor embossed with an English rose. The river anchor represented his home and the English rose, his heart, Sarah. The previous day, he had picked up the ring from his cousin's shop on Nevsky Prospect. The workmanship was spectacular. The river anchor wrapped delicately around the entire circumference of the ring, and the English rose was inset with a resplendent raspberry-red alexandrite stone, a precious Russian gem named after Alexander II himself.

Dmitry arrived at the church at nine o'clock, after picking up four dozen red roses from a greenhouse on the outskirts of town. In May of '79, the Church was not yet open to the public and was still under the control of Saint Isaac's Cathedral, a highly profitable museum. After a generous donation from Dmitry's well-heeled uncle, Viktor Zolkin, the administrators of the church agreed to grant access to Dmitry for exactly one hour, from nine to ten a.m. on the seventh of May.

A riot of color, the interior of the Church harbored seven thousand square meters of Italian marble and more than twenty different Russian minerals, and was adorned with extravagant mosaics based on paintings by Nikolai Bruni, Mikhail Nesterov, Viktor Vasnetsov and Andrei Ryabushkin. That morning, the gilded chandeliers cast a soft glow, augmented by the morning light that streamed in through the large cathedral windows. Surely, this was Heaven on Earth.

Dmitry laid down each rose with care, creating a floral path for his beautiful Sarah to follow.

He glanced down at his antique leather-banded Poljot wristwatch. It was 9:18 a.m. On the note he left for Sarah, he had requested that she open the front door to the Cathedral at exactly 9:20 a.m. The next two minutes seemed to stretch interminably and no matter how hard Dmitry tried, he could not tame his racing heart. It felt as though a thousand wild mustangs were galloping across his very soul.

One minute passed. He watched each second tick by on the watch's second hand as if it were a decade...56, 57, 58, 59...9:20 a.m. He looked to the door. Silence. His heart skipped a beat and an uncomfortably large lump formed in his throat. Sarah was always early to everything. She prided herself on her punctuality.

Dmitry slowly walked the entire length of his rose pathway to the door, with each step echoing his growing fears. 9:25 a.m. *Had she missed the note? Were the directions incorrect? Had she gone to the wrong church? Was she dead in a car accident? Had she fallen in to the Neva River? Had she changed her mind about him?* The last question reverberated loudly, spawning a thousand others. He had always thought that she was far too good for him anyway. He reached for the door handle, forcefully pulling it inward. Much to the surprise of both, Sarah flew by him, landing on the stone floor a few feet away.

"My love!" Dmitry exclaimed, overcome by both shock and joyful relief.

Sarah lay on the floor crying, writhing in pain as she grabbed her ankle, which was already bruised and badly swollen. Dmitry rushed to her side and helped her to her feet. Between sobs, she explained, "I'm so sorry, Dmitry...I fell and sprained...my ankle halfway here...and then I realized...I didn't have any money for a taxi...and I hobbled the rest of the way."

Dmitry had planned an elaborate proposal, but the moment had proven itself far too powerful to be governed by such scripts. He opened the handcrafted wooden ring box, which beautifully presented the ring. He dropped to one knee and blurted out, "Sarah Leigh Appleton, would you do me the honor of marrying me?"

"Yes, yes, yes!" They fell into each other's arms, sobbing with joy.

After that day, they made a vow to return to the Church of the Savior on Spilled Blood every year on their anniversary at 9:20 a.m...and this year, Dmitry was late.

He approached the iron railing that encircled the Church and locked his bike to it. He looked down at his watch: 9:28 a.m. He had just returned from a Nano conference in Moscow that morning and was eagerly anticipating his reunion with Sarah. Fortunately, after thirty-six years of marriage, she had grown to accept Dmitry's habitual tardiness, even on their special day. He pushed through a crowd of tourists milling about at the arched doorway and entered the Church. Hundreds more sightseers crowded the interior. The Church of the Savior on Spilled Blood had re-opened to the public in 1997 as a museum of mosaics, attracting thousands of visitors a year. Sarah always waited for him at the exact spot he had proposed to her. Always. But this year, she was nowhere to be seen. That same gut-wrenching feeling he experienced thirty-six years earlier grabbed him by surprise. *Had she finally come to her senses after all these years?*

He lost consciousness as a razor sharp chest pain dropped him to his knees.

•••

Dust, WV - Base Camp

A life steeped in academia had programmed Gordon to find safety and comfort sitting behind old desks, so that's exactly what he did. It had been a long day with mixed results and he felt as though he needed to pedantically clarify it all. He selected a freshly sharpened pencil from his old "World's Greatest Physics Teacher" mug, which had magically appeared in his tent earlier that day, along with the remainder of his personal effects from his Caltech office.

The mug's bold proclamation had never rung true to him. He knew in his heart that he was far too impatient and distracted to ever truly be the world's greatest teacher of anything. Perhaps this *was* where he really belonged, beholden only to himself and the U.S. Army. He smiled. *No matter how hard one tries to break the mold, the apple really doesn't fall that far from the tree.*

He jotted down a few thoughts on the day:

- Conduit/Object - why has <u>everything</u> with a pulse, within one square mile of the trailer, been dematerialized, except for Caden? Optic nerve?

- Why a pyramid? Mathematical mysticism?

- Zolkin - <u>not the type</u>.

Not surprisingly, Gordon had already absorbed a healthy portion of the Zolkin reference material. There was no mistaking the man's romantic spirit. The attack just didn't compute, and to further complicate matters, Wilkinson had informed Gordon that the ongoing investigation into Zolkin's whereabouts was proceeding slowly. The Russians were tight-lipped.

He knew what had to be done.

•••

Wilkinson was in the midst of his usual evening routine, two fingers of a fine malt scotch accompanied by the revolving vinyl on his Victor Victrola phonograph. Tonight, he was enjoying Krzysztof Penderecki's Symphony No. 2, composed as recently as 1979, but steeped in the romanticism of Bruckner. He took a seat and allowed his eyes to close for a moment.

"Lieutenant General Wilkinson?" a voice inquired, from just outside the tent's entrance.

Wilkinson's eyes snapped to attention. He rose from his desk, smoothing the front of his uniform. "Enter."

Captain Keith Dillon stepped inside the tent, carrying a U.S. Army issued laptop. "May I?" Captain Dillon extended the laptop toward the Wilkinson's desk.

"Certainly," Wilkinson responded as he cleared a space for it.

"There's something I think you should see, sir." He navigated to the WorldOrderUnderground.com webpage, as Wilkinson looked on over his shoulder.

"What in the Sam Hill is that?" The homepage of WorldOrderUnderground.com had fully loaded, revealing a visual cacophony of unnavigable menus, flashing banners and ads.

"It's One World Underground dot com, sir."

"And why do I care?"

"Because of this, sir." Captain Dillon loaded the page with Fletcher's photos accompanied by the anthrax cover story article. Wilkinson examined the images and gave each and every word his full attention.

"You have got to be shittin' me," Wilkinson said, slamming the lid of the laptop case down.

"No, sir. I'm not."

"What do you know about it?"

"Well, sir, it's a popular conspiracy website run by internet radio talk show host Bob Billings. He's already been brought in and he's cooperating. However, it seems that the unidentified individual who provided the content cleverly used a modified form of peer-to-peer sharing to transfer the material, making this very difficult to trace, if not impossible."

Wilkinson felt his anger rise from the pit of his gut. "I want a full accounting of every single person who has set foot within twenty miles of this godforsaken hellhole for the past week. Do you understand?"

"Yes, sir."

"Dismissed."

Captain Dillon turned about-face, before abruptly exiting the tent.

The romantic strains of Penderecki's Symphony No. 2 did little to pacify Wilkinson's swelling fury. He lifted his glass from the desk and hurled it against the forgiving tent wall.

•••

Burbank, CA - Bob Hope International Airport

Fletcher Crisp deplaned on the tarmac of Bob Hope International Airport in Burbank, California, where the unseasonably warm night embraced him like an old familiar friend. After a short stroll down the length of Terminal 1, he stepped out onto the bustling sidewalk and immediately spotted the black Prius. Behind the wheel sat Los Angeles native Harper Crisp, also known as Veritas 213. Harper, twenty-four, was a recent Ph.D. graduate of MIT's Department of Electrical Engineering and Computer Science. History dictated that she should be up in Silicon Valley pulling down six figures, plus healthy stock options and bonuses. Instead, she was here in Burbank picking up her father.

Fletcher landed in the passenger's seat and leaned in to plant a big kiss on Harper's cheek. "You're a sight for sore eyes, love."

She immediately noticed his bandaged hand. "What happened?"

Growing up in a single-parent home, Harper often assumed a mothering role. She was fully aware of the lengths her father would extend himself to uncover the truth, and that was part of the reason she decided to take the assistant professorship in computer science at Caltech. She could live at home, save up some money and keep an eye on her dad.

"Laceration by pyramid."

"Seriously, Dad."

"Oh, I'm quite serious, love." Fletcher withdrew the pyramid from the bag, placed it on his open palm and extended it toward her.

"What is that?" The car swerved into the oncoming lane as the mysterious object held Harper's gaze.

"Eyes on the road," he commanded, grabbing the steering wheel to correct their path.

"Well?"

"That, I'm afraid I don't know. But I do happen to know this girl who works at a certain university where they will be able to find out. I wish I could remember her name...kind of cute if you can get past her footballers' eyes and knobby knees."

"Very funny," Harper replied, throwing an elbow his way. In actuality, Harper was a beauty, though she tried her best to hide it with boyish haircuts, facial piercings and numerous literary and scientific tattoos. "Where did you get it?"

"Gift shop at the airport. Do you like it?" Fletcher never missed an opportunity to put a smile on his daughter's face. She was his world.

"Ha, ha, Dad. Really."

"I found it in the midst of putting out a forest fire on a crest just above the site of the disappearance. True story. Have no idea what it is, but I just have a gut feeling about it. Any ideas?"

She stole a quick second look. "If it doesn't have a processor of some sort inside it, I'm afraid I won't be of much help. There's a guy in the physics department who'd take a look at it for us, though. I think he fancies me."

"Shame about his poor eyesight," Fletcher retorted, before spitting a spent sunflower seed shell out onto the passing pavement.

"And to think I actually missed you."

•••

Highway 52, WV

The pre-dawn light colored the still slumbering horizon an ominous red. Lieutenant General John Wilkinson and Gordon sat side by side in the back of the fully-outfitted black Cadillac Escalade as it sped down southbound Route 52. Wilkinson pressed a button, raising a thick soundproof privacy window that secluded them from the uniformed driver.

"Gordon, you do realize you don't need to do this, right?" Wilkinson's voice softened.

"Yes, John. I gave up on trying to impress generals long ago," Gordon responded coolly. "I've lectured on six of the seven continents and because of that I'm welcome in Iran, China, Russia, you name it... And according to you, my status is 'officially unofficial.' Nobody knows I'm working with the U.S. Army, correct?"

"That's correct, but--"

"But what? There are physics conferences going on in every country, on any given day. It's a perfect cover. You and I both know it. And even if you did send in someone else to find Zolkin, you're still going to need me there to ask all the right questions. It just makes sense."

"Your father would kill me with his bare hands if anything were to happen to you."

"Well, lucky for you he's dead," Gordon replied. He terminated the conversation by pressing the button that lowered the privacy glass.

For the remainder of the journey the two men stared ahead in silence, both wary of the emotion that any further discussion might bring.

CHAPTER EIGHT

St. Petersburg

Saint Petersburg, Russia

SAINT PETERSBURG STATE University. One of the oldest and largest universities in Russia with a teaching staff of nearly seven thousand faculty. Its list of graduates included Russian Prime Minister Vladimir Putin, Russian President Dmitry Medvedev, American novelist Ayn Rand and Nobel Prize winners Ivan Pavlov, Joseph Brodsky and Lev Landau. Though impressive, the list of notable alumni had little to do with Dr. Dmitry Zolkin's decision to take the teaching job.

In 1980, upon the completion of Sarah's Oxford literature degree, Dmitry and Sarah jointly decided to move to Saint Petersburg to begin their married life together. It was Dmitry's home, after all, and Sarah had instantly been charmed by the city's sweeping grandeur. A qualified candidate like Dmitry would have no trouble securing a teaching job at the celebrated university, and though Sarah's still-burgeoning command of Russian would prove an obstacle to her own job search, she had an alternative plan -- to begin work on her first novel. A romance, of course.

They settled into a cozy, bright apartment on Nevsky Prospect. Just a three-minute walk from the Mayakovskaya metro station, the location allowed them to travel freely about the city without the need of a car, as neither of them had ever learned to drive.

A large arched window in their ample living room afforded them a view of the quiet courtyard below and the entire city beyond. It seemed a perfect start.

They readily adjusted to life in their new home. Dmitry accepted a prestigious faculty position in Saint Petersburg State University's physics department. Sarah remained unemployed, but began writing her first novel, *Lost in the City of 101 Islands,* which she very often was. Dmitry was dedicated to both his research and teaching and would often work into the wee hours of the night, exploring new ideas and theories. They both set their work aside on the weekends and intimately came to know every nook and cranny of the city, whether by foot, train or bicycle.

It was during this time that Dmitry first truly explored the theory of "soul energy" or Dusha, which had been the subject of his Oxford doctoral thesis. Having felt the overwhelming power and persistence of love, he was quite certain that the human soul was a potent, viable energy source. He wondered if there really was some higher power and if, perhaps, that higher power harvested and fed upon the lost energy of the soul upon a person's passing? It would explain the creator's desire to inflict upon his creations a lifelong exposure to extremes in love, hate, joy and sorrow. *If the soul is a muscle, one would need to flex it, no?*

His colleagues found the theory embarrassing and a waste of time for a man of such brilliance, but Dmitry persisted. He spent every free moment running the theory over and over in his mind, considering each and every potentiality. But conceptualization and putting the theory to test were two completely different animals. *How does one capture the energy of the soul? And if there is a Heaven, will a worthy soul still pass through the gates or will it be forever trapped in a state of scientific limbo?* Though thrilling, the idea felt akin to challenging God to a chess match. Dmitry fully acknowledged the questionable ethics of working on real-life applications of his Dusha Theory, but he was a scientist first -- and scientific advancements required proof and sacrifice. Besides, if the energy was as powerful as he anticipated, it would be for the good of society as a whole, or so he convinced himself.

Dmitry had heard the rumors regarding the Central Investigation Institute for Special Technology, which operated under the aegis of the KGB. It had previously been referred to as Laboratory 1, Laboratory 12, and the more ominous name, Poison Laboratory of the Soviet Secret Services. The Institute functioned as a covert research and development facility, running poison tests and experiments on Russian state prisoners. Only two years earlier, the Institute and the KGB had facilitated the assassination of dissident Bulgarian writer Georgi Markov, who was shot with a tiny pellet laced with the deadly toxin ricin. Markov had been waiting for a bus in London when he felt a sharp sting in the back of his thigh. He spun around to find a man picking up an umbrella off the ground, who then fled off in a taxi. Markov died three days later. His assassination was commonly referred to as "the umbrella murder."

Dmitry knew the Central Investigation Institute for Special Technology would be interested in the Dusha experiments. If Dmitry's hypothesis proved correct, Dusha could potentially have powerful weapons applications. And while weaponization certainly wasn't his goal, collaborating with the Institute would allow for him to test his theory on animals and then, potentially, human subjects. He mentioned the plan to Sarah only once. She was appalled at the thought of him having anything to do with

KGB or the Institute. If he pursued it, he knew he would not have her support. He dropped the idea.

•••

Saint Petersburg, Russia - Grand Hotel Europe

GORDON HAD SPENT the previous two days in the air. He departed from West Virginia, briefly touched down in Detroit, flew on to Amsterdam, and from there he flew to Saint Petersburg. All totaled, it was about fourteen hours of flight time and a grueling fifteen hours of layover.

During the final leg of his journey, he caught himself staring at a passenger who looked remarkably like his mother. She had the same gentle eyes and familiar smile that led to effortless conversation. Gordon fondly recalled that she would often return home from short jaunts with at least five or six new friends added to her always-growing Christmas card list. The ability to make small talk and connect with complete strangers was a gift he simply hadn't inherited from her. He was more like his father in that regard. People respected him, but no one really considered him a close friend. He'd been to a few weddings, but never as a groomsman or best man. He led a solitary existence and had grown accustomed to it.

When in Saint Petersburg, Gordon typically liked to stay at the five-star Grand Hotel Europe, a fine example of the charm and splendor of nineteenth century tsarist Russia. He inserted his keycard in the security panel of room 305. The Pavarotti Suite. Hues of gold and red dominated the elegant room, but it was the antique grand piano in the living room that made it truly special. Gordon's mother, Margaret, held firmly to the belief that every child should learn to play an instrument. From an early age, Gordon had difficulties forming and maintaining friendships, so it comforted her to know that music would serve as his companion through life's many peaks and valleys. Gordon's first instrument was the trumpet, which soon fell to the wayside after he displayed a proclivity for only practicing ridiculously high and low notes. His music teacher, Mr. Taylor, politely suggested that he might not be a "brass man," and switched him over to piano. Gordon immediately took to the percussive, mathematical feel the piano offered, and to this day, he rarely passed up an opportunity to sit at a vacant bench.

He laid his bag down on the bed and peeled away his outer layer of clothing. The room was five or six degrees colder than he would have liked, but the slight chill helped to mitigate the effects of jet lag crashing down upon him. He took a seat at the piano and began to play Chopin's *Nocturne in E-Flat*, Op. 9, No. 2. Chopin's twenty-one nocturnes were among his favorite piano pieces. The melancholic melody, harmonies and rhythmic broken chords of Op. 9, No. 2, instantly washed his tension away.

As the last note still hung in the air, Gordon rose from the bench and walked over to the floor-to-ceiling living room window. He drew back the heavy gold drapery, revealing a scenic view of Saint Petersburg's snow-covered main avenue, Nevsky Prospect, and the striking Church of the Savior on Spilled Blood. In his well-travelled opinion, there were certainly more beautiful churches and cathedrals in the world, but there was something uniquely special about this one, with its unparalleled mosaic artistry and checkered past. He vaguely recalled that the church had been used as a morgue during WWII, which, given the name, didn't seem that outlandish. Just gazing upon the historical building stirred something deep inside him.

There was a knock on the door. *Odd.* Gordon was ostensibly here for the QuantumCon, but he hadn't yet notified any colleagues of his presence. He answered the door to find an attractive young woman standing before him.

"I have a delivery for you from Dr. Pyotr Sidorov," she said, handing him an unmarked white business envelope.

Gordon pulled a 50-ruble bill from his pocket and handed it to her.

"Thank you, sir. Can I be of any further assistance?"

"No, I'm all set. Thanks." Gordon shut the door and took a seat on the elegantly patterned deep red armchair in his living room. He extracted the letter from its envelope. Typed on Moscow Institute of Physics and Technology letterhead, the letter read:

Dr. Pyotr Sidorov
Moscow Institute of Physics and Technology
Specialized Institute for Quantum Electronics
Mailing address: Russia, 117342, Moscow, ul. Vvedenskogo, 3
Phone: (495) 555-03-89 **Fax:** (495) 555-02-56
E-mail: PSmail@polyus.msk.ru

Dear Gordon,

Thrilled to find you will be attending QuantumCon. I tried ringing you, but it seems you have changed numbers? Would love to buy you that Kvass I owe you. Give me a ring on my cell when you feel up to it.

Sincerely,
Pyotr

Gordon set the letter down on the side table next to him. *That's funny.* He remembered briefly mentioning QuantumCon to Pyotr on their recent call, but he certainly hadn't told him when he would be arriving or where he would be staying. He picked up the phone Wilkinson had given him before he departed. It looked like any other cell, with a dark gray plastic shell and backlit keypad, but unlike other phones, this one relayed every call through the office of U.S. Army Lieutenant General John Wilkinson, and it was carefully monitored day and night. Gordon dialed the number specified in the letter.

Pyotr picked up immediately.

"Gordon! Have I impressed you with my detective work?"

"I didn't know you had it in you, Pyotr. I'll be sure to give you a buzz next time I lose my car keys."

"Well, you did mention that you would be attending QuantumCon, and I seem to remember that you were partial to the Grand Hotel Europe."

"I commend your elephantine memory. Now what about that kvass you owe me?"

"I've got a much better idea. Meet me downstairs in the Caviar Bar and I'll get you properly drunk."

•••

Saint Petersburg, Russia - Caviar Bar

The Caviar Bar and Restaurant was elegantly appointed in a regal palette of deep reds, golds and creamy whites. Not a fan of fish eggs, Gordon opted for a hearty plate of beef Stroganov, while Pyotr indulged in the more fitting Beluga and Osetra caviar. Both men enjoyed shots of cold, crisp fine Russian vodkas with their meals, and the conversation flowed.

Pyotr pried a bit. "So, I've heard a rumor about you, my friend, and I must say, it really surprised me."

"What would that be?" Gordon inquired as he shifted uneasily in his chair.

"An associate of mine from MIT mentioned that you're on sabbatical," Pyotr responded as he lifted a spoonful of Osetra to his lips. "I thought it odd."

"News travels fast. Yes, I'm taking some time away from Caltech. Fully dedicating myself to my writing for a few months."

"Writing? On what?" Pyotr had always been irrationally envious of Gordon's Nobel Prize and no matter how hard he tried, he could never quite seem to disguise it.

"Funnily enough, I had planned on discussing it with you on this trip. I'm afraid I wasn't exactly forthcoming in our last conversation."

"Oh?" Pyotr's curiosity was piqued. He had always known Gordon to be almost brutally direct and honest, not at all the type for intrigue.

"I'm writing a book on Zolkin."

"Dr. Dmitry Zolkin? Why?" Pyotr could not, for the life of him, grasp why Gordon would set aside his groundbreaking research to focus on a man whose reputation and work were both littered with rumor and speculation.

"You don't find his work fascinating?"

"Frankly, no. I find it to be embarrassing, unethical, misleading, irrational, irresponsible...what else? Oh, and dangerous."

"Sounds like a bestseller to me." Gordon laughed and raised a shot glass full of vodka. "To Dmitry."

Pyotr reciprocated, "No, to you and your new career path, my friend."

"So, can I count on your help with my research? You know him about as well as anyone, right?"

"I suppose that's true, but it means little. Dmitry, like most of us, secluded himself with his work."

"What about his wife, Sarah?" Gordon already knew the answer, but was interested to discover what Pyotr had heard.

"Sadly, she went missing at the same time as Dmitry. There are rumors..." Pyotr downed another shot. He was beginning to feel the effects of the vodka.

"Rumors?" Gordon, on the other hand, had drunk only one shot for every three that Pyotr drank and was just sober enough to steer the conversation.

"Well...some people are saying that Sarah discovered the dark side of Dmitry's work and threatened to leave him...they say perhaps he ended her life and then his, but I have never known Dmitry to be a violent man. It seems out of character." Pyotr shook his head and drank yet another shot.

"Any other rumors out there?" Gordon asked, as he indulged in another bite of his mouth-watering Stroganov. It was the first proper meal he'd had in days.

"There are those who believe he was successful with his Dusha studies and experiments, and perhaps a foreign or domestic power found the idea of weaponizing the energy to be highly advantageous. It makes far more sense than a murder and suicide. Think about it, if one were able to capture the power of the soul and it turned out to be a powerful, containable energy, then wouldn't there be an eternally free-flowing supply? For every birth, there is a death, no?" Pyotr posed as he waved down their waiter. "Take it a step further, add a nefarious twist and one could also create and take life in a laboratory setting for the sole purpose of harvesting Dusha. Clone farms."

"Now you've made it sound like a bad Hollywood film, but I suppose you're right. Scientific ethics have always taken a backseat to the research itself and no doubt to the real-world applications of said research," Gordon said as he glanced out the large window overlooking Nevsky Prospect. The snowfall was mesmerizing. "When was the last time you saw Dmitry?"

"About a week before he disappeared. He was in Moscow and we had a meal and far too many drinks together at Kvartira 44."

"Did he seem distraught or distracted in any way?"

"Well, I have never known Dmitry not to be distracted, but no...he didn't seem distraught at all. In fact, just the opposite -- he was excited about an upcoming trip with Sarah to the United States, I believe. Now that I think about it, seems a bit odd given his disappearance around that time. You Yanks don't have him locked up in some cell somewhere, do you?"

"I think the vodka is beginning to talk," laughed Gordon, "and I need to get some sleep, but maybe we can pick this up again tomorrow? I can't tell you how great it is to see you, Pyotr. Really." Gordon rose from his chair, curtailing a prolonged goodbye.

The waiter approached with the guest check holder. Pyotr and Gordon both reached for it simultaneously.

"Gordon, this is on me. You are unemployed, after all," Pyotr chuckled. He found more than a sliver of enjoyment in the truth of the statement.

"Next time, then. Oh...and Pyotr, would you happen to know Dmitry and Sarah's last address? I just want to get a feel for their neighborhood...for the book." Gordon was certainly not the most adept liar, but Pyotr was too drunk to notice or care.

"Sure. It's on Bolshaya Morskaya at the southeast corner bordering St. Isaac's Square. Second building in, on the third floor, I believe."

CHAPTER NINE
Veritas Bellum

North Hollywood, CA - Crisp Residence

FLETCHER CRISP SAT at his desk in the spare bedroom/office of the North Hollywood mid-century style home he shared with his daughter. He navigated to the Veritas Bellum website on his desktop computer. Harper had updated the site with the photos and anthrax cover story yesterday and their web traffic was booming. Veritas had started as a fringe truth movement in the early 1980s, but due to its integrity in investigative reporting, had evolved into the go-to source for international exposés. With no designated leaders, anonymous membership, a rabid fan base and a brilliantly coded secure P2P-like network, it was nearly impossible for the government, or anyone, to penetrate it.

Fletcher had become involved with Veritas following the mysterious disappearance of his beloved wife, Jane, shortly after Harper's birth. Jane had been an aspiring microbiologist and research specialist working on the link between pesticide use and Parkinson's disease. On March 13, 1989, just three days after she was reported missing, her car was found at the bottom of a deep ravine bordering Malibu Canyon Road. Even after an exhaustive three-week search, her body was never found.

Jane had been fully aware of the controversial nature of her work. She knew it had the potential to upset the entire industrial-farming complex, but her early research had proven fruitful and she thought it would be unethical to cease. It was for the greater good.

Fletcher was sure that Jane's death was a result of foul play. The pesticide industry generated over fifty billion dollars a year in sales, and that was an awful lot of money to put in jeopardy.

When Jane disappeared, Veritas contacted Fletcher anonymously and inquired if he would be interested in participating in a story about missing microbiologists who were involved in controversial research. He had never heard of Veritas Bellum, which at that time distributed its printed publication freely through libraries and bookshops, but he was looking for answers and would have agreed to almost anything at that point. He read the article upon its publishing and found it to be both shocking and eye-opening; in fact, the entire issue was.

Soon after, Fletcher entered a dark period of excessive drinking chased down by an unhealthy dose of self-loathing. He was ex-SAS and employed as a security consultant at a prominent firm in Los Angeles. If anyone should have seen the inherent danger of Jane's work, surely he was the one. How could he have missed it?

It was the bright eyes, smiles and giggles of his baby daughter that brought him back from the depths of despair. From that moment on, Fletcher vowed to find the truth at all costs. Through persistence and patience, he slowly became more and more involved with Veritas, leading him right to the inner circle, where he remained today.

Harper's voice drifted down the hallway. "Dad?"

"In the office."

Harper opened the office door just enough to make eye contact with her father.

"Need the pyramid. I'm going to have Kumar take a look today."

"*The* Kumar?" He never missed an opportunity.

"Yes, Dad. *The* Kumar is not only an accomplished actor and civil servant, but also a brilliant astrophysicist who moonlights at Caltech," she teased.

Fletcher unlocked a small fire safe, stowed away in the back corner of the office closet. He removed the pyramid and handed it to Harper.

"I trust I don't need to remind you how valuable this is?"

"I get it."

"Good. Go forth in truth." Fletcher looked after her as she walked away down the hall.

"Harper," he called after her. "Care to pick me up some seeds on your way home tonight? Jumbo --"

"Jumbo. Salted. Sunflower. Seeds," she interjected. She turned briefly toward him and flashed a smile before disappearing around the corner.

Some days she looked more like her mother than others, and this was one of those days. It was both a blessing and a curse.

•••

Pasadena, CA - Caltech Biological Imaging Center

Harper entered the Biological Imaging Center at Caltech to find Kumar, head down, madly typing away on a computer in the far corner of the otherwise vacant lab.

"Kumar, do you have a sec?"

Kumar jumped at the sound of Harper's voice and turned to greet her with a nervous smile.

"Sorry, didn't mean to sneak up on you like that," Harper said as she laid her hand atop Kumar's shoulder. She was fully aware of her feminine charms when she needed to be.

"No worries. What can I do for you?" Kumar put on his best cool guy act in addition to flexing his nonexistent deltoid, which rapidly warmed beneath her gentle touch.

"Well, it's sort of an odd request...I found this object on a hike this past weekend and for the life of me, I can't figure out what it is."

"May I see it?" Kumar looked up at her with his bright chestnut, almond-shaped eyes, catching her off-guard. They left an impression.

She reached into the backpack slung over her left shoulder and pulled out the pyramid. Kumar took it from her and studied it in silence for a moment.

"You're definitely right about it being strange. If I had to guess, I would say it's covered with some sort of nano-based coating. And its density is highly irregular."

Kumar walked over to a BVZ-7600 x-ray machine and placed the pyramid on a table in front of it.

"Oh, and Kumar....I think we should keep this on the down-low. We're both new...don't want our department heads thinking we're using university equipment for silly personal things."

"No problem." Kumar was very proud of his job and planned to keep it. He threw on a lead apron and handed one to Harper, who did the same.

He photographed the pyramid from a few different angles and examined the results on the adjacent monitor. He scratched his head.

"Hmm, that's weird." He tapped the side of the monitor a few times. No change.

"What is it?" Harper inquired, disguising her excitement. Maybe her father's instincts were right after all.

"It's completely radiolucent. It doesn't show up on the x-ray...at all. I don't get it." Kumar was completely befuddled. *How can something with such a high density be permeable to radiation?*

"That does seem odd. Maybe your equipment needs calibration?"

"No, it's been functioning perfectly. Hey, do you mind if I hang on to it and run a few more tests?"

"Sorry, but I'm going to be tied up the rest of the day until pretty late, so I think I'll just take it with me. We should definitely grab a coffee or something some time," she said. She handed him the lead apron and reached for the pyramid.

"Oh...yeah...sure, that would be great." Like a true scientist, Kumar's interest in Harper had been completely displaced by his interest in her enigmatic pyramid.

•••

Saint Petersburg, Russia - Grand Hotel Europe

Gordon emerged from the bathroom, still dripping, with a plush white hotel towel wrapped around his waist. He glanced at the clock atop his bedside table. *Already one o'clock.* Jet lag had stolen half the day from him. He was relieved to have some distance between himself and the prying eyes of Wilkinson.

The previous evening, he had explored QuantumCon in Saint Petersburg's newly built ExpoForum, and he'd encountered many familiar faces, all of whom were interested in the reason for his departure from Caltech. After the first few times through his fictional account, he began to believe it himself. He quickly learned the power of prevarication.

He had planned on a return visit to the convention later that evening, and had purposely set aside the afternoon to explore Dmitry and Sarah's neighborhood.

A quick peek behind his bedroom curtains revealed the same snowy scene that had followed him to bed the previous night. The falling snow, combined with the historical architecture of Saint Petersburg, added a certain gravitas to the already heavy task at hand.

It would be cold wandering the streets all afternoon. He added a sheepskin Cossack hat, wool scarf and brown overcoat to his regular uniform.

He glanced down at a printout of the directions to Dmitry and Sarah's apartment. The distance was just over one mile by foot:

Grand Hotel Europe
Mikhailovskaya Ulitsa, seventh, Saint Petersburg, Russia 191011
1. Head south on Mikhailovskaya Ulitsa toward Nevsky Prospect- 240 ft
2. Turn right onto Nevsky Prospect- 0.5 mi
3. Turn left onto Bol Morskaya Ulitsa - 0.5 mi
4. Turn right onto St. Isaac Square

Gordon stepped out onto the snow-covered sidewalk. The moisture in his nostrils froze instantly upon his first inhalation. A shiver ran up his spine as he pulled his scarf tightly around his neck. Living in Southern California had softened him.

He quickly found his way to Nevsky Prospect. Almost every building on the avenue stood as a monument on a par with a stroll down the Champs-Elysées or a walk along the most elegant streets of Amsterdam, Rome or Venice. Gordon made a point of absorbing and fully appreciating his surroundings. He had been in Saint Petersburg a handful of times, but was often too lost in his own thoughts to truly acknowledge the splendor of the city. It was a welcome distraction.

Gordon smiled as he approached 18 Nevsky Prospect. Looking down upon him from the iconic red, black and white sign on the side of the building was none other than Colonel Sanders. As he passed under the sign, he noticed the quaint Literaturnaya Cafe on the second floor above and made the uncustomary decision to pop in for a quick cup of tea and a warm-up. He had stupidly forgotten to purchase gloves, and what had started as a light snowfall had now developed into a squall, at least by Gordon's somewhat skewed West Coast standards.

He brushed the rapidly accumulating snow from his overcoat and hat before stepping into the building. He climbed the stairs leading up to the cafe, where he was greeted by a hostess who took his hat and coat. She escorted him to a small secluded corner table where he took a seat. A glance around the room revealed a pleasant interior reminiscent of pre-Revolutionary Saint Petersburg: rich burgundy walls, heavy cream-colored drapery and ornate table lamps with green upholstered lampshades. He glanced at the menu, which seemed to have a thousand choices, not usually a good sign for fine dining. He erred on the side of caution and ordered cabbage soup with an Earl Grey tea, both of which arrived in a timely manner.

As Gordon sipped his tea, he casually observed an older Russian gentleman staring at him from a nearby table. He thought nothing of it, but noticed an English newspaper sitting atop an adjacent table next to the man.

"Excuse me sir, is that your paper?"

"No, please take," the old man replied in broken English. "You American?"

Gordon leaned over and grabbed the paper, the *Times of London*. He hadn't read a newspaper in over a week and was curious what might be happening in the outside world. Besides, he always felt as if every person in a restaurant was eying him with pity when he dined alone, and holding a book or newspaper seemed to diffuse their unwanted attention.

"Yes, I am American."

"Would you like to join me...here?" the older gentleman asked, pointing to the chair next to him.

Awkward. Gordon was incapable of turning down such offers. His mind screamed "no," but the echo of his mother's voice in the back of his mind answered "yes" on his behalf.

"Sure," Gordon replied, and with his teacup and soup bowl he made his way over to the gentleman's table.

"My name is Jurek Novokov."

"Gordon. Dr. Gordon B. Gray." The two men shook hands as Gordon settled in opposite Jurek.

"I knew you were here to business." Jurek's English was broken and heavily accented.

"How's that?" Gordon inquired, curiosity piqued.

"Young man here alone, in the middle of winter, all the way from America. No vacation time. You bring a girl here to love this city, no?" Jurek stroked his full gray beard, which seemed to further legitimize his wise insight.

Gordon laughed. "You got me. Yes, I'm here for a physics conference at the Expo."

"Physics?" Jurek inquired with genuine surprise.

"Yes, I'm a physicist. I was a professor at Caltech University in California, but now I'm doing some research for a book on a Russian physicist." Conversation never really flowed with Gordon, it was always too much or too little. He envied people like his mother, who always seemed to know exactly the right thing to say at the right time.

"What physicist?" Jurek inquired with a sense of urgency.

"Dr. Dmitry Zolkin."

Jurek's face went ghost white as his forehead dropped to the table.

"Are you okay, Mr. Novokov?" Gordon placed a concerned hand on the side of Jurek's arm, a forced gesture learned over time. The need for other humans to touch mystified him. He would opt for a salute over a hug, any day.

Jurek picked his head up off the table and stared at Gordon in disbelief.

"I am cousin of Dmitry."

Gordon was dumbfounded. First he had acted on a fleeting instinct to walk in the snow, which led him to an impromptu layover at the Literaturnaya Cafe, which, in turn, led him directly to Jurek. It brought to mind something Einstein had said during his close friend Michele Besso's funeral: "Now Besso has departed from this strange world a little ahead of me. That means nothing. People like us, who believe in physics, know that the distinction between past, present and future is only a stubbornly persistent illusion."

Physicists with psychological or spiritual leanings had long written about synchronicity as a valid experimental concept for exploring the connection between quantum and classical physics. It was all a little new-agey for Gordon, but this experience certainly warranted giving synchronicity a second look.

Gordon soon discovered that Jurek was a jeweler. In fact, he had designed Sarah's engagement ring for Dmitry. Jurek and the rest of the family had been through what he described as "pure hell" for the past six months...interrogations, accusations, spurious rumors and threats. He recounted that nothing had seemed out of the norm before Dmitry's disappearance. In fact, he and Sarah were as happy as any two people could be.

Gordon steered their conversation to Dmitry's Dusha research. Jurek seemed to know very little about it. He mentioned that the Federal Security Service of the Russian Federation (the FSB, formerly known as the KGB) had pressed him and other family members for details on that very subject, but no one had any knowledge of it. After another two and a half cups of tea, Gordon had completely won Jurek's trust -- so much so that he offered to let Gordon have a look around Dmitry and Sarah's apartment, for which he possessed a key. They planned to meet at the residence later that evening.

•••

Pasadena, CA - Caltech

The phone rang and rang and rang. How was it possible her father could be so bad at answering the phone? Harper hung on, fully knowing that eventually he would pick up. It happened on the eighth ring.

"Hello?" Fletcher answered the phone with the presupposition that the person on the other line would either be delivering bad news or trying to sell him something he didn't need. He held the handset at a distance from his ear, which suggested he thought it might be carrying a highly contagious virus or lethal radiation leak.

"Dad."

"Hey, darlin', everything okay?" His tone instantly lightened upon hearing Harper's voice.

"Yeah, yeah...I just wanted to tell you about the pyramid. I had Kumar take a look at it this morning and he ran it through the x-ray machine in the lab."

"And?"

"And it didn't show up. Nothing."

"What do you mean?"

"I mean it is one hundred percent radiolucent. There's nothing on the x-ray. Nada. Zilch. Zip."

"Did he have any idea what it might be?"

"Well, he mentioned a nano-based coating, but then when he x-rayed it, he was completely baffled. He asked to hang on to it, but I declined. Politely."

"That's my girl. Do you have any boyfriends in the nano department?"

"That's funny, Dad. No, I don't. Even if I did, I'd keep it under wraps. The advanced tech behind this thing would set off all sorts of alarms. I'm guessing there aren't too many substances of this density that go undetected by x-ray. A terrorist's holy grail."

"Indeed. Let me put the word out, perhaps we have a nano expert in our midst. Good work, love."

"Okay, Dad. Gotta go, don't wait for dinner -- I'll be late."

Fletcher set the phone back down in the charger and turned to his computer.

Veritas 22.

Fletcher had little contact with him since the article about Sarah. He didn't actually know his real name, or if *he* actually was a *he*, but he knew that Veritas 22 had an impressive breadth of scientific knowledge and access to cooperative high-level scientists. The Veritas article was one of the only investigative pieces on the unexplained disappearance of microbiologists to be published, and it had won Veritas a healthy network of silent support within the science community.

During her junior year at North Hollywood High, Harper had designed a brilliant P2P-like covert communication system called Blacknet, which greatly simplified communication among Veritas members. Only trusted Veritas contributors had access to the actual interface, yet Blacknet was still connected to a global network of Veritas "friends," who allowed a portion of their bandwidth and hard drives to be used for encrypted data storage, making it nearly impossible to infiltrate and trace data.

The Veritas Blacknet interface was bare bones, black screen with a blinking green cursor. Fletcher began typing:

> t<<veritas 22>>
> f<<veritas 103>>
> m<< have a small object from dust, wv that is highly unusual, dense and 100% radiolucent. need a nano expert to examine.>>

The Blacknet syntax was easy to master, even for someone like Fletcher, who had a strong aversion to computers and sitting behind desks. It basically consisted of four characters and an opening tag (<<) and a closing tag (>>). The four characters were t, f, m, and a, which respectively signified to, from, message, and attachment.

Fletcher sat and stared at the blinking cursor, awaiting a response. Impatient, he reached for a classic style Rubik's cube from the desk and began twisting and turning the maddening puzzle. He managed to solve the red side and decided to tackle blue. Over the course of the next ten painful minutes, he managed to complete blue, but completely destroyed the red side in the process. *How does Harper solve this entire thing in under thirty seconds?*

He Googled the world record for solving the cube and the result made his jaw drop: Luke Judd from Australia -- 5.26 seconds!

To make matters worse, he looked like he was fourteen years old. *Bloody ridiculous.* Frustrated and completely disillusioned, he proceeded to disassemble the entire cube and reassemble it with all of the sides intact. *There's more than one way to skin a cat. Take that, Luke Judd.*

His computer beeped. There was a message awaiting him:

t<< veritas 103>>
f<<veritas 22>>
M<<go to po boxes & more. 34568 victory ave, glendale, ca tomorrow (11/5/12) at 9:35pm. rita will be at the counter. tell her it's for po box 2398.>>

Every time he received a communique via Blacknet he felt a little more like James Bond. He had the looks, accent and charm; he was just missing the Aston Martin DB5 in the driveway...and the Bond girl.

•••

Saint Petersburg, Russia - Zolkin Residence

Gordon stood outside Dmitry and Sarah's Imperial style apartment building, admiring its grandiose profusion of columns, windows and pilasters. *Even apartments look like palaces in this city,* Gordon thought, as he shuffled his legs back and forth in a vain attempt to stay warm. The saddle shoes had proven to be a bad choice. The snow continued to fall and his feet were damp and half frozen.

"Gordon, I see you are a timely man, like me. Shall we?" Gordon looked up to find Jurek motioning toward the front door of the beautifully appointed front entrance. They entered the building.

A grand marble staircase accented by a burgundy carpet runner and a gilded railing welcomed them as they passed through the front door. Above, an ornate Rococo-style chandelier swayed gently in a rogue winter draft, casting an eerie shifting pool of light.

Gordon felt something rub against the back of his legs, catching him off guard. He jumped, sending a frightened black cat scurrying past him up the stairs.

"No worry, just cat," Jurek chuckled, clearly amused by Gordon's skittishness.

"Black cat," Gordon whispered to himself, suddenly feeling like the naive horror film victim who ignored all the obvious signs that he was about to meet a gruesome death.

"Up to next," Jurek commanded.

As they ascended the staircase, a shiver ran up Gordon's spine. *It must be forty degrees in this place.* Suddenly, he missed Los Angeles, his Caltech job, his warm office, swaying palm trees, sunny days and In-N-Out Burger.

Gordon followed closely behind Jurek as they weaved through the building's immense corridors. They reached apartment 314. Jurek pulled a key from the pocket of his double-breasted wool pea coat. As he inserted the key in the lock, an elderly neighbor nosily peeked out from behind her door.

"Shoo." Jurek curtly dismissed her as if she was a mere nettlesome mutt. She resigned with a bothered face and slammed the door. "Old bag," Jurek muttered as he and Gordon entered.

The apartment was both pitch black and ice cold. Jurek blindly reached for the side table drawer just to the left of the entrance. He fumbled around for a moment before extracting a matchbook and a long white dinner candle. He lit the candle as he approached the large dining table that rested before them and proceeded to light the six-pillared candelabra centerpiece, which cast just enough light to make the room navigable.

Gordon's eyes quickly adjusted to the dim glow that revealed a large and richly decorated living space with fifteen-foot ceilings, ornate crown molding and a large window with a breathtaking night view of St. Isaac's Square and the golden-domed cathedral beyond.

"No electricity. I pay for apartment rent while Dmitry is gone, but no utilities. Dmitry will owe me too much when he returns! Follow me." Jurek picked up the candelabra and led Gordon down the hallway.

They entered the first door on their right. *Yikes.* Clearly, the room had once functioned as an office, but was now in a complete state of disarray with papers, books, photos and cables scattered about on the floor. A vintage Smith Corona typewriter rested on one of the desks and a computer monitor on the other. Cables dangled from the back of the monitor, a clear indication that someone had, not so delicately, removed the PC that was once attached.

"FSB are not so good at cleaning up," Jurek remarked.

"Looks like they got what they wanted."

"Just about, but not quite."

Jurek walked over to a waist-high wooden bookcase sitting beneath the window. All its books had been thrown from the shelves and lay in disarray on the floor. Jurek reached under the bottom of the right side of the case and slid the entire outer veneer up and out, revealing a hidden cavity. The workmanship was absolutely flawless, with no indication of a seam. The cavity was very narrow, but deep enough to hide one black leather journal. Jurek picked it up and handed it to Gordon.

"Here, you read. Physics. I make case for Dmitry, you like?"

"You are a true craftsman, Jurek."

"There's good market for items like this in Russia, where found secrets serve as death sentences. I am first a businessman and two, I am an artist." Jurek smiled. "Read, go on." Jurek held the candelabra over the journal and gestured for Gordon to open it. Gordon took a cursory look. From what he could decipher, it was the Dusha research...written in Russian.

"You understand book? Everyone in family look. No one understand."

"Yes, it's very important physics research. I will need to have it translated. Why did you risk leaving it here?"

"FSB search here twice. They never find. I hide in my home, they might find, no?"

"I see. May I take this with me?"

"Will help you find Dmitry?"

"I believe it will."

"You keep, my friend." Jurek grabbed Gordon's arms and stared directly into his eyes. "Bring home Dmitry and Sarah. Please."

"I will do my best, Jurek. Thank you for entrusting me with --"

A loud bang on the front door stopped Gordon mid-sentence. Jurek instinctively lifted his index finger to his lips, shushing Gordon. He blew out the six candles in one long exhalation, while Gordon hastily jammed the journal down the front waistband of his trousers. They froze in place.

Gordon felt as though his heart might break through his chest wall with each resounding beat. He was sure it could be heard all the way out in the hallway. Perhaps he was destined to play the naive victim after all?

They hung suspended on the cusp of discovery. A second loud bang caught Gordon by surprise. He stepped back, tripped over a cable on the floor, barely catching himself by grabbing the typewriter, which tottered perilously over the edge of the desk. Jurek reflexively dropped the candelabra, took hold of Gordon and steadied the typewriter in one seamless motion. Surely, Gordon had given them away. They awaited a response.

A woman shouted something in Russian. A wave of anxiety washed over Gordon. He looked to Jurek for his next cue. Jurek smiled, took a deep breath and put his hand to his heart.

"Breathe, my friend. It is a drunk husband stumbling in the hallway and an angry wife. In Russia, we call that happily married."

Gordon laughed out loud. He was certain he had never felt such relief in his life.

"We leave while our luck is still good, yes?"

Gordon nodded in agreement, and the two men departed in silence.

CHAPTER TEN

The Past Returns

Seven Months Earlier - Undisclosed Location

DMITRY RUBBED HIS bleary eyes as he awoke in the shadowy room. Everything was a blur. He held his shapeless hand in front of his face and watched it sharpen as his focus slowly returned. His nails were filthy. He picked at them as he surveyed his surroundings from atop a squalid paper-thin mattress on a rusty steel-spring cot.

At 20' by 20', the cheerless room was palatial compared to his previous holding cell. A small barred window let in just enough light to fight back the shadows. The colorless cement floor and walls echoed the chill that penetrated his tired bones. A squat toilet was provided in the corner opposite him, next to a reinforced door which allowed the sole means of entrance and exit for the cell. A small drain rested in the center of the floor, above which a heavy chain hung down from the ceiling. Though he longed for water, he prayed he had seen the last of the fire hose.

He assessed his physical condition. His mouth was so dry that his gluey tongue felt like an unwelcome foreign object in his mouth. He attempted to sit upright, but his emaciated musculature wasn't equal to the task. He glanced down at his weakened body. Soiled, torn clothing hung from his skeletal frame.

A paralyzing thirst and hunger crippled him, driving his thoughts to the edge of madness. If given the ultimatum, he would willingly opt to kill a man for a glass of water or morsel of food. This primal sense of self-preservation pushed any consideration of Sarah's whereabouts and well-being far from his mind.

"Help." What felt like a roar to him left his lips as a mere whisper. Dmitry made a second attempt to push himself upright. He made it halfway before losing his grip on the side of the cot and he came crashing down on the unforgiving floor. The cement was ice cold on his back and stole his breath from him. Dmitry waved his arms back and forth trying to draw the attention of whomever might be observing him.

No response. He grabbed the side of the cot and tried to pull himself back up onto the mattress. It was no use. He was spent. Resigned, he slumped back down to the ground and lay waiting for whatever fate had in store for him.

After what seemed like hours, Dmitry heard the distinct sound of men's dress shoes walking down the hallway leading to his door. *Click, clack, click, clack.* Dmitry's breathing shallowed and his heart raced in anticipation of what was coming next.

The green door swung open revealing a pleasant-faced, impeccably dressed white male, who walked directly over to Dmitry. The man crouched down, slipped his arms underneath Dmitry's fetid armpits, and pulled him back up to the cot. As he took a step back, he brushed away imagined filth from the arms of his gray suit jacket and straightened his tie.

"Water," Dmitry muttered, expending his remaining energy.

"You are thirsty?" replied the man. It was an accent Dmitry did not recognize.

"Please." Dmitry's pleading eyes spoke louder than his hushed words.

The man turned abruptly and exited the room. Dmitry heard the sound of his footsteps fade as he walked away, down the corridor. Then silence. Dmitry feared the man would not return. He wanted to cry, but tears required bodily fluids and his were all but depleted.

He helplessly stared at the open door and waited until the sound of the man's footsteps resumed, amplifying with his increasing proximity. The man entered the room carrying a tall glass of water. He approached Dmitry, took a seat next to him on the mattress and gingerly placed a hand behind Dmitry's neck as he lifted his head toward the glass. Dmitry's bone-dry lips cracked as he opened his mouth to receive the water. After a mere mouthful the man pulled the glass away.

"More...please."

The man jerked his hand away from the back of Dmitry's neck allowing his head to fall back to the cot. Dmitry stared up at him in pain.

"Water," Dmitry whispered, pleading.

The man held up the glass as if he were going to pour water into Dmitry's mouth, before suddenly swinging the glass to the side and emptying it on the floor a full three feet away from the cot. The man answered Dmitry's desperate eyes with an ice cold stare, then departed, locking the door in his wake.

Dmitry used every ounce of strength to roll over on the narrow cot, forcing himself to fall to the floor. Unable to break his fall, he impacted with a resounding thump. He dragged his limp body over to the quickly expanding puddle and extended his sandpaper tongue, and lapped at the water like a caged animal.

•••

Saint Petersburg, Russia - Bus #3

Gordon rode the number three bus back to the Grand Hotel Europe. The scare in Dmitry's apartment had left him feeling jittery. He neurotically felt for the journal in the waistband of his trousers every few seconds, as his eyes dashed furtively about the bus.

An elderly woman near the front of the bus kept turning around to stare at him. He couldn't recall if she had boarded at the Mikhailovskaya Ulitsa stop, with him, or if she was already seated when he boarded. Was she the old lady from the apartment next door? He couldn't recall her face either. Was she following him? Was this all a trap?

Gordon was so hyper-aware that the slightest sounds were beginning to make him jump in his seat. *Calm down. Think. Be sensible.* He glanced up toward the front of the bus again. The woman was looking directly at him with her focused, beady eyes. She looked as though she wanted to tell him something. Now he was almost certain that it was the woman from the apartment. Was she an FSB spy? He felt certain he would meet the same fate as Dmitry and Sarah. In a moment of panic, Gordon picked up his cell and dialed.

Wilkinson answered almost immediately, "Gordon, everything okay?"

"I think I'm being followed. I'm not sure what to do."

"Where are you?"

"On the number three bus heading back to the hotel. I just came from Dmitry's apartment."

"You were in his apartment? Why didn't you call earlier? I could have had someone meet you there."

"I don't know, I guess...I, uh--"

"Never mind. How did you get in?"

"I met his cousin Jurek in a cafe, by pure coincidence. Apparently his cousin has been taking care of the apartment for him."

"Are you sure? Was he there before you arrived?"

"I...I can't remember."

"Well, did he approach you or was it vice versa?"

"He approached me." *Uh-oh*. Gordon quickly deduced where the line of questioning was leading.

"Are you being followed?"

"Not that I'm aware of. There's an old woman on the bus who keeps staring at me, though. I think she saw me enter Dmitry's apartment with Jurek."

"Don't get off at your stop. What does this Jurek know?"

"He knows my name and that I'm a physicist here for the QuantumCon and also that I am writing a book on Zolkin. Oh, and he gave me one of Dmitry's notebooks."

"Is QuantumCon still open?"

"Yes, the closing party is tonight."

"Good. Get off the bus at the stop for QuantumCon. Go into the Expo and stay on the main floor. Make sure you're surrounded by as many people as possible at all times. I'll have someone meet you there. How long before you arrive?"

"Next stop. Four or five minutes."

"I'll call back with instructions," Wilkinson said, before abruptly terminating the call.

Gordon already felt better. He breathed a little deeper as he rested his head on the icy window. The rhythm of the passing cars combined with the heavy falling snow was calming.

A black Mercedes sedan pulled up alongside him, traveling at the same speed as the bus. The other vehicles seemed to fly by the car. Gordon tried to get a look at the driver, but the snow and nightfall provided impenetrable cover. *It's nothing,* he thought.

He lifted his head from the window and shifted his gaze ahead. The old woman was still staring at him.

The bus slowed as it approached the Expo stop. Gordon rose from his seat and walked forward toward the front exit. As he passed the old woman, she reached out and grabbed his arm. He went rigid with anxiety. Their eyes met. She shook her head *no*. Gordon panicked. He broke his arm free of her grasp and rushed off the bus, almost tripping over his own feet on the snow-covered sidewalk.

During his short ride, the storm had developed further. The wind whipped against his bare face, and snow clung to his eyelashes. Gordon glanced back at the woman's window. She was still shaking her head no. Suddenly, she stopped and pointed directly behind him. Gordon swung his head around. Two well-dressed thick-chested men grabbed him by each arm, patting him down with their free hands. The larger of the two, distinguished by a finely manicured black beard, found and confiscated his cell phone.

"Help!" Gordon shouted back toward the bus, but it was pointless; the doors were closing and his scream was swallowed by the blustery storm. The two men lifted him inches above the ground as they effortlessly conveyed him back toward the Mercedes. The bearded man opened the back door, forced Gordon's head down, and stuffed him into the back seat of the sedan.

"Hello, Gordon."

It was his father.

•••

Burbank, CA - Mini-Mall

Fletcher pulled into the parking spot directly in front of PO Boxes & More. It was a small storefront harbored within a typical Los Angeles street corner mini-mall. A "Closed" sign hung from the front door, but Fletcher spied a dim light at the back of the shop that indicated otherwise. He checked his watch. *Five minutes early. Promptness is a lonely business.*

The parking lot was empty, save for a few cars parked in front of the Green Machine, one of LA's ubiquitous marijuana dispensaries. The messenger bag on the passenger seat caught Fletcher's eye. *Time for just one more peek.* He removed the pyramid and placed it on the flat palm of his right hand. It was a simple, unadorned object, but try as he might, he just couldn't seem to take his eyes off it.

An LAPD squad car pulled in behind Fletcher and idled with its lights on. Fletcher coolly replaced the pyramid in the messenger bag and gently tossed the bag on the floor. His plates and license were both clean, but the timing aroused his suspicions, and he anxiously anticipated the inevitable knock on the window. After what felt like an eternity, the officer exited the squad car and approached Fletcher, lightly tapping on the window with a heavy black flashlight that could easily double as a bludgeon. Fletcher obediently rolled down his window.

"Yes, Officer?"

"License, registration and proof of insurance, please." The officer's flashlight scanned the interior of the car, as Fletcher tendered the requested documents. The probing beam lingered on the messenger bag just a little too long for Fletcher's liking.

"May I ask what the problem is, Officer?"

"We've had some issues with customers of the dispensary smoking marijuana in this parking lot. What's your business?"

"I'm just here to collect my friend Rita who works in that shop," Fletcher answered, pointing to the storefront directly in front of him.

"Wait here please." The officer walked back toward his squad car, speaking into a handheld radio, just out of earshot.

Fletcher looked back at the storefront. A woman in the front window was watching the scene unfold. She briefly made eye contact with Fletcher before exiting the shop and walking toward his car.

The officer approached and handed Fletcher his documents.

"What's he done now?" Rita asked as she brazenly placed her hand on the officer's arm. Her Eastern European cheekbones, coy smile and gamine figure provided a welcome distraction.

"You know this man, Miss?" The officer shined his flashlight in Fletcher's face.

"Yes sir, and he's late...again!" Rita responded enthusiastically. Oscars have been awarded for lesser performances.

The officer smiled. "You're free to go, Mr. Crisp. Sorry for the inconvenience."

"Not a problem, Officer."

Fletcher picked up the messenger bag from the floor and exited the car. Rita hugged him warmly, and they entered the store hand-in-hand.

"Thank you," Fletcher said, genuinely relieved.

Rita yanked her hand free of his grasp. "For what?" Rita's suddenly acerbic tone and frosty demeanor caught Fletcher off guard.

"For the hug." *If there's one thing that works on women, it's humor.* Fletcher spied just a glimmer of a smile somewhere beneath Rita's stony facade.

"Do you have the package?"

Ouch.

"Yes, but seriously, thanks for coming to my rescue out there."

"Wasn't rescuing you. I hate repeating myself. Do you have the package?"

Fletcher opened his messenger bag and extracted the pyramid. He passed it over to Rita. "This is for P.O. Box 2398."

"I think we're well past that now."

Rita took the pyramid, turned her back to him and walked out of sight.

Fletcher called after her, "That's it? Don't suppose I can take you out to dinner sometime?"

The dim light in the back of the shop switched off. Fletcher walked toward the front door, saying to himself, "I'll take that as a maybe."

●●●

Saint Petersburg, Russia - QuantumCon

Gordon hadn't seen his father, General Thomas B. Gray, in three years, two months and four days. He looked the same, yet different. His facial structure was off, as if he had been disassembled and put back together slightly askew. Gordon simply couldn't recall his father having such pronounced cheekbones or such a finely-shaped nose. His cropped hair was the same rich golden brown, but his eyes looked different...blue, when Gordon knew them to be hazel. The subtle evolution was surprisingly unsettling, though not as unnerving as a face-to-face meeting with your father, three years after his supposed death.

Gordon didn't know what to say or do. The General had never been particularly demonstrative, so a hug seemed unlikely.

The car began to gently rock up and down in rhythm with Gordon's nervous knee.

"Gordon, you need to listen to me very closely. I'm sure you have many questions, but I'm afraid they must wait. We've been following you since your arrival in Russia. You cannot trust the people you think you can trust. What are your orders?"

Silence. Fractions of unfiltered memories, questions, answers and doubts clouded Gordon's mind. He opened his mouth to speak, but his tongue was trapped in a state of paralysis. The General recognized the lost expression on his son's face and placed a paternal hand on Gordon's knee. The simple gesture brought Gordon back to the moment. The car ceased rocking.

"Well...ah...I've been told by John...ah, Lieutenant General Wilkinson, to enter QuantumCon inside the Expo and to proceed to the main floor show, where the closing party -- Dad?"

"Yes?"

"Is Mom alive?" The question existed long before it was spoken and its departure came as a huge relief to Gordon.

"Gordon, you need to focus. Your life is in danger. Did Jurek give you anything?"

"This." Gordon pulled the journal from his waistband and handed it to his father. "But Jurek is FSB."

"No, the drunken man and woman you heard shouting in the hallway of Dmitry's building were FSB and they are waiting for you in your hotel room right now."

"But, John told me --."

"Forget John, he knows only the story they tell him."

"So the journal is real?"

"As real as this moment. Who knows what we will find in there, but in one day you managed to secure what we have been seeking for the past six months."

Gordon allowed himself to indulge in a moment of pride, before immediately hurtling back into his anxiety-riddled reality.

"What should I do?"

"Follow John's directives. His men will see that you're safe from FSB. Mention the journal to no one. You must go now."

"That's it?" It was not exactly the reunion he had hoped for.

"Give him back the cell."

The bearded man deftly reassembled Gordon's phone before handing it back to him.

"We'll be the ones monitoring your calls now. I'll be nearby." His father motioned toward the door. "Go."

As Gordon exited the car, the phone rang.

"Hello?"

"Gordon, are you at the Expo yet?" Wilkinson sounded genuinely concerned.

"Walking in now."

"And the woman?"

"Still on the bus. I think I may have overreacted, I'm sorry."

"Nothing to be sorry about. I have two men waiting at the Stoli mixer side bar. They will escort you back to your hotel room, where they will have just a few questions for you. Okay?"

"I guess." The choked sound of Gordon's voice betrayed his feelings of doubt.

"Gordon, I know these men personally. You're in good hands. You know you can trust me."

Gordon wanted to say, "Well, actually, a man we all believed to be dead for the past three years informed me that I can trust no one," but instead he responded, "I know, John. Thank you."

"Get in there, they're waiting," he said, before ending the call.

Gordon entered the Expo and quickly realized that he had left his QuantumCon credentials back in the hotel. An overgrown security guard at the entrance to the main floor stopped him.

"Need to see your badge, sir."

Gordon fumbled around in his pockets, pretending to search for his credentials. "I'm sorry, but I seem to have forgotten my badge back at the hotel."

"Sorry, but we can't let you in without it, sir." The security guard crossed his muscular arms, suggesting the conversation was over.

"But I'm a Nobel Award winner in physics, surely that's enough to get me in?"

"And I'm Albert Einstein. You still need a badge. I'm going to need you to step away from the door, sir."

The guard placed his hands on Gordon's shoulders and gently shifted him to the side so that other attendees could freely enter.

"Dr. Gray?"

Gordon spun around to find a middle-aged American male looking at him with a surprised expression.

"Yes?"

The man offered his hand to Gordon. "Bob Barchie. I'm responsible for organizing this whole mess," he said as he made a broad sweeping gesture, encompassing the entire Expo Center. "Is there a problem here?" Bob asked the now-sheepish security guard.

"This gentleman doesn't have a badge, Mr. Barchie. Just following protocol."

"This gentleman happens to be Dr. Gordon B. Gray. He is the youngest Nobel Laureate of all time and he's my guest."

"Yes, sir." The guard stepped aside, allowing them both to pass.

"I wish I had known you would be attending the conference, Gordon. It would have been an honor to have you speak."

"Thank you, yes, it was all quite last-minute, really. Would you happen to know where the Stoli Bar is?"

"Certainly, west side of the hall in the north corner. Under the disco ball, I believe. I would love to join you for a drink, if you have the time."

"I'm so sorry, I'm already late for a meeting, but perhaps we can schedule a dinner while I'm in town?" Gordon offered, as he handed Bob a business card.

"Yes, certainly. I'll give you a call," Bob replied, doing his best to disguise his obvious disappointment.

"Sounds great. And thanks for stepping in back there."

Gordon departed abruptly, heading toward the northwest corner of the hall. Barchie watched him walk away, with an unmistakable wistful expression.

The convention floor had been transformed into a quasi-nightclub, with dimmed lights, sponsored bars, DJs and dancing girls. Physicists aren't particularly renowned for their moves on the dance floor, so the whole thing had eroded into a bit of a scientific embarrassment, with drunken physicists, hired girls, a seizure-inducing light show and a day-glow DJ blasting bad dub step. The comedic scene allowed Gordon to forget his predicament for a moment and served as reminder of why he never attended convention parties.

As he approached the Stoli bar, he immediately spotted John's men. The first was wearing a black bespoke suit and the other a similar style gray one. It was their tailored attire that gave them away. Every other attendee seemed to be wearing ill-fitting clothing extracted from an early '90s Midwest time capsule. Gordon made eye contact with the black-suited man, who subtly nodded toward the entrance.

On cue, Gordon turned and retraced his path back to the front of the hall. Head down, he focused on his classic coffee-colored saddle shoes, allowing him to avoid any further discussions with admirers and drunken associates.

He tried not to consider the unanswered question he had asked his father in the car, but it kept prying its way back into his already crowded thoughts. Based on his father's hesitation, he knew the answer was "no."

Gordon ached for his mother at that moment. The visceral heart pains he had experienced upon learning of her death returned all at once. The day had touched upon every one of his emotions. It was certainly a departure from his usual cerebral routine. Though daunting, there was something thrilling about it all; he felt his blood coursing through his veins and each breath tunneling through the passageways of his lungs. He felt present and alive.

Gordon left the Expo and headed back in the direction of the Grand Hotel Europe. He never once turned to check on John's men, who followed at a safe distance behind him. His brain was flooded with thoughts of Jurek, Dmitry, John, the journal, the woman on the bus, and of course, his mother and father. How was it possible that less than a week ago he was living an uneventful existence as a college professor? His life suddenly felt unrecognizable.

Lost in thought, the walk to the Grand Hotel Europe seemed to pass by in a mere moment. He walked through the lobby without making eye contact with anyone and boarded the open elevator. A pleasant-looking young woman in a hotel uniform stood just inside the door patiently awaiting its departure. As the elevator doors were about to close a voice called out, "Hold that, please."

The hotel employee held the door and the gentlemen in the black and gray suits both entered the elevator. Gordon noticed that the hotel employee had already pressed the button for his floor, the third.

"What floor?" the woman asked of the two gentlemen.

"Already pressed, guess we're neighbors," the gentleman in the black suit responded, in an unexpectedly thick Southern accent.

The elevator doors closed and the four trapped souls rose to meet their fate.

•••

Six Months Earlier - Undisclosed Location

Dmitry gently swung back and forth, suspended from the heavy chain that hung down from the ceiling. With his arms fully extended above his head and his feet hovering inches above the cement floor, he was in excruciating pain. Filthy and emaciated, he bore no resemblance to his former self.

His captor stood directly in front of him, flanked by a hulking man with a thick chocolate beard and clean-shaven head.

"The answer is simple, Dmitry. The next time you see your wife she'll either be breathing or not. The choice is yours."

"I already told you," Dmitry pleaded, struggling to find the strength to even speak. "My theories failed in the laboratory. My work was shut down by the KGB. I swear to you."

"We believe you are lying to us, Dmitry. We believe it was your little experiment that took out the Institute along with the entire city block."

"I wasn't even working that night. I left early for a dinner with Sarah. You can ask her yourself. Dr. Belikov was alone."

"I'm afraid Sarah is in no condition to be answering questions right now, and Dr. Belikov is dead. Unless you are experiencing some sense of urgency to join him, I would suggest that now is a good time to start cooperating, Dmitry."

"What have you done to Sarah?" Dmitry struggled against the chains, but the resulting swinging motion caused him even greater pain.

"She probably has another few days left before she will die of dehydration. She seems so thirsty," he laughed.

"What is it that you want?" Dmitry asked, slowly feeling his resolve slip away.

"We inherited a device, so to speak. The device is very, very special, but it requires a power source beyond what we are currently capable of supplying. That is where you come in."

"Will I see Sarah if I help you?"

"Sarah will see a glass of water if you help us. How's that for a start?"

"If you let her die, I will never speak. There will be nothing of me left to torture."

"That's very poetic, Dmitry, but I'm afraid you are in no position to be making demands."

His questioner exited the room through the fortified door, allowing it to slam shut in his wake.

The large bearded man spat in Dmitry's face, effortlessly lifting him far above his head. Dmitry's bound hands were unhooked from the chain and he collapsed to the cement floor, where he lay sobbing like a motherless child.

•••

Saint Petersburg, Russia - Grand Hotel Europe

Gordon, Wilkinson's men, and the female hotel employee all exited the elevator together, their destinies inextricably tangled like an ancient Rasta's dreadlock. A palpable feeling of tension clouded the air.

Gordon was at the head of the pack, which only served to heighten his anxiety. He stopped to tie his shoe so that the others were forced to pass him. The woman in the hotel uniform brushed by and continued down the hall, with the man in black following closely at her heels. The man in gray lingered behind Gordon, pretending to check his phone.

After triple-knotting his shoelaces Gordon rose and proceeded to room 305. He pulled out his keycard and inserted it in the digital keypad. As the light flashed green, the man in gray gently pinned Gordon back against the wall, motioned for him to stay put and surged past him into the room. Gordon remained in the hallway, knowing full well that there were FSB agents inside, awaiting his return. As he stood next to the door, he glanced down the hallway and saw the man in black and the hotel employee both disappear around the corner at the far end of the hall. Gordon was alone.

He listened intently for what felt like hours; his room remained silent. Gordon always had difficulty judging the passing of time, especially under stressful conditions where moments seemed to stretch to minutes. He had no idea if he'd been standing against the wall for ten seconds or two hours. On an impulse, he entered the room...his instincts had served him well earlier in the day.

He walked down the narrow unlit corridor that led to the living room. As he reached the halfway point, a jarring thunderous chord sounded from the piano. He reeled back in horror, and every muscle in his body went rigid. The dissonant chord resonated ominously, followed by two loud thuds. Then silence. Gordon inched along as if walking a tightrope strung between the world's tallest buildings.

He tiptoed into the living room. The tiniest sliver of moonlight peeked in through the curtains, barely revealing the two bodies lying on the floor near the grand piano. An unsettling quiet gurgling sound emanated from one of them. Gordon approached the man in gray; the sound was coming from his slit throat, which simultaneously gushed blood and leaked every breath he attempted to inhale.

He looked up at Gordon and used his last moment of life to warn him. "Run," he whispered.

Gordon didn't waste a single moment. He tore back through the living room and down the corridor. As he erupted through the doorway of his suite into the hotel's hallway, he launched into the woman from the elevator, who took flight and violently impacted with the opposite wall. Her limp body crashed to the ground and a snub-nosed pistol flew from her hand. Gordon picked up the gun, a silent Russian MSP, and ran down the hall. He burst through the fire exit door, nearly stumbling over the body. The neck of the man in black was bent at a peculiar angle, and his glazed eyes were wide open and fixed on the ceiling.

Gordon took the fire escape stairs five at a time and reached ground level in what seemed mere seconds. He pushed the fire exit door open and spilled directly out onto the snow-covered sidewalk. He looked down the street in both directions. The now-waning snowstorm had carpeted the entire city in a foot and a half of pristine snow. He found a misplaced moment of serenity in the virginal white landscape. The stillness. His mind wandered and he imagined liquid nitrogen frozen pumpkins falling to the ground in slow motion, releasing the most perfect of triboluminescent sparks. His ringing phone reeled him back to the chaos.

"Gordon?" It was his father.

"They're all dead." The tension, fear and anxiety coursing through his veins decayed as quickly as the sound of his voice. Fatigue hit him like a Joe Louis right cross to the jaw. Suddenly, his legs felt leaden and incapable of taking another step. The pistol escaped his weakened grasp and fell to the snowy sidewalk. He almost wanted it to all end, right here, right now.

"Gordon, stay with me. There should be a taxi parked about a hundred yards due east of the hotel entrance. Do you see it?"

"Yes." It was the only taxi on the street.

"Get in it. The driver knows where to go. When this call ends, remove the battery and destroy your phone."

"Will I see you again?"

The line went dead.

CHAPTER ELEVEN

The Pyramid

North Hollywood, CA - Crisp Residence

FLETCHER STRUGGLED, RED-FACED, dangling from a chin-up bar mounted in the entranceway to his modestly-sized living room. He had already done eighteen pull-ups, but he considered his morning a failure if he didn't make it to twenty-five. He managed to get through nineteen, twenty and twenty-one, before the computer alert chimed. He swung off the bar, walked down the short hallway and entered his office. A blinking green cursor awaited his response.

> t<<veritas 22>>
> f<<veritas 103>>
> m<<pyramid is coated with a nanomesh coating which appears to alter electromagnetic radiation incident on the pyramid. the coating is made of carbon nanotubes with a length equal to the wavelength of the electromagnetic radiation incident on the pyramid. exhibits capability to alter electromagnetic radiation, including mitigating, intensifying, or absorbing and re-transmitting electromagnetic radiation. united states origins. running more tests. will inform.>>

Fletcher re-read the message more than once, hoping that it would eventually start to make some sense, but his mind never really progressed past the word 'nanomesh.' Googling the word led him directly to its Wikipedia page:

> The **nanomesh** is a new inorganic nanostructured two-dimensional material, similar to graphene. It was discovered in 2003 at the University of Zurich, Switzerland.
>
> It consists of a single layer of boron (B) and nitrogen (N) atoms, which forms by self-assembly a highly regular mesh after high-temperature exposure of a clean rhodium[1] or ruthenium[2] surface to borazine under ultra-high vacuum.

And so on...

It was even more confusing than the message from Veritas 22. Fletcher resigned himself to the fact that the subject matter simply extended beyond his rather rudimentary grasp of the sciences. It made him think of Jane. If she was here, she would surely be able to explain all of this to him in a manner he would understand.

Her patience had been extraordinary.

Fletcher recalled the night they met – it was August 23, 1985 at the Horse and Carriage, an expat pub in Sherman Oaks, California. He was visiting the U.S., interviewing with private security firms. His shattered femur forced him out of the British SAS on disability, and he was seeking a cushy job in the States, where the girls were prettier, the summers longer, and the pay higher. It was his last night in LA and he had arranged to meet a few mates along with some California blondes they had charmed at the beach earlier in the week. The drinking began in earnest early in the evening and they were all fully intoxicated by sunset.

Jane was enjoying the last of her summer break with a few collegiate, intellectual types at a nearby table, when Fletcher's stopgap girlfriend began to gag in an attempt to hold back a fountain of vomit. Fletcher, his mates and the other girls were in no state to care for anyone beyond themselves. Jane, ever kind-spirited, escorted the girl (whose name Fletcher couldn't even recall) to the bathroom, where she proceeded to throw up at least a half dozen times. Jane stayed with her the entire time, offering reassuring words as she held back the girl's long blonde locks.

When they finally re-emerged from the bathroom, Fletcher was the only remaining member of his party. Jane said goodbye to her friends, who all looked at her like she had lost her mind, then offered to drive both the drunken girl and the car-less Fletcher to their respective destinations.

Fletcher had sobered up quickly. He carried his blonde friend to Jane's car, a timeworn Toyota Corolla, parked a short distance from the pub. He and Jane engaged in some pleasant chit-chat and soon discovered they were both leaving town the following day, Jane to resume her studies at Cal Berkeley and Fletcher to return to England. Fletcher Sherlock-ed his semi-conscious blonde friend's home address by rifling through her purse and extracting her California driver's license. *Candy Goldman. Not even twenty-one.* As they pulled up to a new-money mansion in the hills of Encino, Fletcher realized he would have to face Candy's parents.

Jane could see his mounting concern. "Why don't you just let me walk her to the door?"

"Do I look that frightened of Mr. --" Fletcher gazed down at the girl's last name, "Goldman?"

"Frankly, yes."

"How about you pretend to be my girlfriend and we can just be a couple of good Samaritans from the pub?" Fletcher offered.

"Unlikely, but we can give it a shot."

They knocked on the massive door, with Candy draped between them. Much to Fletcher's relief, her mother answered. She thanked them profusely and invited them in for a cup of coffee. Fletcher and Jane politely declined, opting to escape while luck was still on their side.

They returned to the car. It was just the two of them now. The odd circumstances had cemented a quick bond between them and the conversation flowed. As Jane pulled up outside the apartment where Fletcher was staying, she had the strange urge to just drive away with him and never look back. Instead, they sat in her car, talking for hours.

Jane learned that Fletcher liked pubs, rugby, football, mountain climbing, flying helis, and Clint Eastwood movies, while she preferred the more refined symphonies, theater, tennis, chess, and Woody Allen films. It appeared they had nothing in common, yet their attraction was unmistakable. Jane pulled away from the front of the apartment four hours later at two a.m., not knowing if she would ever see him again.

She tossed and turned the rest of the night, regretting that she hadn't been more forward with Fletcher. They had exchanged addresses, but how likely was it that they would become pen pals? It sounded stupid even considering it. After about four hours of sleep, she peeled her eyes open, made a strong pot of coffee and finished packing her things for Berkeley. Her father dropped her off at LAX and she made her way to Terminal 3, Gate 13. An hour early, she sat and studied a chapter from one of her biology textbooks.

"Jane Meyer, please report to the desk at Gate 13."

Jane looked up from her book. She couldn't quite believe her eyes. Fletcher was standing at the Gate 13 desk scanning the room. As their eyes met, they both started laughing. She left her things at her seat and just barely held herself back from running directly into his arms. *That would be silly, right?*

He met her halfway.

"Shouldn't you be in the International Terminal?" Jane asked, hardly able to contain her excitement.

"Technically, yes. But I missed my flight."

"What happened?"

"Well, I just spent the last two hours running through Terminal 1 and Terminal 2 trying to track you down. You forgot something."

"What?" Jane couldn't imagine what he could have been referring to.

"This." Fletcher gently placed his hands on either side of her face and kissed her unsuspecting lips. It was the most perfectly romantic thing that had ever happened to her. She wanted to scream with joy. One kiss turned into two, which turned into three and before long, the whole terminal was cheering them on.

Fletcher cleared the memory from his mind with a quick shake of his head. He knew where that kind of thinking led, and it ended at the bottom of a bottle followed by a week of not wanting to get out of bed. Many years ago he'd promised Harper that he would not allow himself to engage in such self-destructive behavior anymore. Occasionally he faltered, but a man like Fletcher needed to drink his demons away every now and then.

He looked back at the blinking green cursor. *Best leave this one to Harper.* He returned to his pull-up bar, where he continued his morning routine...twenty-two, twenty-three, twenty-four, twenty-five.

•••

Fatino, Russia - Farmhouse

Gordon and the taxi driver had not spoken during their nine-hour journey. What had started as an awkward silence became their natural state. Gordon felt certain that spoken words would merely bounce off the impenetrable barrier that had grown between them. He had little desire to test the theory.

The silence allowed Gordon an hour or two of light sleep, followed by hours of heavy reflection. It seemed that every stray thought led back to his mother. His gut told him she was dead. Even without knowing the circumstances, he blamed his father for her death. Why was he the one who survived?

The world sailed by, an endless blanket of white, broken by snow-covered trees and the odd house. After nine hours of traveling south on the M10, they were deeply ensconced in the Russian countryside. Finally, the driver exited the freeway and turned up a freshly-plowed narrow dirt road. Gordon was hungry, tired and confused. He hoped his father would be waiting at their destination. He needed answers.

As the car reached the crest of the sloping hill, an old farmhouse came into view. The taxi stopped a few feet short of the front door. The driver remained in his seat with the engine running and his eyes locked on the house. Gordon assumed this was his cue to exit. He stepped out into the bitter early morning air, which involuntarily stole his first breath. He made his way along a freshly shoveled path to the front door and knocked. Footsteps approached, deliberate and sure.

The front door opened. It was his father.

"Son." the General pulled Gordon through the door and held him in a tight embrace. An unspoken understanding bound them -- someone was missing from this reunion. Gordon tried desperately to hold back the tears, but it was a battle not easily won.

The General released Gordon and stepped back to take a proper look at him. There was no mistaking the adoration he felt for his son.

"I'm so proud of you, Gordon." The General pulled a handkerchief from his pocket and wiped away the tears that silently streamed down Gordon's face.

Gordon had been waiting his whole life to hear those words spoken by his father. Their absence had driven him to succeed.

"I guess you know I have some questions?"

"And I'm ready for them all. Come have a seat." His father led him to a long wooden table with communal bench style seating. Gordon took a place opposite his father and looked around the small rustic farmhouse. An antique wood stove in the open-style living room threw off a hospitable warm glow. A worn sofa, an armchair and a few scattered side tables and shelves completed the minimalist furnishings.

The General poured two shots of Peter the Great's Zarskaya vodka. Gordon raised his glass.

"Budem zdorovy," the General said as their glasses clinked.

"I didn't know you speak Russian."

The General poured two more shots. "When in Rome."

"Tell me about Mom. Everything."

The General took a mournful deep breath as if he were about to relive the dreaded moment. "We were heading out to

Uncle Mike's for Christmas. Mom looked beautiful, she had on that red dress she loved so much. There was a car pulled over on the side of the road just before you cross the Colorado River heading into California...on the I-40. The driver was a man, about forty-five years old...he flagged us down. He was dressed in business attire...I didn't even think twice about whether to stop or not. I pulled over, told Mom to wait in the car and I got out to help him. I walked over to his car and he seemed friendly enough. He said his radiator had overheated and asked if I had any water or coolant. I bent over the car engine to take a look, and that was the last I remember until I woke up sitting in the driver's seat of my car...in the river." The General swallowed hard. He had little experience recounting the tale, and even three years later it still felt raw.

"Was Mom next to you...when you woke up?" Gordon reached across the table and placed his hand on his father's arm. It was a small gesture, but it helped his father continue.

"No...she was gone. I came to and the car was fully submerged and filling up with water rapidly. Your mom's window was rolled down and she was gone. I undid my seatbelt and tried opening my door and window, but they were both jammed, so I swam out the open window on her side. The water was murky, like swimming through pea soup, but I just kept at it." The General poured himself yet another shot and threw it down. "We had just had some bad storms, so the river was flowing fast and it was cold. I kept looking for her, but I was drifting with the current and I couldn't see a thing. I swear I looked for hours and I damn near died of hypothermia." The General looked to Gordon for a sign of approval.

"Mom couldn't have been in any better hands."

"That's not the whole story, Gordon." The General hung his head.

"What do you mean?"

"I mean, I knew something was up. I stumbled upon something at work that I wasn't supposed to see. Nobody was supposed to see it. Nobody. It was unthinkable." The General shook his head. "I didn't know what to do and I brought it to the attention of the wrong guy. He told me to forget about it, but I guess he could sense that was just not going to happen. Everything took a turn there. I was followed. I'm pretty sure they were keeping tabs on Mom too. I never told her. I never should have told anyone. She'd be here today. It's my fault."

"What was it, Dad?"

"Almost four years ago, I discovered that a cabal within our federal government was planning a dirty bomb attack on the Qualcomm Stadium on Super Bowl Sunday. The fingerprint on the bomb was going to point to Iran. I'm assuming the plan was to use that intel as a pretext to go to war."

"Dad, you know I would never doubt your word, but that's a serious accusation. The U.S. government killing its own citizens?" Gordon had never been a political guy. He came from a long line of Republicans, but chose to register as an Independent and embarrassingly, hadn't even bothered to vote in the last election. Despite his disinterest in politics, growing up on a military base had given him a heightened sense of patriotism. The scenario his father had just related to him seemed unimaginable.

"Believe me, it's not something I ever expected to see. I spent my whole life working to protect the citizens of the United States and then I find that a contingent within our own government is planning to kill them?"

"Why didn't you tell Mom?"

"Because your mom was too good and too trusting. Hearing something like that would have destroyed her entire belief system…I suppose it did anyway."

Gordon rose from the bench, rounded the table and took a seat next to his father. He pulled his father's head to his chest. The General collapsed. The pain he had suppressed for years surfaced. Gordon had never seen his father like this. An emotionally repellent man, the General, was now sobbing in his arms. It was an odd feeling, a child consoling a parent.

After a prolonged embrace, the General pulled away, hanging his head in shame. Crying with both poise and grace required practice -- something he had little of. The General sniffled as he roughly wiped away the tears on his shirt sleeve.

Gordon did his best to overlook the emotional outburst, aimlessly glancing around the room. It seemed the noble thing to do. "So Dad, where have you been all this time?"

"A better question is, where haven't I been? I went to Mexico for a while after the incident. I anonymously alerted the FBI to the Super Bowl suitcase nuke and I supplied just enough intel to be taken seriously. Security was so tight by the time the Bowl came around, you couldn't get a pocket knife past security. I've spent every waking moment looking for Mom and hunting down the men responsible for her death…I've watched your life unfold from afar. I just want you to know that you've given me my only moments of joy and pride over the past three years. I'm so proud of you, and you know how proud Mom would have been."

The General lifted his bleary-eyed gaze, seeking his son's affirmation. Gordon simply offered a quick nod. His head was a befogged mess of emotions and questions. It was as if his mouth was a tiny door that simply couldn't accommodate the deluge of sentences waiting to exit. The room fell into a clumsy silence, eventually broken by the General.

"Son?"

"Sorry. It's a lot to absorb -- Mom, the Super Bowl, the government. So what is this mess I got myself wrapped up in?"

"It runs deep. My investigation led me to an organization called Veritas Bellum. I found we had mutual interests. The disappearance of Dmitry Zolkin and his wife Sarah popped up on our radar almost immediately. Veritas has a long history of exposing suspicious deaths and disappearances of prominent scientists and Dr. Zolkin certainly fit the profile. You made the association between Zolkin and the Dust, West Virginia disappearance for us. It wasn't something that anyone else had connected. We assumed Zolkin was killed after he discontinued his work at the Central Investigation Institute for Special Technology. Once FSB, always FSB."

"Can I trust John?"

"John is a pawn who thinks he's a king. He's stuck in the middle of a much bigger battle that he knows nothing about."

"Is that a 'no'?"

"It's a 'don't trust pawns'...or kings, for that matter."

"Do you have the journal here, Dad?"

The General rose from the bench and walked over to a small side table next to a tattered old armchair. He opened the top drawer and pulled out Dmitry's journal and a typed translation. "The original in Russian, and a translation."

Gordon began to read.

•••

The Year 1986 - Russia

On April 26, 1986, the Chernobyl nuclear power plant's reactor number four suffered a catastrophic power increase, leading to explosions in its core, which released large quantities of radioactive contamination into the atmosphere, spreading over much of the western Soviet Union and Europe. Nuclear scientists had previously assured Gorbachev and Soviet leadership that their nuclear reactors were completely safe, leading to finger pointing and a general distrust in the technology. The KGB was tasked with collecting the best minds in the USSR and directing their energies toward solving their country's looming power crisis. The KGB plucked the leading scientists from the Moscow Institute of Physics and Technology, Moscow Power Engineering Institute, Moscow State University, Tomsk Polytechnic University and Saint Petersburg University.

Dr. Dmitry Zoltov's name appeared very near the top of the recruitment list. He had been a professor at Saint Petersburg State University in the physics department for six years, and his polarizing theoretical work was widely known. Due to the unyielding demands of Soviet leadership, the post-Chernobyl recruitment process was actually a compulsory enlistment. "No" simply wasn't an option and before long, Dmitry was conducting his research out of the Saint Petersburg branch of the KGB's Central Investigation Institute for Special Technology. Dmitry was quite familiar with Sarah's disdain for the KGB and he made the difficult choice to withhold the details of his involvement from her.

His teaching schedule was cut in half to just two morning classes and his afternoons and evenings were spent at his new research lab, #22, at the Institute. The KGB's willingness to cater to his every whim and desire appealed to Dmitry's hungry ego. It was a research scientist's dream.

His Dusha experiments began at a very basic level. He believed that every living creature had a soul, so he started small. Hundreds of mice entered Dmitry's laboratory alive and left dead over the course of those first few months. Fellow researchers at the Institute, who already thought Dmitry's work odd, referred to him as the "The Grim Squeaker" due to the high volume of mouse corpses produced by his research.

Those doomed mice were connected to every machine, probe, wire, contraption and gadget both known and unknown to man. Ultimately, their means of execution was a 150 mg/kg dose of sodium pentobarbital and they spent the last five minutes of their lives slowly slipping into a coma-like state, followed by a quiet death. All in the name of science, or at least that's what Dmitry kept telling himself.

As a physicist, Dmitry had spent very little time working with creatures, whether living or deceased, and playing the role of executioner, combined with the lack of positive results, began to wear him down. His remedy was vodka and his self-prescribed dosage was high.

Sarah saw the signs immediately. It was so unlike Dmitry to lose his patience with her. When she confronted him one evening, he completely broke down and told her everything. At first she could barely contain her furor. How could he lie to her about something like this? Her feelings of anger and betrayal soon gave way to reason, when she realized he had little choice but to work with the KGB. She made him vow to never withhold anything from her again, no matter the perceived consequence.

Coming clean with Sarah lifted a huge weight from Dmitry's shoulders and offered him a fresh perspective on his research. He began experimenting with a modified version of Kirlian photography, a technique that had been around since the late 1930s, when Russian engineer Semyon Kirlian accidentally discovered this particular phenomenon in his lab. In Kirlian photography, the subject is in direct contact with a film placed upon a charged metal plate. The resulting photograph depicts the subject's bioenergy or aura, which presents itself as a fuzzy glow around the subject. In one famous experiment, a section of a leaf was torn away after the first photograph was taken, and a faint image of the missing section remained when a second photograph was taken -- almost as if the soul, or Dusha, of a living thing outlived its own shell.

Dmitry developed a high-speed version of electrophotography in order to determine the exact time Dusha left the body upon death. The mice in the experiments were outfitted with a wireless device called a Neuroprobe, which measured their brain activity in real-time. After the sodium pentobarbital was administered, the mice generally succumbed within five minutes. Dmitry considered their clinical death to be at the moment they ceased to have brain activity. Combining the electrophotography with the Neuroprobe data proved to Dmitry that there was a distinct change in the mice's auras when photographed before and immediately after death. Interestingly, he found that the shift in aura occurred at exactly 0.33 seconds before brain activity flatlined, in 99% of the mice. Dmitry considered this shift to be the result of the soul departing the body and believed it may help explain near-death experiences.

The 0.33-second time discrepancy, in which the body continued living beyond the presence of the soul, fascinated Dmitry. Were the soul and the brain still in communication during that third of a second? Dmitry was not a religious man, but a spiritual one, yes, clearly...perhaps what appeared to be 0.33 seconds here on Earth was really an eternity for the soul? What if in that fraction of a second, the soul as a separate entity still had access to all of the memories stored within the human shell? Those who lived to love would be eternally rewarded with the beautiful memories of their lives, while those who dwelled in states of hate, fear and envy would be subject to reliving those experiences for eternity. *Heaven and Hell.*

Still, none of this explained where the Dusha went upon death. The spiritual implications were powerful, but did not represent the type of power the KGB was interested in. They demanded results and decided that Dmitry had had enough time "playing" with mice.

On one unseasonably cold, clear, sunny day in July, Dmitry cycled from his office in the department of physics at Saint Petersburg State University to his lab at the Institute. By this point he knew all of the security guards very well and had established the friendly shorthand chit-chat, as one does over time. But after an icy reception from Vlad, the security guard on duty, he knew something was wrong. He dared to hope -- *perhaps Vlad is just having a bad morning?*

As Dmitry walked down the hall to his lab, he realized his fellow scientists' lab doors were all closed. *Odd.* Like Dmitry, most of the scientists were not there by choice, and worked long hours on highly experimental work that was often tedious and unfruitful. An open door to a lab was an invitation for passers-by to come in and break the tedium, if just for a moment. There were always at least one or two open at any given moment.

As Dmitry inserted the key in the door to his lab, he found it was already unlocked. *Strange.* He pushed open the door to discover he was not alone.

"Ah, Dr. Zoltov. I hope you don't mind I let myself in? My name is Grigori Vasilevich." Wearing all black, Grigori stood six foot four, with a jaw and body both apparently carved from cold steel.

"What can I do for you, Mr. Vasilevich?"

"Grigori, please." Grigori walked around the lab handling objects and shifting papers around as if he owned the place. "Your research has caught the eye of one of my comrades. Like you, he is also a doctor. He wishes to facilitate your research and can provide you with a supply of human volunteers for your studies."

"Sir, it would be highly unethical and inhumane to conduct my studies on humans."

"Ethics and humanity are luxuries we cannot afford. These men have a debt to pay to society and you will simply be collecting it." Grigori stopped directly in front of Dmitry, uncomfortably close.

Dmitry looked directly into Grigori's lifeless gray eyes. "What if I don't wish to proceed?"

"I think your wife -- Sarah, is it? I think it would be a shame if she were to drown. She does seem to love writing on that park bench along the Neva. In fact, I thought I saw her there this morning."

"I see." Dmitry knew this fight had only one possible winner.

"Your first specimen will be waiting for you here tomorrow, accompanied by Dr. Belikov, of course."

Dmitry's heart sank. Belikov was more commonly known as "Dr. Toxin." The Soviet Poison Lab was Belikov's hospital and his survival rates hovered around zero percent. Belikov was known to be a brilliant, ruthless man, and if Dmitry was forced to work with him, he felt certain he would have no choice but to do as he was told.

Dmitry returned home that evening and anxiously recounted the turn of events to Sarah. She begged him to leave Russia with her while they still could, but he knew it was already too late for that. The KGB would find them no matter where they might travel. He assured her they would both be fine if he simply cooperated. So he did.

Belikov greeted him the following morning and each morning after that -- until the incident.

Dmitry's initial impressions of Belikov were surprisingly positive. He was a delicate man with fine features, a gentle voice, a warm smile and a spectacular bedside manner. Every man who rolled into Lab 22 on a hospital gurney knew he would not roll out alive, yet under Belikov's care, they remained calm throughout the process. Dmitry wanted to hate Belikov, but he just couldn't. The man was brilliant, kind and cultured. Dmitry's initial feelings of horror at the thought of conducting research on humans slowly evaporated into acceptance. The first few deaths were difficult to watch, but he soon became accustomed to death's constant presence, which lingered like an unwanted guest at the end of a party. The human mind is funny that way. No matter the horror, one can only be shocked a handful of times before the numbing begins.

With the addition of an equally brilliant counterpart to help elucidate his many theories, Dmitry's Dusha studies progressed rapidly. The comparatively rudimentary Kirlian photography and EEGs were surpassed and replaced by theoretical work in quantum physics and Dusha traps. Their early experimentation suggested that Dusha might possess similar energy potential to and characteristics of anti-matter, but anti-matter was little understood and posed unique challenges itself.

When the electrons, protons and neutrons of which our universe is composed were created, many of their anti-twins, or positrons, antiprotons and antineutrons, were also made. In theory, a galaxy like ours -- but composed entirely of anti-matter -- could have evolved elsewhere in our vast universe. Our anti-twin. But when matter and anti-matter meet, they completely destroy each other, leaving behind the pure energy they were composed of. Physicists refer to this as "annihilation." The reaction of just half a gram of antimatter with half a gram of matter would produce a level of destruction equal to the Hiroshima bomb. But unlike anti-matter, Dusha did not react with other matter. Dmitry and Belikov believed that Dusha was self-reactive. Dmitry estimated the amount of Dusha released by a single person upon death was approximately one-tenth of a gram, far less than the Hiroshima bomb, but enough to power a thousand Russian homes for an entire year. A solution to Russia's looming energy crisis.

Dmitry designed a quantum trap or "bottle" in which the subjects could be encased just before their death, the theory being that the field within the "bottle" would isolate the elusive Dusha and allow for its containment.

Belikov and Dmitry's experiments continued. Dozens of men passed through the "bottle," with no success.

One evening, volunteer 134 was injected with the usual dosage of sodium pentobarbital. The typical time of death always rested somewhere between five to ten minutes, but volunteer 134 kept hanging on. The procedure for powering up the "bottle" was complicated and time-consuming, so rather than removing volunteer 134 and injecting him with a higher dose, Dmitry and Belikov decided to wait it out. After all, volunteer 134's vital signs were diminishing and in theory it shouldn't have taken much longer. Yet one hour later, volunteer 134's heart was still beating.

Dmitry had plans to take Sarah out that evening for a special dinner to celebrate the publication of her second novel, *Gossamer Threads*. Belikov had a stack of paperwork to attend to, so he ordered Dmitry to go home and enjoy the evening with his beautiful wife. Dmitry left at 7:15. At 7:36, in a series of ear-deafening blasts accompanied by a blinding blue light, the Institute blew up, leaving thirty-eight presumed dead and an entire block of Saint Petersburg cratered. One might even describe the scene as a complete annihilation. Of the thirty-eight missing people, not a single body was found.

With the recent disaster at Chernobyl, the Soviets could not weather the kind of scrutiny this incident was sure to bring. The KGB research program at the Institute was terminated the following morning.

•••

Fatino, Russia - Farmhouse

Gordon looked up from the last page of the translated printout of Dmitry's journal, which ended abruptly with the Saint Petersburg explosion. It was hardly a smoking gun.

Instinctively, Gordon wondered if Dmitry knew something about volunteer 134 that he hadn't documented. *Had the trap worked on volunteer #134? Had his Dusha leveled an entire city block?* It was a possibility, but Gordon was a scientist and science required definitive proof.

Gordon set the printout down on the small side table next to the threadbare armchair. He sat back and allowed his eyes to shut for a moment. In one short week, his life had turned upside down. It was a lot to take in for a guy who liked to wear the same tie, shirt, jacket and pants every day. He had narrowly escaped an assassination by the FSB and was now entrenched in no man's land between the U.S. government and an intellectual truth movement. Gordon longed to sit behind his desk at Caltech where answers always came easily -- but it was too late for all that now.

He rose from the armchair and returned to the kitchen table where he found his father, still drinking.

"Don't you think you've had enough?" Gordon took the liter of vodka from his Father's hands. *It's an odd feeling, parenting one's parent.*

"I've had enough for the past three years, but that hasn't stopped me yet." The General's speech was slurred and his exaggerated arm movements looked like those of a mad conductor. It was another first for Gordon, seeing his father in this state. He had known the man to have an occasional scotch now and then, but it never seemed to affect him. This was ugly. In the past three hours, his father had become far too human and far too fallible.

"Believe me, Dad, I'd join you if I though we could drink this colossal mess under the table, but we've got some work to do if we're going to win this truth war of yours." Gordon walked over to the kitchen sink and filled a tall glass with water. "Drink this."

The General emptied the glass and slammed it down on the table as if he had just completed some kind of juvenile drinking challenge.

"Dad, I could really use you right now. I feel a little lost in all this and I don't really know where to begin," Gordon pleaded as he took a seat next to his Father.

"You're a better man than me, Gordon."

"Dad-"

"No, it's true. I've known it since you were a little boy. Your mom knew it too. She deserves all the credit; I was never there, and when I was, I didn't give you what you needed."

"Okay. Here's the deal, Dad. We're going to cut this pity party short, you're going to take a cold shower and have a few cups of coffee before we get to work. Got it?" Gordon rose from the bench and pulled his father up with him. "Go hit the shower. I'll have coffee waiting for you. Go." Gordon gently shoved him in the direction of the bathroom. It felt good to be the one giving orders for a change.

Gordon rummaged through an old pine cupboard in the kitchen and found a couple of mugs. A dusty coffeemaker rested on the counter. Gordon removed the pot and gave it a quick rinse. He filled the reservoir and replaced the pot in the cradle. *Coffee, where are you hiding?* He found a tin of Maxwell House in the freezer. *Seriously, Maxwell House? This is what we're exporting to the Russians? No wonder they hate us.* Gordon dumped half the tin in the top of the machine and flipped the switch.

The sound of the shower stopped after two short minutes. Navy shower. Once a soldier, always a soldier.

The General appeared back in the kitchen, looking better than when he left.

"Sorry, Gordon. Seeing you brings your mom back."

"No apology necessary, Dad. Seeing you brings *you* back, and for that I am thankful." Gordon poured his father a mug of coffee. He looked in the fridge for some milk or cream, but only found vodka, smoked salmon and caviar.

He handed his father the mug. "Looks like we need to do some grocery shopping."

"I'll pick up some things later. I'm afraid you won't be going out to do much of anything." The General opened his laptop and navigated to the *Saint Petersburg Times* website.

Gordon took a seat next to his father and looked at the screen. His Nobel Prize publicity photo stared back at him from the front page.

FOUR DIE IN TRAGIC HOTEL FIRE - US. NOBEL
LAUREATE AMONG DEAD
By Alex Telkin
The Saint Petersburg Times
Published: November 6, 2015 (Issue # 1784)

U.S. Nobel Laureate wunderkind, Dr. Gordon B. Gray,
23, was one of four victims believed to have perished in a
tragic fire late Thursday evening at the Grand Hotel
Europe. The identities of the other three victims have not
yet been released pending notification of the victims'
families. Dr. Gray was the youngest Nobel Laureate in the
history of the award. The cause of the fire is yet unknown.
This is a developing story, check back for updates.

"Guess we're both dead now." Gordon's weak attempt at
humor failed to disguise his concern. It was a message. He wouldn't
be returning to the U.S. alive, at least if the Russians had any say in
the matter.

"On the bright side, they aren't framing you for the
murders." The General almost smiled.

"Yes, that is good news, I suppose." Well, at least his father
felt well enough to make light of the situation. Gordon rose to pour
himself a cup of coffee. "Won't John demand the body and an
independent investigation?"

"John can demand the keys to the Winter Palace, but he'll
still get whatever the FSB wants to give him. It was a fire, so you're
just a pile of ashes. The Russians are brilliant with this sort of
thing."

"Creating dead bodies?"

"Creating stories around dead bodies." The General walked back to the bathroom and re-emerged carrying a Panadol pill pack. He popped three capsules through the foil, tossed them in his mouth and chased them down with a slug of coffee.

"So what's next?"

"We find Dmitry."

"Does Veritas have any leads?"

"I just learned that we have an object retrieved from the site of the disappearance in West Virginia."

"The pyramid?"

"Yes, how did you know?" the General inquired, surprised.

"We uncovered it in a grid search in the woods surrounding the trailer. Well, actually, we uncovered the location it was in before it was stolen from the crime scene. I believe it acts as a window or perhaps targeting device for whatever weapon caused the dematerialization. Where is it?"

"It was with an associate of yours at Caltech, but it's in a lab in Houston right now."

"Caltech? You have someone at Caltech?"

"Technically, I'm not supposed to know this, but yes, we have a young woman there who is something of a computer whiz. Her father is the one who found the pyramid. He's Ex-SAS."

"And you trust these people."

"With my life."

"Who's the woman at Caltech?" Gordon mentally reviewed the names of the computer department faculty, but drew a blank.

"We make it a point not to know each other's names. I know them as Veritas 103 and Veritas 213."

"What's your number?"

"151."

"Is 007 available?"

The General laughed. It felt like the first time in a long while. "I thought you'd be more the 'pi with a repeating decimal' type."

"It's actually an infinite decimal, Dad, but I appreciate the reference."

"You're the expert. It always mystified your mother and me...your command of math. She barely got through algebra and I can just about count all my fingers and toes."

"I've often wondered, too." Gordon said as he walked over to the kitchen window. He felt an eerie stillness in the air as he gazed at the untouched snow that surrounded them. "Are we okay here, Dad?"

"Well, this is a Veritas safe house, but as you know, safety is relative. You're certainly safer than you were. The next house is two miles away, and people mind their own business down here."

"Do you know of any trips Dmitry and Sarah took right before their disappearance? An associate of mine in Saint Petersburg mentioned something about a trip to the U.S.?"

"Dr. Pyotr Sidorov?"

"How long have you been following me?"

"I never stopped. Pyotr has friends in the FSB. I can't be sure, but I think he's the one who sold you out."

"I've known him since I was a kid, Dad. I find it hard to believe. He knows Dmitry well."

"Maybe a little too well?"

"They were friends. He had dinner with Dmitry a week before he disappeared." Gordon sighed with frustration. "It must be tough not trusting anyone. Hell of a way to live." Gordon grabbed his coat from over the back of the armchair. "I need some fresh air."

"Don't go far."

The old door rattled as it slammed shut behind Gordon.

•••

Houston, Texas - Sidewalk Cafe

Veritas 22 sat outside a nondescript sidewalk cafe nursing a soy latte. Nothing about her appearance particularly stood out, other than the oversized Jackie O sunglasses that seemed to cover half of her petite face. She glanced down at her watch impatiently.

An anxious looking man approached her table, cradling a messenger bag in his arms. Bill Gates looked dangerous, compared to this guy.

"The rain in Spain..." The man's voice crackled with nervous energy, almost collapsing in on itself.

Veritas 22 looked up from her latte and completed his phrase: "Tastes better than champagne." She gestured for him to take the empty seat opposite her.

"Phew, I was worried you weren't the right person and I was going to look like a total jackass. I've never even seen *My Fair Lady*," he said, settling in.

"A fine film." Veritas 22 sensed the man's anxiety and extended a warm smile to calm him.

"So, do you just want me to tell you what I know? How does this work?" Clearly not a conversationalist.

"Yes, that would be great."

"The nanomesh is mine...well, in the sense that it bears the signature of my research. My work is in cloaking. This particular nanomesh disguises whatever's beneath the coating from x-ray. I'm working on a variant that will also be invisible to the human eye. We've had some success testing in water, but I still have --"

Veritas 22 interrupted him mid-sentence. "That sounds fascinating. Do you mind if I ask you a few questions?"

"Not at all, go ahead," he replied with a newfound confidence. Talking about his work instantly set him at ease. Bolstered, he eyed Veritas 22 like a side of beef in a butcher's display. *Not bad. Dinner, maybe?*

"Do you have any idea what the object might be capable of?"

"No. It seems to have...well...gone quiet, if you will. I'm getting nothing from it. Perhaps a single-use application? The pyramid shell is made of lonsdaleite. Harder than diamonds and it comes from space...meteors. There's a deposit at the Diablo Canyon Crater in Arizona, but the main haul of lonsdaleite came from Tunguska in Russia. You know, the Tunguska event?"

"Yes, I am quite familiar with it."

In fact, it had been something of an obsession of Veritas 22's in her younger days. She had always been intrigued by the mystery surrounding the Tunguska event. At 7:14 a.m. on June 30, 1908, an enormously powerful explosion occurred near the Podkamennaya Tunguska River in what is now Krasnoyarsk Krai, Russia. Russian settlers in the hills northwest of Lake Baikal described seeing a column of blueish light, nearly as bright as the sun, moving across the sky. About ten minutes later, there was a flash in the sky followed by sounds similar to artillery fire. The sounds were accompanied by a shock wave that knocked people off their feet and shattered windows hundreds of miles away -- the explosion typically referred to as the Tunguska event. Most scientists believe it was caused by an asteroid that entered Earth's atmosphere at about 33,500 miles per hour. During its quick plunge, the 220-million-pound space rock heated the air surrounding it to 44,500 degrees Fahrenheit. At a height of about 28,000 feet, the combination of pressure and heat caused the asteroid to fragment and annihilate itself, producing a fireball and releasing energy equivalent to about one hundred and eighty-five Hiroshima bombs. Other theories suggested the involvement of aliens, anti-matter, black holes or Nikola Tesla, but carried little credence within the scientific community.

"Who would have access to your nanomesh research?"

"Anyone who subscribes to the *Journal of Nano Letters*. I published last year. They would need access to the proper facilities and equipment to produce the same results, of course."

"Naturally. Okay, well, thank you for your time. You've been very helpful. You can leave the bag on your chair."

The scientist had hoped to continue the conversation and perhaps inquire about Veritas 22's dinner plans, but her premature dismissal caught him off-guard and he reverted back to his initial nervous state. "Umm....yea, sure no problem. Okay...bye." He made a swift exit.

Veritas 22 called after him, "The bag."

The man returned and left the messenger bag sitting on the chair next to her.

"Sorry about that." He waved awkwardly, and departed.

Veritas 22 picked up the bag from the chair and verified its contents.

The pyramid was right where it needed to be.

•••

Houston, Texas - Motel

Veritas 22 logged on to Blacknet and typed the following message to both General Thomas B. Gray and Fletcher Crisp:

t<<veritas 103, 151>>
f<<veritas 22>>
m<< nanomesh is a dead end. pyramid is made of lonsdaleite. two main sources: tunguska event in

krasnoyarsk krai, russia and diablo canyon crater in arizona. seeking info on collectors.>>

She read the message over once before pressing return. Veritas 22 rose from behind the motel desk and walked over to the king-size bed in the middle of the room. She lay back on the far left side of the bed and stared up at the whirring ceiling fan. Out of old habit, she reached her arm over to the right side of the bed, but there was no one there. She closed her eyes and dozed off.

CHAPTER TWELVE

Escape

Fatino, Russia - Farmhouse

THE GENERAL WAS concerned. He wanted to give his son space, but too much time had lapsed and he knew Gordon was ill-equipped for the sub-zero temperatures. He grabbed his anorak from the back bedroom and walked outside. The previous day's snowstorm had left a perfect white canvas and the crisp air smelled as fresh as line dried sheets. The General wasn't much for moments, but he appreciated the stark beauty of this one.

Tracking Gordon in these conditions was easy; there was one set of footprints heading out and none returning. It appeared that Gordon had ventured out back toward the woods that flanked the east side of the property. The General made a note to get Gordon a pair of boots, as the footprints in the snow indicated he was still wearing a dress shoe. *In fact, the kid needs a new wardrobe altogether.*

The crunchiness of the freshly fallen snow underfoot resonated all the way up through his bones to his teeth. It almost tickled. As the General looked toward the tree line, a beautiful ten-point buck emerged from the woods and stopped about a hundred yards in front of him. It brought to mind Christmas, a day that had been marked by self-loathing and pity for the past three years.

Perhaps he and Gordon would be able to spend it together this year?

A brittle branch snapped under the weight of the General's foot as he moved forward, frightening the buck who tore off across the wide open field. Gradually, Gordon's outline emerged through the trees in the distance. The General called out to him.

"Gordon!"

Gordon turned toward the sound of his father's voice. His feet and hands were numb and wet, and he felt idiotic for storming off like a child. *Still can't face your problems.* Over the years, more than a few women had pointed out this flaw to him.

Gordon waved. "Over here."

The General waved back. It made Gordon feel even more ridiculous. His first few hours back with his father and he had already reverted to old childish behavior. His father had been through a great deal. Who was he to question his judgment? Maybe Pyotr was FSB. He certainly always seemed to have access to more money than most scientists Gordon had dealt with. His father had just been trying to protect him. He owed him an apology.

The General continued walking toward his son. He loved that Gordon had inherited his wife's fiery temper and Irish eyes. He tried to put himself in his son's shoes: one minute, he was sitting pretty behind a cozy desk in California, the next he was in the middle of a triple homicide in Russia. Add in a reunion with your dead father, and you've got a hell of a week. He had always been too tough on Gordon, even as a boy. *Not many people get a second chance*, the General reminded himself. He vowed to change. He placed each of his footsteps in the exact prints left by his son, not exactly walking in someone's shoes, but nonetheless a step in the right direction. His untied bootlace caught his eye. As the General paused to tie it, a perfect silence embraced him.

Gordon neared the very edge of the tree line. He could see clouds of breath rise above his father, who appeared to be tying his boot.

Suddenly, a booming gunshot shattered the silence. A flock of birds soared up from their nearby roosts, startling Gordon. Panicked, he looked over to his father who was still posed in a crouched position. *Just a hunter.*

"Dad?" he called out expectantly.

The answer was not what he had hoped for. The General's limp body collapsed into the blanket of snow, revealing a blood-splattered canvas.

Gordon's heart pounded and his breaths shortened. He looked in the direction of the gunfire. No sign of a shooter for what seemed miles.

Gordon fought his instinct to flee and ran directly for his father, fully realizing that he would be the next target. As he neared, Gordon could clearly see the fatal wound, a clean shot through the middle of the forehead, which exited through a gaping hole in the back of his Father's skull. There was no need to check for a pulse.

A second shot rang out. Gordon felt a scorching heat on the side of his face. Reflexively, his hand touched his cheek. It was wet with blood. He assumed he would meet the same fate as his father. It seemed appropriate that they should die side by side in this field together. He waited for it all to end, but rather than collapsing to the ground, he remained upright. *Final reflexes? The soul's last stand?* He reached up to his face again and felt a deep gash across the side of his cheek. Had the bullet just grazed him? He looked over to the patch of trees again: still nothing.

A third shot sent a surge of adrenaline coursing through Gordon's veins. This time, he ran as fast as his legs could carry him toward the house about three hundred yards away. *Only three football fields. One thing at a time.*

He keenly anticipated the sound of another gunshot, and his inevitable tumble to a snowy grave seemed imminent. Ridiculously, in that moment of primal fear and survival, all he could think about was Peter Falk telling him to "serpentine." *Humor and tragedy. Odd bedfellows.*

Despite the fact that he had spent a great deal of his life sitting behind a desk, Gordon had always made an effort to maintain a healthy exercise regime, but the snow was deep and he found himself struggling to stay erect. A fall would mean the difference between life and death. He deftly managed to retrace his father's steps back to the house without a single spill.

Gordon noticed the rusted sky blue car parked in the gravel driveway. A Russian-made Lada.

He blasted through the front door with a renewed focus. *The keys.* The kitchen counters were bare except for the coffee maker. He grabbed Dmitry's journal and the translation from the side table next to the armchair and shoved them in his blazer pocket. He pulled out the side table drawer with such force that its meager contents, a matchbook and a TV remote control, spilled onto the floor. *No keys.*

He ran to his father's bedroom at the back of the house. A chest of drawers flanked the left wall. Gordon rummaged through them in a panicked frenzy, throwing their unsought contents to the floor. He found his father's passport and shoved it in his pocket. It suddenly occurred to him that his father must have the keys on his person.

He rushed back through the house toward the main room, smashing his shoulder on the bedroom doorjamb as he exited. *Dammit.* Gordon reflexively grabbed his shoulder as a sharp pain shot up his right side. His jacket felt wet. He looked down and saw that he was covered in blood. He ran to the kitchen counter, grabbed a dish towel and held it up to the deep gash on his face.

He glanced at the dining table. *The computer.* Gordon picked it up before bounding back out into the snow.

He paused in front of the house. *What is that?* A foreign sound slowly began to increase in volume. An engine. He felt the relevance of time like never before. *No room for false steps.* He rushed around the side of the house. His father lay dead a couple hundred yards in front of him.

The sound was getting louder. He soon identified the source, a snowmobile, racing toward him from about a mile away. *What kind of man can make a shot from that distance?*

Gordon was moving so fast he almost tripped over his father's dead body, which had already taken on an eerie blueish tinge. He riffled through his father's jacket pockets. *Cigarettes? When did he start smoking?* He moved on to his trouser pockets. His father's body was positioned awkwardly, so Gordon roughly pushed his father's chest back in order to gain access to the front pockets. The General's body stiffly fell to one side, leaving behind a congealing pool of blood and splattering of brain matter.

Gordon retched at the horrific sight.

He wiped away the acrid bile on his sleeve and continued checking the right pocket. *A wallet.* Gordon stowed it in his jacket. His father's left side was still buried in the snow. He broke through the frozen crust with his bare hands to access his father's left pocket.

The throaty roar of the snowmobile engine grew louder.

Gordon narrowed his attention to the search for the keys. He could feel something from outside the pocket. He forced his hand in and found a set of keys. *Please be for the car. Please be for the car.*

Gordon stole one last look at his father and then raced back toward the house. There were too many variables in play right now. *Is one of these the car key? Will the car even start?* The sound of the snowmobile was getting louder. His mother's voice came to him: "One thing at a time, Gordon." A sudden focus washed over him. His peripheral world blurred, leaving a crystal clear image of the car before him.

Gordon sprinted to the driver's side of the car and yanked the door handle. The car was unlocked, but the door was frozen shut. Gordon kicked it as hard as his wet frozen foot would allow. It didn't budge. He tried the backseat passenger side door -- it opened. He scrambled in and awkwardly climbed into the driver's seat. He pulled the key ring from his pocket. There were five or six keys; all of them suspect.

"C'mon, Dad. Help me out here. One more time." The sound of the snowmobile grew louder. He looked at the keys -- all color-coded. He chose the light blue key and inserted it in the ignition. Perfect fit. The car cranked over, but it didn't want to start.

Gordon looked in the rearview mirror. The assassin was clearly coming into view now. The snowmobile stopped and the assassin aimed his long sniper rifle directly at Gordon, who ducked just as a shot rang out. The rear window shattered and the bullet passed straight through the driver's seat headrest, clanging as it fell to the metal floor. The snowmobile engine revved. Gordon stole another glance in the rearview mirror. The man rapidly approached, only about two hundred yards out now. *Seconds away.* Gordon pumped the fuel pedal and turned the key again, careful to keep his head tucked down below the dash. The engine caught. He threw the manual transmission into reverse and slammed down on the gas pedal. The front wheels spun uselessly in the high snow. He was going nowhere. Gordon slammed the car into drive. *C'mon.* The car surged forward, lodging its front bumper in a high snow bank. He threw the car back in reverse again. This time, the wheels caught and the car swung out wide as it reversed. As he jerked the wheel hard to the right, the car fishtailed out to the left, pointing him directly down the long drive. Gordon hit the gas and accelerated forward. He glanced back at the snowmobile in the rearview mirror. The gap widened.

The long driveway spilled directly onto the main road. *Left or right?* As he braked, the wheel pulled hard to the left. Surrendering to fate, he took a sharp left and sped off.

An endless forest of white birch trees lined both sides of the road. One blurred into the next as Gordon sped away, leaving the snowmobile far behind.

Map! His father always kept one. With one hand on the wheel, Gordon reached across the passenger seat and unlatched the glove compartment. A shiny black Russian GSh-18 pistol fell to the floor, just beyond his reach. He had never fired a gun before and hoped to keep it that way. *No map.* He surveyed the road ahead. Miles of nothing. It was a strange feeling, driving with no destination. For the first time in his life, Gordon had literally handed fate the wheel.

Gordon's soaring adrenaline had masked the pain...until now. His cheek throbbed in time with his elevated heart rate. A quick look in the rearview mirror revealed a six-inch gash running from the corner of his mouth to his ear on the right side of his face. The blood flow was slowing, but the wound would require medical attention sooner than later.

A highway sign provided his first indication of direction -- 223 kilometers to Moscow, a three-hour drive. He checked for a pursuit vehicle in the rearview mirror. The assassin surely must have seen him make the left turn. At best, he would have a thirty-minute jump on his pursuer. The M1 traffic had picked up since he'd left Fatino and the old sky blue Lada was beginning to feel more and more like a moving target. Not to mention the blown-out rear window, which was easily winning the battle with the Lada's underpowered heater.

Shivering, Gordon pulled his father's wallet from his pocket and swung it open. His third-grade school portrait stared back at him, right next to an old photo of his parents, taken on their honeymoon in Miami. He had never seen them look happier. His breathing quickened as an unfamiliar burning rage took hold, abolishing every ounce of remaining sentiment. Given the chance, he would not hesitate to kill the man who murdered his father. He opened the billfold and found it stuffed with a dozen 5,000-ruble bank notes. A small fortune by Russian standards. *A parting gift.*

A road sign pointing in the direction of a town called Gagarin caught his eye. Gordon had always been a space travel enthusiast and cosmonaut Yuri Gagarin had been the first human to journey into outer space. Gagarin's famous quote, "I could have gone on flying through space forever," was one of Gordon's favorites.

Surely, it was a sign. He exited.

The town of Gagarin unfolded before him, a provincial backwater with a smattering of multi-story buildings and a healthy population of vehicles running to and from the M1. *Certainly large enough to warrant a hospital or clinic of some sort.*

A commemorative statue of Gagarin welcomed him, casually posed with a jacket draped over one shoulder and the other arm fully extended as if he were about to take flight. Just the first, of six or seven additional Gagarin memorials and museums he would pass on the way to the town center. All fitting humble tributes to a provincial Russian boy who rose to worldwide fame.

As he drove through the business district, he came upon a nondescript brick building marked by a sign with a white background and a red cross. He pulled into the lot, parking in the designated area along the side of the building. He grabbed his father's computer from the passenger seat and walked to the front entrance.

There were two rules he had always been told to abide by while in Russia: 1) avoid drinking the tap water, and 2) avoid the hospitals at all cost. Rules usually comforted Gordon, but today they stood in his way.

Gordon approached the reception area, where a young woman dressed in a traditional nurse's uniform was in charge of the front desk. She was completely unfazed by his blood-splattered clothing and seeping wound. Barely acknowledging him, she mumbled something in Russian and pushed a form his way. Gordon looked down at the paper, which was, naturally, written in Russian.

"English? You speak English?"

The girl shook her head no. Gordon looked around the waiting area; there were four elderly patients, all of whom looked impoverished and ill. Nonetheless, Gordon addressed them. "Does anyone speak English?" A chorus of blank stares answered his question.

He turned back to the girl at the desk and pointed to his cheek. "Doctor, need doctor." Gordon pulled out his wallet and held up his rubles. "Rubles for doctor." Suddenly more interested, the girl nodded her head and pointed to a door at the end of a dingy gray hallway.

He knocked on the door. A diminutive gentlemen of about sixty-five answered and gestured for him to enter. Wearing a near-white lab coat, he was the closest thing to a doctor Gordon had seen in the building.

His concerned expression set Gordon at ease.

"Do you speak English?"

"Yes, little. Dr. Batkin."

Gordon sighed with relief and eagerly shook his hand. "Jerry. I cut my face in a hunting accident. I have rubles." Gordon handed the doctor a 5,000-ruble banknote, a fortune to a man whose salary was a meager twenty-three thousand rubles a year.

The Doctor nodded as he scrutinized Gordon's appearance. Gordon was wearing his standard uniform, white shirt, maroon tie, tweed jacket and flannel trousers, all of which were covered in blood. Additionally, he appeared to have a death grip on a laptop, an atypical hunting accessory. Dr. Batkin hadn't graduated at the top of his class, but it seemed fairly obvious this man hadn't been out hunting moose.

"I see, hunting." The doctor played along, motioning for Gordon to lie back on the examination table. He slipped on a pair of surgical gloves and examined the wound. Gordon's adrenaline surge had long since passed and his entire sensory system seemed focused on the raw nerve endings in his check. He flinched at the gentlest of touches.

"I can sew and give antibiotic, but you will have scar. Yes?"

"Yes, okay."

"Did you have success?"

"Excuse me?"

"Hunting success?"

"No, I'm afraid I didn't," Gordon replied, dreading where the line of questioning was leading.

"Please excuse me for a minute?"

"Yes, sure." Dr. Batkin left the room. Gordon feared he was notifying the local police, or even worse, FSB. He heard him speaking to someone out in the hall, but Gordon's understanding of Russian didn't extend far beyond *da, nyet,* and *spasiba.* He would have to take his chances.

Moments later, Dr. Batkin returned carrying a rather menacing long needle. Gordon *hated* needles. Needles, and spiders. As a child growing up in the Arizona desert, he had once found a tarantula waiting for him in a baseball glove, abruptly marking the end of his sporting career.

"For pain."

"No, I take pain. No needle." Gordon waved the needle away. Fear of needles aside, how was he to know Dr. Batkin wasn't going to drug him and turn him over to the FSB? He firmly shook his head no.

"Yes, shot. It's okay. You need. No move." The doctor mimicked Gordon's earlier flinching.

Gordon glanced up at Dr. Batkin. He had soft eyes, the kind that can't lie. Too exhausted for a debate, Gordon conceded.

The doctor injected the needle in the area just to the left side of Gordon's wound. The warm numbing sensation of the shot provided almost instantaneous relief.

Devoid of all ceremony, the doctor picked up the suturing needle and began stitching Gordon's cheek. The wound was deep and would require multiple layers of stitches. Gordon didn't feel a thing, beyond a slight tugging sensation every time the doctor pulled a suture tight. The rhythmic nature of the work was almost comforting. Gordon's eyes grew heavy. He hadn't had a wink of sleep since the long cab ride from Saint Petersburg. His mind began to wander. *It was the cabbie.* Gordon was certain it was the driver who had tipped off the FSB or whomever it was that murdered his father. He struggled against every blink, but his fatigue-laden eyelids eventually won the battle. He fell into a deep sleep.

•••

Los Angeles, CA - High Rise

Fletcher walked down a long window-lined corridor near the top of a Los Angeles high rise, flanked by sweeping views extending from downtown all the way to the Pacific Ocean. He pulled his cell phone from the pocket of his fitted two-button suit jacket and dialed a familiar number.

Harper greeted him curtly. "Hi, Dad, everything okay? I have like two minutes before I need to be in class,"

"Yes, love, everything's fine. I just wanted to give you a quick update on the pyramid. Apparently, the nanomush is a dead end." Fletcher opened the fire exit door at the end of the hallway, ascended one flight of stairs and stepped out onto the roof of the building. A helipad sat before him, surrounded by the skyscrapers of downtown Los Angeles.

"Mesh, Dad. It's nanomesh."

"Exactly, the nanomush," Fletcher persisted, smiling into the phone. "However, they did find it's made of a rare mineral called lonsdaleite."

"The hardest substance on Earth, but actually from outer space. Found at meteor sites," Harper stated smugly.

"My very own little Miss Encyclopedia Britannica."

"Why, thank you. The apple falls far from the tree. Anything else?"

"That's it. We sit tight for a bit."

A helicopter approached the rooftop. The sound was near deafening.

"What is that?" Harper pulled her distorting phone away from her ear.

"Helicopter...client...gotta go." Fletcher's voice broke up with the sonic distortion from the approaching chopper. He ended the call and placed the phone back in his pocket. As the helicopter touched down, he ran to the rear cabin, opened the door for a young impeccably dressed Middle Eastern man, and offered his arm as the man stepped down. With heads tucked, the new arrival and Fletcher jogged over to the rooftop door and disappeared through the stairwell.

•••

Gagarin, Russia - Clinic

Gordon jolted awake in a pitch black room, blanketed in a cold sweat. He touched his throbbing cheek to find it had been bandaged. *Where am I?* He blindly set his feet down on the ground and gently pushed forward, feeling for a wall or a light switch. A loud metallic crashing sound rang out as he tripped over a bucket that sent him hurtling to the floor.

"What the --?" Gordon slowly picked himself up and continued inching forward.

Suddenly the door swung open, flooding the room with light. Gordon's eyes took a moment to adjust, before focusing in on the slender silhouette at the door. Dr. Batkin.

"You have good sleep?"

"Where am I?"

"Closet. You fall sleep. No wake up. I have patients to see, so move you to closet." The doctor flicked on the lights, revealing stainless steel medical equipment, cleaning agents and a mop and bucket. It was indeed a closet.

Gordon looked down at his watch. Two and a half hours had lapsed. He panicked, realizing he was no longer in possession of his father's laptop.

"You okay?" Dr. Batkin inquired, clearly puzzled by Gordon's agitated expression.

"My computer?" Gordon typed manically on the air with his fingers.

"Ah, yes. Come." Gordon followed Dr. Batkin back to his office, where his laptop sat undisturbed on the desk.

"I leave. You come. You shower. My wife make soup. Clean clothes. Yes?"

Gordon's stomach growled loudly, answering on his behalf. He nodded in the affirmative.

"You take these." Dr. Batkin handed him two bottles of pills. "One pain, one antibiotics. You take now. Three times day." He handed Gordon a glass of tap water. Gordon stared at the glass. *1) avoid drinking Russian tap water, and 2) avoid Russian hospitals at all cost.* Gordon shrugged his shoulders, threw one pill from each container in his mouth and washed them back with the forbidden tap water.

"Thank you. Do you have Wi-Fi? For the computer. Internet?" Gordon fired up the laptop and opened a browser window to show the doctor.

"No computer home. Daughter teacher at school has. She take you after soup. Yes?"

"Yes, thank you. Why are you helping me?"

"Help? I like American. You pay me, wife happy. Make life very good," Dr. Batkin responded with a broad smile and a friendly pat on the back. "Come."

Gordon followed behind the doctor as he exited the clinic and approached his car in the parking lot. It was in even worse condition than Gordon's Lada. Gordon smiled.

"Dr. Batkin. May I buy your car? I will give you my car and more money?" Gordon pointed to his Lada at the back of the parking lot, as he reached in his wallet and pulled out ten thousand rubles.

"Yes, yes. Your car now," Dr. Batkin eagerly accepted. He and Gordon exchanged keys. "You follow me, yes?" Gordon nodded as he walked over to his new 1976 burnt orange Mosvitch 412, set his laptop down on the seat next to him and turned the key. The engine reluctantly sputtered to life. Gordon followed Dr. Batkin through the colorless town to his modest three-room home on the outskirts of Gagarin.

Dr. Batkin's wife met them at the door. She outweighed her husband by a good hundred pounds and looked like she would just as soon snap Gordon in two as feed him.

"Thank you for your hospitality." Gordon extended his hand to Mrs. Batkin, who instead, welcomed him with a cold stare. He lowered his arm and offered her a wide berth as he entered the Batkin's home. The homey smell of cooked cabbage enveloped him, warming his insides and stirring his dormant taste buds. It was not an unwelcome feeling.

"She not speak English. We can call her 'old hag!'" Dr. Batkin's laugh was so infectious, Gordon couldn't help but join in.

Mrs. Batkin may not have understood English, but she certainly understood her husband. She picked up a frying pan and slammed it down on the counter. Both men fell silent. She took the lid off of a large pot of cabbage soup simmering on the stove, picked up a bowl, dipped it in the pot and extended it to Gordon. Gordon approached her, humbly accepting the bowl.

"Thank you." Gordon bowed his head slightly, hoping to further demonstrate his appreciation. She scowled at him, before begrudgingly ladling a second bowl for her husband.

"Come." Gordon followed Dr. Batkin to the small dining table in the adjacent room, where they both took a seat.

"I thought you said your wife was happy," Gordon remarked with a frightened expression on his face.

"You should see when mad!" Dr. Batkin looked toward the kitchen, just as his wife stuck her head around the corner to give him the evil eye. He quickly directed his gaze back to Gordon.

Both men enjoyed the peppery soup accompanied by a few glasses of cheap vodka. Gordon's cheek was tender, but the painkiller combined with the alcohol proved a highly effective analgesic.

Dr. Batkin reached in his waistband, pulled out a spent .338 Lapua Magnum and laid it on the table.

"Hunting?"

Gordon regarded him quizzically.

"From car floor. Hunting for cars?"

Thankfully, the vodka had gone straight to Dr. Batkin's head. He started laughing uncontrollably. Once again, Gordon couldn't help but join in. Perhaps it was the painkillers or the vodka; either way, it was the most relaxed he had felt in the past week.

"I was hoping to shoot a Ferrari, but all I got was a Lada!" Gordon exclaimed gleefully.

"A Lada nothing!"

Mrs. Batkin entered the room carrying the pot from the stove and slammed it down on the table next to the laughing men. She violently ladled the cabbage soup into Gordon's empty bowl, spilling it over the sides, almost burning his hand.

"Thank you," Gordon remarked with a straight face as he gazed into her eyes. The scowl almost broke, but not quite. She turned away sharply and filled her husband's bowl before heading back to the kitchen.

"She like you. I can tell."

"I'm not going to lie. I'm a little afraid of her," Gordon replied.

"Me too. So, Mr. Jerry, the American hunter, where do you go next?"

"I honestly don't know yet. I've run into a few problems here in Russia and I'm waiting for friends to help me. That's why I need the internet. For my computer."

"You sleep here tonight on couch. Tomorrow my daughter will take to school and computer wifi there. I insist."

The plush blanket resting at the foot of the comfy couch was all it took to convince Gordon."Yes. I would appreciate that."

"Then we keep drinking. Good for pain." Dr. Batkin pointed to Gordon's cheek, before pouring two more shots. "Take clothes off and wife will wash."

Dr. Batkin called out to his wife in Russian. She left the kitchen and walked to the back of the house, returning with a rather large dressing gown. She handed the gown to Gordon.

"You wear to sleep. Take off clothes. Shower. Bathroom. Not wet face." Dr. Batkin pointed to a door in the hallway. Gordon obediently did as he was told.

The bathroom was the size of a broom closet and featured a vintage squat toilet, sink and half shower.

Gordon removed his clothing and lifted his nose in disgust. The pungent smell that had been trailing him was coming from his own body. He turned on the shower and stepped in, careful to keep his head out of the direct stream.

The warm water felt heavenly against his weary body. Long showers had always been a guilty pleasure. Growing up, they had also been a daily source of conflict. The General never tired of lecturing him on the virtues of the under-two-minute "Navy shower" as opposed to Gordon's fifteen-minute "Hollywood shower." It was just one of many areas where they didn't see eye to eye.

Dad. The horrifying image of his murdered father laying alone in the snowy field, flashed before his eyes. With no identification, Gordon wondered what would happen to the body. A proper burial seemed unlikely. Gordon was not a religious man, but as he stood there in the shower, he prayed for his parents to be reunited somewhere, wherever that might be.

Gordon washed his face gently, careful not to wet the bandage, and scrubbed the blood from his torso and limbs. He already felt better, though a bit woozy from the vodka and painkillers. He stepped out of the shower and examined his reflection in the small mirror over the sink. He barely recognized the person staring back, with dark circles under both eyes, preternatural crow's feet and a massive white bandage covering an entire side of his face, he felt as if he was meeting his older self in some sort of cosmic time warp. Unsettling.

He ran his fingers through his damp wavy dark locks, pushing them to one side before stepping into the ridiculously large sleeping gown. *If only the women of Caltech could see me now.* He laughed at the absolute bizarre universe he had stumbled into.

He left the bathroom carrying his folded dirty clothes and handed them to Mrs. Batkin, who had apparently been standing guard outside the bathroom door. "Thank you."

Mrs. Batkin looked him up and down and erupted in a deep thunderous roar. She brushed past him carrying his dirty laundry and disappeared into the bathroom.

A blushing Gordon rejoined Dr. Batkin at the dining table.

"I told you she like you."

CHAPTER THIRTEEN

New Day

Gagarin, Russia - Batkin Residence

THE CLANG OF pots and pans combined with the mouth-watering aroma of a traditional Russian breakfast roused Gordon. As he pushed himself upright on his makeshift bed, his uncooperative eyes refused to open beyond a mere squint. A blistering headache, a bad case of cotton-mouth and a throbbing cheek wound welcomed him to the day. He asked himself the eternal hangover question: *Why?*

His cleaned and ironed clothing lay neatly folded on the coffee table in front of him. Mrs. Batkin had even managed to remove the blood stains from his blazer and shirt, without the aid of a washing machine. Gordon smiled to himself – perhaps she did like him after all.

After dressing for the day, Gordon and Dr. Batkin enjoyed a breakfast of blini served with sour cream, and tea. It was delicious and just what he needed to fight the vodka-induced haze. They ate in silence...apparently, Gordon wasn't the only one suffering from a hangover.

After an awkward, prolonged goodbye hug from Mrs. Batkin, he and Dr. Batkin departed for his daughter's school. As he made his way out to the vehicles, Gordon couldn't help but notice that the rear window of his former Lada had already been repaired with a heavy clear sheet of plastic and some duct tape. *Duct tape -- holds the universe together.*

Gordon followed behind Dr. Batkin in his newly acquired Mosvitch 412, and they made an uneventful drive to the Gagarin Elementary School.

•••

Gagarin, Russia - Elementary School

The first grade classroom was cozy, with baby blue and white walls, worn brown vinyl flooring and two-student desks arranged in neat rows. Colorful educational posters adorned the walls, and Russian toys and children's books filled a bookcase at the back of the room. A kind-faced woman of about twenty-five sat behind the large desk positioned at the front of the empty classroom.

"Papa! Rad tebya videt." The woman rose from her wooden chair to greet her father with a welcoming hug.

"Meet my American friend, Mr. Jerry." Dr. Batkin pulled away from his daughter's embrace, placed his hand on Gordon's back and gently nudged him forward.

"Hello, Mr. Jerry. My name is Anna," she said transitioning effortlessly to English, as she offered her hand to Gordon.

"It's a pleasure to meet you, Anna."

"It is also a pleasure to meet you," Anna replied.

"Mr. Jerry needs computer internet," Dr. Batkin said, pointing to the laptop Gordon carried in his left hand.

"I see. Please come with me." Anna preceded the men down the narrow corridor leading to the small teacher's lounge at the end of the hallway. As they entered the lounge, Anna pointed to a wireless router sitting on a window ledge on the far side of the room. "Wi-Fi. Please make yourself comfortable."

"Well, my friend Mr. Jerry, I must work. So goodbye." Dr. Batkin left Gordon with a heartfelt hug and a robust back slap.

"Thank you for everything, Dr. Batkin. I owe you one."

"Agggh," Dr. Batkin waved his hand as if to say, "It's nothing." "You remember take medicine. Wear your Russian scar proudly!"

Dr. Batkin and Anna exited the room together, conversing quietly in their native tongue.

Gordon took a seat at a large communal table in the center of the room and powered up his father's laptop. The battery charge was just below 75%. He had a few hours of usage left before he would need to find a power supply.

The Blacknet network window was still open, just as his father had left it. Gordon read his last message:

t<<veritas 103, 151>>
f<<veritas 22>>
m<< nanomesh is a dead end. pyramid is made of lonsdaleite. two main sources: tunguska event in krasnoyarsk krai, russia and diablo canyon crater in arizona. seeking info on collectors.>>

Gordon selected the school's open Wi-Fi network and waited for the laptop to connect. A green cursor began to blink, drawing his attention. He examined the Blacknet syntax. *Simple enough.* He typed:

t<<veritas 103, 22>>
f<<veritas 151>>
m<<151 is dead. this is his son gordon. i am in trouble in russia. please advise.>>

He glanced around the teacher's lounge. Not so different from its U.S. counterparts...window, water cooler, table, cheap artwork, a few potted plants, microwave and a dry erase board. The electric blue walls seemed an odd choice, but after taking in the drab industrial view the sole window offered, he could understand the need to infuse a bit of color.

The sound of Anna's approaching footsteps broke the silence. Gordon turned toward the door.

"Is everything okay?" Anna inquired from the doorway.

"Yes, thank you. Perfect. I really appreciate all your family has done for me."

"You more than doubled my father's yearly salary in one day. It's a good way to make friends in Russia." It was difficult for Gordon to read the tone of her voice and her stoic face revealed nothing. "I have some work to do before my students arrive. You know where my classroom is if you require any further assistance," she said before departing.

Gordon shook his head. *Women...the great unsolved mystery.*

Gordon turned his attention back to the laptop where a message awaited him. His heart skipped a beat in anticipation.

t<<veritas 151, 103>>
f<<veritas 22>>
m<<place your thumb on the biometric sensor at the bottom righthand corner of the laptop and await a response.>>

Gordon placed his right thumb on what appeared to be a standard thumbprint reader and held it there. Moments later, the print reader slid open and Gordon felt a slight pinch on the underside of his thumb. He pulled his hand away from the pad and observed a blood drop forming on the tip of his thumb. He looked back to the screen and its green blinking cursor.

t<<veritas 151, 103>>
f<<veritas 22>>
m<<thank you gordon. your identity has been confirmed. what happened to your father? where are you?>>

Gordon typed.

t<<veritas 22, 103>>
f<<veritas 151>>
m<<i believe the cabbie who transported me to the country house must have tipped off the fsb or whomever it was that shot my father in the field behind the house. i barely escaped with my life. i am in a town called gagarin about 200km west of moscow. i saw the message regarding the lonsdaleite. i may be able to help track down the source. i have no passport and little money. please advise.>>

t<<veritas 151, 103>>
f<<veritas 22>>
m<<make your way to moscow. go to the internet cafe at chayanova street 18. you will be met with documents and money tomorrow at 2pm. pursue your lonsdaleite lead. discreetly.>>

Gordon shut down the laptop. The directive returned his focus. He walked down the hall to Anna's classroom and gently knocked on the closed door.

"Come in."

Gordon entered. Anna was sitting at her desk correcting homework. She barely acknowledged his presence.

"I'm sorry to bother you, but would it be possible to use the phone in the teacher's lounge? I need to call St. Petersburg."

Anna looked up from her papers.

"I know who you are."

"Excuse me?"

"I said, I know who you are. The young physicist. Correct?"

"I...uh," Gordon stammered.

"We do have newspapers here in Gagarin, you know. Your photo was in the paper after the fire at the hotel. Did you kill those men?"

"No, no, I swear to you. Two of those men were there to protect me and the other man was an FSB agent. I am just a physicist."

"Then why do you need protection? And why does the FSB want you?"

"A Russian physicist who may have a very dangerous weapon is missing and my government sent me here to try to find him, before that weapon is used again."

"What is this weapon?"

"The weapon makes people dematerialize, disappear. It's been used on small villages in China and the U.S."

"Sounds impossible."

"Yes, it does, but I assure you it is very real."

"Why isn't your government helping you now?"

"Because I'm not sure who I can and can't trust. Yesterday I saw my father murdered before my eyes, and as you can see I came pretty close myself." Gordon gestured to his bandaged face.

"Just an inch to the right and we wouldn't be talking right now. Are you going to report me?"

"To who? The FSB? I loathe the FSB and everything they stand for."

"Thank you," Gordon replied, relieved.

"You are welcome and yes, you may use the phone." Anna looked back down at the paperwork, cueing Gordon's exit.

Gordon retraced his steps back down the hallway that was now beginning to fill with elementary school children, all of whom eyed him with suspicion. A simple reminder of how odd he must look with a huge bandage covering one side of his face. He entered the teacher's lounge, closed the door and sat back down at the communal table. He opened the browser on his father's laptop and typed *Jurek Novokov* into the Google search box.

Novokov Fine Jewelers - Nevsky Prospect 45, Saint Petersburg, Russia - 3102784203

Gordon jotted down the info on a slip of paper, walked to the rotary phone sitting on the windowsill next to the potted cactus and Wi-Fi router, picked up the handset and dialed the number.

"Dóbry utra," a man answered in Russian.

"Hello, do you speak English?" Gordon asked, easily identifying Jurek's voice.

"Yes, little."

"May I speak to the jeweler Jurek Novokov?"

"This is he."

"Hello, Mr. Novokov. My name is Jerry Cosby and I would like to order an engagement ring. You did some work for a friend of mine in Moscow, which my wife-to-be really adores. I have a design in mind."

"Yes, go on."

"I would like a gold anchor that wraps around the finger, with an English rose on the front."

"I see." Jurek had suspected he was speaking to the "dead" young American physicist, but now he was certain. Only a man writing a book on his cousin Dmitry would know such details.

"My fiancée has requested that the rose be made of a type of mineral called lonsdaleite. It's rare, would you be able to track it down?"

"Yes, that is something I can find."

"I'm traveling from Austria today, but I will check back with you tomorrow and we can discuss this further. I'm very pleased to have spoken to you. Your work is beautiful."

"Thank you."

Gordon hung up the phone, opened his father's wallet and withdrew one 5,000-ruble banknote. He rummaged through a supply drawer in the corner of the room, found an envelope and inserted the money in it. A row of wooden mail receptacles addressed with each of the teacher's names lined the wall next to the door. Anna's was the first. He placed the envelope inside it before quietly departing from the school.

•••

Burbank, CA - Bob Hope Airport

Harper Crisp turned into the entrance of the Bob Hope Airport in Burbank. Fletcher rode shotgun, his ballistic nylon duffel bag perched on his lap.

"Thanks for the lift, love."

"I really don't see why you're the one dealing with this," Harper pleaded.

"The kid needs help and I have a lot of respect for his father, who would have done the same thing for you, I'm sure."

"But we have people in Moscow who can deal with this kind of thing."

"Just like the cabbie in Saint Petersburg who led them right to Veritas 151?"

"You don't know that. It could even be this guy Gordon, for all you know."

"I would think you would display a little more loyalty toward a fellow Caltech professor," Fletcher quipped, doing his best to lighten the tone of the conversation.

"Former Caltech professor. You really trust him? Do I need to remind you that he was working for the US Army -- the same guys who orchestrated the Crimm cover-up?"

"His father was friends with Wilkinson, and I'm sure he thought he could trust him."

"Whatever." Harper pulled to a stop outside the terminal, coldly turning her gaze away from her father. She knew her behavior was childish, but he was all she had left.

"You're not going to let me leave with that kind of a goodbye, are you?" Fletcher leaned his cheek in close for a goodbye kiss. Harper turned back toward him and rolled her eyes. He was relentless and it was nearly impossible to stay mad at him.

"Fine." She gave him a quick peck on the cheek. "But if this Gordon guy gets you in any trouble, I will kill him myself, with my bare hands."

"That's my girl. Love you. I'll be in touch."

"Be safe." Harper looked him directly in the eyes for just a moment, before shifting her gaze back ahead. She hated teary goodbyes as much as her father did. It was his cue to exit.

Bag in hand, Fletcher walked down the busy sidewalk. Harper's eyes followed him with each step. Her father always turned to wave just before entering the terminal -- it was a silly unspoken thing they shared. As Fletcher was about to pass through the door, she smiled in anticipation, but today was different -- her father didn't look back.

•••

Moscow, Russia - The Savany Motel

Gordon crawled along on the M1 in his ailing Mosvitch 412. The steering wheel rattled out of control anytime he accelerated over fifty miles an hour. Progress was slow.

Even with the icy conditions, drivers flew by Gordon doing far in excess of the 90kph speed limit. President Medvedev had once described Russian drivers as "undisciplined and criminally careless" and Gordon had to agree. He had been on the road for two and a half hours and had witnessed three major accidents. It wasn't difficult to understand the widespread use of dashboard cams on Russian roads.

While the Mosvitch was certainly warmer than the windowless Lada, Gordon soon discovered that when he cranked the heater, the radio came on at full volume. Naturally, the radio's volume knob happened to be missing. Gordon found that by tuning in between channels, the blaring static sound was almost tolerable. He turned the heat off every fifteen minutes, until the windows began to freeze up, at which point he cranked it back up for another two or three minutes. It seemed an odd form of sensory torture, but it served as a healthy distraction from dwelling on the murder of his father, as well as the unusual nature of his current predicament. He had no clue who would be meeting him in Moscow. A dead man's trust was guiding him now.

Gordon entered the Moscow city limits and approached what appeared to be a budget motel, The Savarny. He parked the Mosvitch in the almost vacant parking lot, grabbed his laptop from the passenger seat and walked into the small front lobby where the unfriendly face of the middle-aged desk attendant failed to greet him.

"Hello, do you speak English?"

"Little." The man didn't even look up from the computer keyboard he was busily typing away on.

"How much for a room?"

"Seven hundred rubles. I need ID," the man replied, still immersed in his computer activities.

"I'm afraid I was robbed and my wallet was stolen. Can I perhaps pay a little more for the room?" Gordon proffered, hoping his luck with bribery would continue.

"No ID and room costs seven thousand rubles."

"How about five?" Gordon handed the man a crisp 5,000-ruble note. The attendant eyed Gordon with disdain, before reluctantly grabbing the bill.

"Okay, but no bathroom in your suite."

Gordon nodded.

The man pushed a hotel registration book and a pen toward Gordon. "You fill out."

Gordon registered under the assumed name, Jerry Cosby; a baffling marriage of two iconic American comedians' names, Jerry Seinfeld and Bill Cosby. He glanced back up as the attendant slammed down a key with the number 21 engraved on it. *A real key, old school.*

"Upstairs. Left." The attendant practically spat the directions in Gordon's face.

Gordon ascended the stairs at the back of the lobby, turning as instructed. Room 21 was the first door on the left. He inserted the key and entered the darkened chamber. He flicked on the light switch, illuminating the 12' x 12' room. "Suite" was perhaps a bit too grand a word. The decor was Russian Imperialism meets the 1970s, with heavy gold drapery, a fake potted fern, faded green carpeting, gold print bedspread, cherry veneer headboard and a gold lamp with a mint green pleated upholstered shade. Gordon sat on the corner of the queen-size bed and the entire mattress sprang up behind him. He was far too tired to care.

He disrobed, crawled under the covers and closed his eyes.

CHAPTER FOURTEEN

Moscow

Somewhere Over The North Pacific Ocean

FLETCHER SAT RECLINED in his seat, sipping a gin and tonic and dining on a surprisingly tasty take on boeuf bourguignon. An attractive middle-aged blonde sat next to him. Fletcher could already see the telltale signs of interest. She had already dropped her cloth napkin twice, presumably so she could lean his way, casually brushing up against his leg like an attention-starved kitten.

She dropped it again. *Time for action.*

"You need a leash for that one," Fletcher joked, breaking the ice. It was a long flight and some conversation might speed it along.

"I'm so sorry, but it just doesn't want to stay in one place."

"Not a problem." Fletcher leaned over and picked it up for her, allowing for a nice view of her lean, sculpted legs. He handed her back the napkin.

"Thank you. Melanie Johnson," Melanie responded, extending her hand.

"Fletcher Crisp."

"Are you traveling to Moscow for business or pleasure?"

Fletcher admired her direct approach. "I'm a spy. So a bit of both, I suppose."

"Ooooh, a spy. Shouldn't you be drinking martinis?" she giggled coquettishly.

"Afraid gin's my sin," he replied, holding up his glass.

"Cheers," she said as she lifted her glass of Napa Valley chardonnay to meet his. "So where do spies stay in Russia these days?"

"If I told you that, I'm afraid I would have to kill you. You?" Fletcher smiled.

"I'm at the Ararat Park Hyatt," she replied all too eagerly.

"Ahh, yes, the low-rent district," he said, smiling. "And what brings you to Moscow?"

"I'm in the exporting business. I sell oil and gas field equipment."

"Ahh, CIA," Fletcher retorted, causing Melanie to almost double over with laughter. "Perhaps we should meet this evening to exchange intel over a few dry martinis?"

"I'd like that. There's a lovely bar in the Park Hyatt. If you'll excuse me, I need to map out the upcoming invasion of Iran." Melanie smiled, pointing to her laptop.

"Of course." Fletcher removed the eye mask from the complimentary traveler package wedged in the seat back. His military training had left him well-versed in the economy of sleep.

•••

Moscow, Russia - The Savany Motel

Gordon felt good. He had slept for fifteen hours straight and the intense throbbing in his cheek had settled down to a tolerable dull ache. He removed the soiled bandage from his wound in front of the full-length dressing mirror in the corner of the room. The first image that came to mind was *Frankenstein*. He barely recognized the face staring back at him. It was an odd sensation, appearing a stranger to oneself. He counted thirty stitches on the surface, plus whatever had been done underneath. He would be wearing this scar to the grave.

He redressed the wound with some supplies he had picked up earlier that morning, opting for two extra-large skin-colored Band-aids instead of the more conspicuous white gauze Dr. Batkin had used. His appearance improved dramatically.

Gordon rummaged through his pockets in search of the slip of paper he'd written Jurek's number on. Every time he opened the billfold, his mother's eyes were there, staring back at him. He couldn't understand how his father could live with the constant reminder. He removed the photo and gently tucked it behind his father's credit cards which all bore the assumed name, John Wayne. He had never really considered his father's sense of humor before that moment, but clearly there had been one lurking in the depths.

He pulled out the slip of paper with Jurek's number on it, which had been tucked in between two 5,000-ruble notes.

Novokov Fine Jewelers - Nevsky Prospect 45, Saint Petersburg, Russia - 3102784203

Jurek picked up immediately. "Dóbry dyen."

"Mr. Novokov?"

"Yes, this is he."

"Hello, this is Jerry Cosby, we spoke yesterday about a ring for my future wife."

"Yes, I remember. She want lonsdaleite?"

"That's correct. Did you manage to have any luck tracking some down?"

"Some. There is collector in Moscow who may be able to assist you. His name is Konstantin Chekhov."

"Thank you. I am in Moscow and I will negotiate the price with him directly. I will be in touch."

"Good luck, my friend."

Gordon grabbed his laptop, walked downstairs and exited through the lobby. The distracted desk attendant didn't even look up from his newspaper. It made Gordon homesick for the smiling faces that greeted him every morning at his local Starbucks. He was developing a newfound appreciation for the small things, including good old American customer service.

He approached his Mosvitch 412. *Strange.* The driver's window was rolled halfway down. He was certain he hadn't left it that way. He hopped in the car, set his laptop down on the passenger seat and looked around. Everything appeared to be in its right place. No bodies in the back seat. Still apprehensive, Gordon departed for the internet cafe at Chayanova Street 18 in downtown Moscow.

•••

Moscow, Russia - Moscow Domodedovo Airport

Fletcher grabbed his duffel bag from the overhead bin and stood in the aisle waiting for the front passenger door of the Boeing 777 to open. Still seated, Melanie, who had been asleep for most of the journey, rubbed her eyes and ran her fingers through her long silky ash-blonde hair. She glanced up at Fletcher.

"Wow. Guess I was tired."

"I'll say. I've never heard such snoring in my life...and the drooling...it's a wonder they let you sit in first class," Fletcher joked with a warm smile and a wink.

Melanie, still groggy, wasn't quite ready for humor. He recognized her slightly annoyed expression as the same one Harper regularly displayed before she had her first cup of morning coffee.

"Kidding, of course. You didn't make a peep," Fletcher replied.

"Sorry, my sense of humor takes at least an hour to wake up after my eyes are open. Can I bother you to grab my bag for me?"

"Certainly." Fletcher grabbed the only other bag in the overhead compartment and handed it to her as she rose to join him in the aisle. They de-planed together and walked side by side down the long concourse on their way to the airport exit.

"Alas, this is where we part. Have a safe journey into town." Fletcher headed directly for customs as she continued on to baggage claim.

"I'll be waiting for that drink later," she called after him, with a wink.

"Save me a seat," Fletcher smoothly replied, unfazed by his uncanny ability to charm and disarm.

•••

Moscow, Russia - Cafemax

Gordon glanced around the Cafemax, Moscow's immense twenty-four hour Internet cafe. Before him lay endless rows of stations with back-to-back computer terminals mounted in modern looking wooden cubicle style desks. Three hundred in total, offering little privacy, beyond a short wooden barrier separating each terminal.

Gordon walked to the very back of the sparsely populated room and sat down at the end of a vacant row. He logged on to the computer with the credentials provided at the front desk and navigated to the *Los Angeles Times* front page. He had hoped to see some mention of his demise there, but alas, his death was already old news. He fought the urge to Google his own name, as he felt certain the computers were under state surveillance.

Just seeing the *Times* logo made him pine for home. He missed his daily morning routine of sitting down with the paper and a cup of coffee. Would anything ever feel normal again? Would he even be able to return to the U.S.? The future held many unanswered questions. Familiar feelings of anxiety began to creep up on him. "One thing at a time, Gordon," -- his mother's voice was always close.

Fletcher entered the Cafemax internet café and purchased an hour of computer time for sixty rubles. He immediately spied Gordon sitting at the back of the cafe. He might as well have been wearing a bull's-eye on his back. The dozen or so other occupants were all between the ages of twelve and sixteen, with the majority of them clustered together playing video games.

Fletcher walked to the back row and took a seat at the station next to Gordon.

"Any idea how to get this damn thing to work?" Fletcher asked, futilely tapping away at the keys.

Gordon was so wrapped up in his own thoughts, he hadn't even noticed Fletcher's approach. He glanced over, understanding immediately that this was the man his father had said he could trust with his life. His presence was already a comfort.

"Just enter in the code from the slip of paper they gave you," Gordon replied, with a smile. Gordon had no idea what to expect from his Veritas contact, but Fletcher's humorous introduction was certainly a welcome surprise.

"I see they didn't award you that Nobel for nothing." Fletcher entered the code in the login window and opened the browser. He navigated to eBay and entered the search word "airsickness bags." Fletcher had a collection of over twelve hundred barf bags from two hundred and three different airlines. There were a few Russian airline bags he would still love to acquire. *When in Rome.*

"So, I'm new to this whole thing. You know who I am, but do I refer to you by your number? Should I keep looking at my screen?" Gordon inquired, with his eyes locked on his monitor. Gordon's experience with clandestine meetings was limited to what he'd seen in the cinema, and films never seemed to address these awkward introductions.

"I'm Fletcher, Fletcher Crisp. And, yes, just keep surfing along. I myself am looking to add to my airsickness bag collection. eBay. My Russian's not so good. Thank God for pictures."

"I collect physics jokes," Gordon replied with a straight face. Gordon began collecting jokes on his twelfth birthday. He found that all kids loved jokes and it was an easy way for him to start a conversation or to be accepted in a group of kids that otherwise might have found him odd or standoffish. To this day, he still pulled out his favorites at cocktail parties. Never one to talk about the weather, jokes had always functioned as his icebreaker of choice. Everyone liked an excuse to have a good laugh.

"Let's hear what you've got," Fletcher replied, as he admired a vintage Pulkovo Airlines sickness bag.

"A six-year-old boy spots Albert Einstein walking down the street and decides to try out his favorite joke on him: 'Mr. Einstein! Why did the chicken cross the road?' To which Einstein replied, 'My young burgeoning mind, zee question does not have a definite answer. Vether zee chicken crossed zee road or zee road crossed zee chicken depends on your frame of reference.'" Gordon chuckled. He felt like he got a little closer to perfecting Einstein's heavy German accent every time he told the joke. He stole a glance in Fletcher's direction. No reaction.

Fletcher failed to see the humor in Gordon's joke. "I'm more of a 'horse walks into a bar' kind of joke guy." He had spent his entire career surrounded by some of the toughest men on the planet and now everywhere he looked, he was surrounded by nerds. Harper often liked to remind him that "nerds rule the world." *Perhaps, but armed with jokes like this, it would be a short reign.*

"Observations are observer-dependent." Gordon typically unleashed his jokes at university functions and cocktail parties and was unaccustomed to having to explain their punch lines.

"Is that the punch line?"

"Observations are relative...dependent on the point of view of the observer. Did you find the men responsible for my father's murder?" Segues had never been Gordon's strong suit. He never understood the need to ease people into a different conversational subject.

"I'm afraid I don't have any information for you. We operate in a way that prevents a person from knowing too much about any one thing. I can assure you that someone is dealing with it, but my mission is to secure you and find Dr. Dmitry Zoltov, hopefully with your assistance. There's rumor of another disappearance. Mexico this time."

"Same circumstances?"

"Yes, small village of fifty-six people, blue light."

"We need to follow up on a lead I have. There's a man here in Moscow named Konstantin Chekhov who is a lonsdaleite collector."

"Is anyone following you?"

"I haven't seen anyone, but it's not exactly something I'm accustomed to looking for. The driver's side window on my car was open this morning, but nothing was missing."

"You must not return to the motel or your car when you leave here. Did you leave anything in either of those places?"

Gordon held up the laptop. "This is all I have left."

"I'm afraid I've been instructed to take that from you." Fletcher shifted his gaze from the screen to meet Gordon's probing stare.

"It's all I have left of my dad."

"I assure you that anything personal of your father's will be backed up to another drive."

"I know my father trusted all of you and that means a lot to me, but he's dead. It was one of your people that drove me to the farmhouse and for all I know they led whomever it was that murdered my father directly to us. I'm keeping the laptop," Gordon replied, surprised by his steely resolve and confident tone. *Where has this guy been hiding the last 23 years?*

"Listen, I get it, but if that drops into the wrong hands, we're looking at a serious problem. I'm not letting you out of my sight from here on out. I'm afraid we're going to be bunking together as well. How about you let me transport it back to the hotel? It's within walking distance of here -- the Ararat Park Hyatt. You're going to make a left when you hit the sidewalk and the hotel is about half a mile down the street, on the north side. I'm going to follow you from a distance. I need to make sure you aren't being followed. Clear?"

Gordon nodded his head.

"Hop to it. We're in suite number 524. I'll be right behind you."

Gordon arose, with the laptop in his right hand.

"Ahem, the laptop. Leave it on your seat."

Gordon ignored Fletcher's directive. If anyone wanted to gain his trust from now on, it would need to be on his terms.

Fletcher shook his head as Gordon walked away. He admired the kid's chutzpah. He would have done the exact same thing given the circumstances.

Gordon exited the cafe and made a sharp left turn. The snowfall had resumed and the temperature was falling with it. The rush of ice cold air felt good against his wounded cheek. It helped to clear his busy mind. As he traversed the sidewalk that was full of shoppers and business people going about their daily business, Gordon walked with a peace he hadn't felt since arriving in Russia.

Fletcher tailed Gordon from a safe distance. He scanned the road, the sidewalks, the rooftops and the windows in the surrounding buildings. Nothing caught his eye. He hoped Gordon wasn't going to be even more difficult to manage than he had anticipated. After all, he was fully aware of the complexities of dealing with young intelligent types. His thoughts turned to Harper and his paternal instinct kicked in. *You're safe now, kid.*

•••

Gagarin, Russia - Batkin Residence

From behind the couch, it appeared that Dr. and Mrs. Batkin were settling in for an uncustomary evening of snuggling on the couch. The TV was tuned to the popular Russian sitcom, *Intern,* and the room was warmed by a cozy fire burning in the rustic fireplace at their backs.

But all was not as tranquil as it seemed. The canned TV laughter was a little too loud and the Batkins were sitting a little too still.

The view from the front of the couch told a different story altogether. The Batkins' wrists and ankles were bound with duct tape, and their mouths were sealed shut too. Both Dr. and Mrs. Batkin's eyes were wide open, frozen in a moment of eternal terror. The blood had begun to congeal around the bullet holes that marked the center of each of their foreheads and the end of their lives.

CHAPTER FIFTEEN

A Divorce

Five Months Earlier - Undisclosed Location

DMITRY AWOKE TO the squeaking sound of the rusty iron wheels, as the bearded man rolled the old hospital bed into his room. His ears had grown accustomed to the solitude of his captivity, and what he may have once considered a minor annoyance now felt like a full-on auditory assault. He defensively covered his ears with his hands as he looked at the diminutive figure lying lifelessly on the bed across the room from where he lay.

It can't be. Dmitry rubbed his eyes in disbelief; surely his dehydration and starvation were playing tricks on his mind.

The bearded man pushed the bed to the wall directly opposite Dmitry's cot, then made his way back to the door. Just before exiting he remarked casually, "I believe you two know each other." It was the first time the bearded man had spoken to him. His gravelly baritone was rougher than sandpaper on a sunburn.

Dmitry glanced at the inanimate figure on the bed. *Could it be?* The sheets stirred and his fellow captive turned to meet his gaze.

Her creamy white complexion had been replaced by a deathly pallor and her moon-sized hazel eyes seemed to have recessed into the back of her sockets. The warm, easy smile that had once lifted his spirits on the darkest of days -- gone. His burdened heart fell to the pit of his stomach. Was it love or pity that he was feeling? He couldn't be sure.

"Sarah?" Dmitry inquired, taken aback by the fragility of his own voice.

She nodded, imperceptibly. His English Rose.

He had expected to feel different upon their reunion. Love, not pity and confusion. *Where has it gone?*

At that moment, Dmitry's sartorially refined captor entered the room carrying a serving platter and one tall glass of ice cold water.

"I see the two of you have been reintroduced. I have special treat for one of you," he said, lifting the silver dome off the serving platter. *An English roast.* The heavenly smell of buttery carrots, crispy potatoes and fall-off-the-fork beef sent a rhapsodic shiver from Dmitry's head to his toes. Elated, he laughed aloud, almost uncontrollably.

"Only one of you will dine this evening and I'm afraid to say, the other will not...ever again," he said as he carried the tray to Sarah's bedside. "Ladies first."

"No," Dmitry shouted, not so much in protest of the ultimatum, but in protest of the pecking order. Why should *she* decide their fate? Once the object of his affection, Sarah was now just another obstacle to overcome. He wanted to survive desperately...at any cost. He turned away from her, too ashamed and frightened to see her reaction.

Their captor smiled, lifting the glass to Sarah's cracked, parched mouth. He allowed a single mouthful of water to enter before asking, "More?"

Sarah turned her vacant gaze away from Dmitry to meet that of her captor. Fully depleting her energy reserves, she forcefully spat the water back in his face.

"The lady hath spoken."

The man rose from her bedside, carrying the serving platter to Dmitry, who managed to sit upright under his own steam. It was the most he had moved in a week. He readily accepted the platter and buried his face in the dinner like a jackal to a corpse. Before he finished the meal, Sarah had passed.

The human mind deals with trauma in mysterious ways.

The first few weeks after her death were the roughest. As Dmitry's captors slowly re-introduced him to the pleasures of modern comforts -- regular meals, warm showers, clean clothing, a room to call his own -- his mental clarity returned, forcing him to face his savage behavior. At first, he could barely muster the energy to speak, eat and move, too ashamed and despondent to even attempt to take his own life...but, slowly, day by day, his perception shifted.

When his body had strengthened enough, they moved him to a remote underground facility which housed a lab that far surpassed any other he had ever seen. They accommodated his every request, no matter the cost. His progress was fast and productive. His old ego emerged, the one that had long hungered to be acknowledged for his work in theoretical physics. His peers had once ridiculed his Dusha theories, but that would all change.

In a bizarre twist of fate, he came to resent the time he had spent with Sarah. It had been time away from his work. Work that would change the world.

•••

Moscow, Russia - The Conservatory Lounge & Bar

The Conservatory Lounge & Bar sat on the tenth floor of Moscow's Ararat Park Hyatt, a contemporary luxury hotel in the heart of the city. With floor to ceiling windows, the lounge offered expansive views over Red Square, the renovated Bolshoi Theatre and the Kremlin. The crowd was fashionable and the alcohol flowing.

Melanie Johnson sat at the bar next to self-proclaimed American music impresario Scotty Grazier, who, although in his late forties, dressed like the much younger artists he managed.

"Yeah, so first I was like, 'Do you know who I am?' and then, you know... I'm a former Marine, so I told the guy I would kick his ass if he didn't hand over the microphone."

Melanie was so thoroughly unimpressed, she could barely muster a response. "Did he?"

"Did he what?" Scotty threw back his fourth shot of Moscow's own high-end Kauffman vodka, oblivious to the thread of his own meandering monologue.

"Did he hand you -- never mind." Melanie looked around the room for a savior. She had come for one reason only, to reconnect with Fletcher, but at this point, anyone would do. Though attractive, Melanie was ten to fifteen years older than most of the other women in the room. She immediately regretted not opting for the shorter skirt and lower-cut top. She'd have to dig herself out of this hole.

"Please excuse me, but I have an early morning."

"Yeah, sure." Before the words had even exited his mouth, he had already moved on to his next victim. A Russian model, available by the hour...perhaps the language barrier would work in his favor this time.

As Melanie walked back toward the lounge entrance, she felt a finger gently tap her shoulder.

"Leaving so soon?" asked a gravelly voice in a familiar English accent.

Melanie turned to find Fletcher standing behind her with a reluctant-looking, yet boyishly handsome, guest in tow.

She almost exploded with delight. "Fletcher!"

"Allow me to introduce my friend --." Fletcher looked back at Gordon. They hadn't discussed names in the room. In fact, they hadn't discussed much of anything. Once they made it back to the hotel safely, Gordon had lapsed into an uncommunicative state. He would need time to mourn his father's death, in his own way. Both men were exhausted, but neither could sleep. Fletcher decided a field trip to the bar was in order, and Gordon acquiesced.

"Jerry. Jerry Cosby." Gordon offered his hand to Melanie.

"Nice to meet you Jerry Cosby. Ouch," she exclaimed, pointing to the two jumbo-sized Band-Aids covering his cheek.

"Shaving accident," Gordon replied with a warm smile.

"I didn't see you on the flight."

"No, I flew in a few days ago."

"Are you a spy, too?" she asked, giggling suggestively.

Gordon did not yet have a drink in hand, which thankfully prevented him from spraying it all over her face.

Fletcher, amused by Gordon's shell-shocked reaction, interceded. "The spies will return with drinks in hand. Why don't you grab us that table over by the window? Chardonnay, right?"

"Yes, please," Melanie responded, flipping her hair back suggestively as she sashayed her way through the buzzing room.

Fletcher grabbed Gordon's arm and directed him toward the bar. "For a guy who collects jokes, you certainly don't have a very keen sense of humor, mate. The spy thing was a joke. Women love spies, James Bond, that kind of thing. Shaken, not stirred. Get the picture?"

"Sorry. She caught me by surprise."

"I'll say. What's your poison?" Fletcher asked, waving the bartender over.

"I would kill for a Yoo-hoo right now," Gordon replied, dead serious. He had picked up a Yoo-hoo habit at Caltech and was craving the sugary kick.

"A what who?"

"Yoo-hoo, it's a chocolaty beverage."

Fletcher rolled his eyes as he turned back to the bartender who was patiently awaiting their order. "Two gin and tonics, a glass of the house chardonnay and an empty coffee mug, please."

Gordon regarded Fletcher with a quizzical expression on his face.

Fletcher pulled the bag of jumbo sunflower seeds from his cargo pants pocket. "Seeds."

"Odd habit," Gordon said, smiling.

"Says the kid who orders a Yoo-hoo at a bar. Just one and we head back up, okay? Don't say anything stupid at the table."

"So what's my backstory?"

Fletcher looked Gordon up and down. "Dressed like that, I would say a freshman English lit major." He was wearing the uniform... tweed jacket, gray flannel trousers, white shirt and maroon tie.

Gordon looked down at his clothes and laughed. "And you?" he asked playfully as he considered Fletcher's wardrobe...cargo pants, black polo shirt, trainers and a pullover. "P.E. teacher?"

"Well, look at that, you do have a sense of humor." Fletcher slapped him on the back and handed him a gin and tonic. "Cheers, mate."

Fletcher extended his glass to meet Gordon's. *The kid was definitely odd, but endearing.* He wondered what Harper would think of Gordon. Her boyfriends had been few and far between, and Fletcher was beginning to worry that he was the reason she had problems establishing long-term relationships.

"I get the feeling you don't get out much," Fletcher said as he nudged Gordon away from the lively bar back toward Melanie's table.

"I'm not much of a bar guy. Actually, I spend a lot of time with whiteboards and computers."

"Really?" Fletcher made no attempt to curtail his sarcasm. "If there's one thing you need to learn tonight, it's to never leave a pretty lady waiting in a bar full of men."

The two men pushed and shoved their way through the shoulder-to-shoulder crowd. The table by the window was occupied -- but not by Melanie.

She was nowhere to be seen.

•••

Moments Earlier - The Conservatory Lounge & Bar

Melanie smiled to herself as she approached the window-side table. *This was going to be easy.* Tasked with infiltrating Veritas Bellum, it was less than four months on the job and she had already wedged her foot in the door. *Surely, the so-called truth movement could use an oil industry insider?* With no knowledge of Veritas's direct connection to the mass disappearances, Melanie had no clue she had stepped into a buzzing hornet's nest.

As she placed her hand on the seat back of the chair, a tall, fit young man in a flashy suit gently swept it aside.

"Please, allow me," he offered politely.

Melanie's training and experience told her not to trust the strikingly handsome man, but his impossibly blue eyes and chiseled jawline spoke to her more loudly. What harm could it do? Fletcher was a mere thirty feet away and besides, her ego could use a little boost after the earlier fiasco.

She allowed the handsome stranger to push her chair in.

As she turned to thank her new friend, she was greeted by a sharp burning sensation on the side of her neck.

Everything went black.

Melanie's body collapsed in on itself like a rag doll. The young man caught her in his arms, holding her firmly against his side. He effortlessly guided her lifeless body across the crowded bar.

He answered questioning looks from fellow revelers by simply raising his cupped hand to his mouth and tipping his head back, suggesting that his flopsy friend had imbibed one drink too many. The gesture was more than enough to elicit sympathetic glances and knowing smiles from all he passed. It was always so easy with women. He hoped for the same result with the Englishman and the young scientist.

•••

Fort Huachuca, AZ - Wilkinson Residence

Lieutenant General John Wilkinson's last contact with Gordon had been exactly eighty-one and a half hours ago and each second that had since passed felt like an eternity. Gordon had trusted him and that trust had cost him his life. Wilkinson had lost men in battle, but this was personal. He succumbed to self-pity for only a moment before allowing the pain to re-emerge as a vengeful rage. *Someone will pay.*

The incident had not passed unnoticed. It was a colossal diplomatic screw-up. Behind closed doors, the Russians were throwing around words like "espionage" and "assassin", further setting back already strained U.S.-Russian relations. Wilkinson had been summoned by the president himself, and their brief conversation involved more finger-pointing than actual words.

The Russians had cemented a giant wall of obfuscation around the incident. Information was controlled and conflicting.

The charred corpses of the two CIA agents Wilkinson had sent to escort Gordon back to the hotel were en route back to the U.S., but the whereabouts of Gordon's remains had become something of a mystery. The Russians claimed all that remained of Gordon was mere ash, but the facts just didn't add up.

Gordon's phone had "gone quiet" after he last spoke with Wilkinson outside of QuantumCon, but the satellite positioning data continued until it terminated just outside the western fire exit of the Grand Europe Hotel. Wilkinson retraced each of Gordon's steps after their last conversation and it just didn't make sense. *Too many questions.*

Wilkinson sat behind his home-office desk, nursing a coffee and staring at the positioning data on the printout in front of him. He felt helpless. The higher-ups were well aware of his emotional ties to the case -- and there was no room for emotion in international diplomacy. The Russians were upset about the tightening Iranian oil sanctions and weren't opposed to using Gordon's case as a bargaining chip. The whole thing was a mess. Wilkinson was officially put on leave for a few weeks until things "cooled down." There was little he could do but hope.

CHAPTER SIXTEEN

The Gemologist

Moscow, Russia - Chekhov Residence

KONSTANTIN CHEKHOV PLACED the portable phone back in its cradle atop his desk. It was an unusual call. He couldn't remember the last time someone had made such a specific inquiry about lonsdaleite, or even the last time he had conversed with an American, for that matter. At eighty-three, he was retired from the Moscow Gemological Institute, the school he'd co-founded, and outside of occasional interview requests, his phone rarely rang with business inquiries anymore.

He looked up from his desk and gazed around his expansive woody den. Dozens of eyes stared back at him. Raccoons, deer, squirrel, bear, antelope, zebra and hippo...lifeless, they consumed every inch of his wall space. *Watching the watcher.* Konstantin couldn't recall when his love of taxidermy had first taken hold, but it was second only to his love of gemology and had become an all-consuming hobby. Through the years, his pursuit of rare gems and beasts had often gone hand in hand. A purist through and through, Konstantin only mounted animals he had hunted and killed himself, and he'd travelled the world in search of his next trophies.

The call. Odd. He opened his desk drawer, reached under it and peeled back the tape that held the key. He arose from his desk and walked over to a large metal cabinet with dozens of small alphabetized drawers. Konstantin unlocked the "L" drawer and gently pulled it open.

Sitting there in the middle of the drawer was a small black pyramid.

•••

Moscow, Russia - Patriarshy Pond

Konstantin's instructions had been simple. Come alone and meet at the green park bench along the west side of Patriarshy Pond in downtown Moscow's affluent Presnensky district.

Fletcher wasn't about to let Gordon out of his sight, so they travelled the short two kilometer distance by foot and subway, allowing him to safely tail Gordon, unnoticed by any other observers.

Still shaken by the incident at the bar the previous evening, Fletcher had only allowed himself light catnaps during the night. Though sleep-deprived, his senses were sharp and tuned. He'd made up his mind that nothing was happening to the kid on his watch.

As he approached the pond, Gordon walked by a seated statue of Russia's most beloved fabulist, Ivan Krylov. Coincidentally, Ivan had been a good friend of Alexander Pushkin's. Pushkin had amusingly modified Krylov's description of "an ass of most honest principles" (*The Ass and the Peasant*) to provide the opening of his romantic novel in verse, *Evgenii Onegin*. So well-known were Krylov's fables that readers were immediately alerted and amused by *Onegin's* first line, "My uncle, of most honest principles."

Gordon passed couples young and old, individuals and clusters of friends, as he walked the icy perimeter. It was large for a pond, but even from the opposite bank, Gordon could clearly see the diminutive figure on the bench, awaiting his arrival. With a manicured neon white beard and full head of matching hair, Konstantin Chekhov certainly cut a striking figure.

As Gordon walked the circumference of the pond, he brushed by two lovers lost in an impetuous kiss on the snowy bank. Funny how someone else's happiness can make you feel so bad about your own failures, he thought. His wistful gaze lingered on the young couple: so fully absorbed in one another, they didn't even notice his passing. He walked on toward the bench.

It was an unsettling feeling, knowing you are being watched. He couldn't see them, but he could feel Fletcher's eyes on the back of his head. If it had been anyone else but Fletcher, Gordon felt certain it would have driven him mad, but the Englishman was special -- his mere presence empowered Gordon. As he neared the bench, he felt nothing....no fear, pain or anxiety. He had a job to do.

"Dr. Chekhov."

"Yes, Mr. Cosby, I presume. A bit younger than I had anticipated."

Gordon extended his hand. "Jerry. And I'm older then I look."

"Indeed, so how can I help you? Our phone call was less than illuminating."

"I apologize for my rather vague inquiry, but I had hoped we would be able to meet in person for a private discussion."

"I am a discreet man and expect the same in return."

Gordon nodded in agreement. "Understood. What can you tell me about lonsdaleite?"

"Well, it's a rare hexagonal diamond found in its natural state at meteorite sites. Most notably, Canyon Diablo in the United

States, Goalpara in India and the Allan Hills meteorite in Antarctica."

"And Tunguska?"

Konstantin looked surprised by the question. "Tunguska, yes, there too."

"Have you ever come across any of the Tunguska lonsdaleite?"

"My grandfather, Gregor Chekhov, was the first mineralogist on site."

"The 1921 expedition?"

"No, much earlier than that." The event occurred in 1908, but due to the remote destination and turbulent political climate, a documented Russian expedition didn't reach Tunguska until over a decade later in 1921.

A prolonged silence hung in the air, allowing Gordon's mind the freedom to explore unproven theories and wild suspicions. His naive black and white view of the world had been replaced by one painted in a multitude of grays. Konstantin's distant gaze did little to dissuade his wandering thoughts.

Konstantin broke the silence. "Perhaps we can circumvent the lengthy prologue and begin with the chapter that is of an interest to us both?" Like Gordon, Konstantin had little time for dancing around truths.

"I have some questions about a pyramid-shaped object composed of lonsdaleite," Gordon replied, more than happy to skip the pleasantries.

Konstantin couldn't quite believe his ears. Stone-faced, he contained his excitement. "I see. Tell me more about the object."

"Well, it's black and measures about three inches across its base and about two inches high." Gordon carefully mapped out the dimensions and shape with his index fingers.

There was no question, it was identical to the pyramid Konstantin had been given by his grandfather, mere hours before his death.

"Do you have the object in your possession?" Konstantin inquired.

"No." Gordon dared not tell him he hadn't even actually laid eyes on it. "Have you ever seen anything matching the description?"

Konstantin was faced with a choice. Lies or the truth? The mysterious pyramid had served as a dead end for far too long.

"My grandfather gave me an item fitting that description...before he passed." Konstantin was a hardened man, not prone to displays of emotion, but his grandfather held a special place in his heart. Gregor had practically raised him. He directed his damp eyes downward to avoid Gordon's scrutiny.

"May I see it?"

"Well, I suppose that is the question. Isn't it?" Konstantin looked Gordon squarely in the face. He had dealt with enough liars in his life to recognize Gordon's honest eyes. "Let's start with your real name, shall we?"

"My name is Gordon, Dr. Gordon B. Gray." It was a huge relief to hear the words leave his mouth. A simple confirmation of his own existence. "There are people who want me dead and I may have put you in danger by arranging this meeting."

"Danger is relative. I cannot swim, so the pond poses a bigger threat to my well-being at the moment than you do, I'm afraid."

Gordon smiled. Konstantin's gentle demeanor calmed him.

An image flashed before Konstantin's eyes. It was the smile, he recognized. The Russian papers had all used a photo of

Gordon taken at a Caltech function honoring his Nobel Prize win. Gordon hated posing for photos and almost never smiled on command, except in this particular portrait. Of all the press photos he had posed for in his life, it was odd that would be the one to find its way into the Russian papers.

"The dead young physicist."

"Yes, that is correct," Gordon stated flatly with little hesitation.

"Why would anyone want to kill a young Nobel Award-winning physicist?"

A snowball flew directly into the back of Gordon's head. Startled, he leapt to his feet and swung around to find a teen boy walking toward the bench. "Prastee meenya pozhalosta," the boy said, with a sheepish expression on his face.

"He's asking for your forgiveness," Konstantin translated.

Gordon waved his hand as if to say "no problem" and smiled at the boy, who ran back toward his amused friends. Gordon returned to the bench.

"Sorry. I have an exaggerated startle reflex."

"So it seems. Shall we continue this conversation at my house this evening?"

"Yes. I would like that."

"Will you be bringing your friend?" Konstantin gestured in the direction of Fletcher, who was sitting on the bank of the pond, about a hundred yards from the bench.

Gordon responded with a forced quizzical expression. He was a terrible liar.

"He can't take his eyes off you. I've seen collectors peer at precious gems with less admiration."

•••

Three Months Earlier - Undisclosed Location

The room was white. Too white. The glare reflecting off the floor and walls was enough to pinpoint the most cavernous of pupils.

Men and women dressed in sterile white lab coats entered and exited the immense room through a capsule-shaped glass-walled tube. The reverberation of delicate footsteps and an ominous industrial hum provided the soundtrack in the otherwise eerily quiet workspace.

At first glance, the immense wall looked like some sort of a Kubrickian futuristic sci-fi morgue with hundreds, if not thousands, of corpse drawers covering it. A longer second glance revealed the entire wall was in motion, with the drawers rotating through a series of labyrinthic formations, with no apparent rhyme or reason. Each drawer had a transparent door illuminated by a penetrating green LED projection that displayed a series of four continuously changing numbers. Behind the numbers it was still possible to make out the shaved heads of the unfortunate "volunteers" as they lay awaiting their final breaths, each head cradled in a stainless steel haloed contraption whose prongs anchored deep within their skulls.

Lab technicians stood in silence before the wall as if it were some sort of sacred shrine, busily typing away on their small handheld computer devices. Occasionally, as a drawer rotated down to the bottom row, a technician approached it and pressed a small red button situated in the upper right corner of each drawer, instantaneously causing the body within to disappear. It happened so rapidly that it was impossible to tell if the body was ejected into some sort of compartment behind the wall, or if indeed it just disappeared into the ether. After a drawer emptied, its thick, transparent door sprung open, signaling its availability for a new occupant. Shortly thereafter, a technician would roll in another sedated body on a surgical cart, position it in front of the now vacant drawer and wait for the automated entry process to begin. The efficiency and grandeur of the entire operation was both breathtakingly beautiful and macabre at the same time.

Suddenly, an earsplitting alarm shattered the muted rhythm of the workspace. A red alert light flashed on and off above the west wall, casting an ominous glow upon the room and the panicked occupants below. The dozen or so lab technicians in the room all raced for the ballistic glass-walled walkway at the room's exit, ignoring emergency protocol as they pushed and shoved their way in.

Meanwhile, one drawer near the top of the stack had begun flashing a series of red numbers on its LED readout at a seizure-inducing rate. The wall's other drawers all shifted to allow the flashing one to return to the bottom row.

After the last technician had forced his way through the crowded capsule's doorway, one calm individual pushed his way through and coolly approached the wall. It was Dmitry. He had regained a few pounds as well as his old ruddy complexion, his bedraggled beard a distant memory.

He stood in front of the suspect corpse drawer, which had now made its way down to the center of the first row. Unflustered, he observed the continuously streaming data on the front of its door. Dmitry pulled a handheld computer device from his white lab coat and began to type. The combination of the deafening alarm and the obnoxious red alert light had no apparent effect on him whatsoever. He entered one final string of data into the handheld computer device and walked away from the flashing drawer. The alarm and alert light both ceased and the drawers resumed their normal patterns of motion.

Slowly, the still-anxious technicians began to filter back into the room, and resumed their automatous duties.

CHAPTER SEVENTEEN

Hack The Hacker

Pasadena, CA - Caltech

HARPER SAT AT her desk, throwing an aged piece of Silly Putty against the wall of her insignificantly-sized cubicle. A framed 5" x 7" photo of her mother and father rested on the edge of her desk, providing the spartan nest's sole connection to humanity. Like Gordon, Harper displayed a lack of talent for decorating and could care less what that said about her.

She hadn't heard from her father since he left for Russia. The lack of communication was unlike him and she was sick of waiting. She grabbed her backpack and skateboard before proceeding to the exit of the Annenberg Building, home to the Department of Computing and Mathematical Sciences, and her cubicle.

She threw the board down on the cement sidewalk immediately outside the door and skated off toward the Bridge Building.

The tone on campus since the reporting of Gordon's death was decidedly dour. Nerds were unnatural mourners and Harper found the candlelight vigils and public memorials nauseating. She blamed Gordon for her father's absence and held no regard for his poster boy status.

She hopped off her board in front of the Bridge Building and bounded up the stairs leading to the entrance. The hallways were dark and empty...and the smooth floors looked too good to pass up. Harper dropped her board and carved down the hall.

Gordon's old office remained untouched, the academic equivalent of retiring the jersey of a superstar athlete. Flowers and notes from his many admirers decorated the hallway outside his door. She looked down at the doorknob. *Disgusting.* A lace brassiere hung from it. She picked it up and flung it to the side. She had seen Gordon's Nobel photo plastered everywhere and she frankly didn't see the appeal. *Too boyish. Looked like he could play the preppy, brainy one in a boy band.*

She pulled a man-size multi-tool from her backpack and took the liberty of picking the lock on Gordon's door, a skill she inherited from her father. She quietly shut the door behind her and took a quick look around. Gordon's Nobel Prize still hung on the wall behind his desk and a few textbooks remained on the bookshelf. A desktop computer sat on a small portable table just to the left of his desk. It proved far too great a temptation.

Harper powered up the computer, breezing by the weak security. As a rebellious young teen, she had fallen in with an international hacking collective composed of a bunch of wayward twenty- and thirty-something-year-old guys who found joy in messing with right-wing politicians, greedy corporations and oppressive regimes. Harmless stuff, until they decided to post the NIN video for *Closer* on the homepage of the UK Conservatives Party. One sloppy mistake led the Conservative Party's hired team of computer security specialists straight back to thirteen-year-old prodigy, Harper Crisp. Her gravely disappointed father had been forced to call in a favor with an old SAS team member, who at the time was in the employ of MI5. They let her off with a slap on the wrist. The security firm was so impressed by Harper's work, they offered her an internship right on the spot. As a form of punishment, Fletcher forced her to take the position. She put in a full summer's work and received an invaluable education in computer security and the best ways to circumvent it.

She nosed through the files on his hard drive. The guy was squeaky clean, boringly so...physics, physics and more physics. Harper missed the edgier nature of her East Coast MIT friends, whose intelligence didn't preclude a keen sense of pop culture and an appreciation of mischief making.

She'd grown up in Los Angeles, but never really felt like she belonged. Though she was unconventionally pretty herself, she found the LA obsession with looks and celebrity to be mind-numbing. One only needed a modicum of knowledge to stand out among the sea of pedestrian intellects.

Harper browsed through a few photos on his hard drive, stopping to admire one of Gordon standing in a cap and gown, holding his diploma. Having been briefed on his family situation, she imagined Gordon's now-deceased parents standing behind the camera and proudly smiling at him as they snapped away. At least she and Gordon had that in common. *Motherless souls were rudderless souls.*

A flashing prompt demanded her attention. A flash of panic squeezed the oxygen from her lungs. *Sloppy, Harper. Sloppy.*

"Hello."

Her cyber presence had clearly been detected. She shifted nervously in her seat. *How did this person know she wasn't just an associate backing up Gordon's files?* She instantly reverted to her younger teen self who sat nervously on the edge of her bed awaiting a lecture from her disappointed father. *Was he in danger?*

"Hello," she replied; each letter seemed to take a lifetime to type.

After a moment's pause, the blinking cursor returned with the response, "Looking for something? Gordon perhaps?"

"Gordon is dead," she replied.

"You like to play games. Me too. We shall be fast friends."

"Who are you?"

"I am a man of no consequence. A mere cog in the machine. Much like you, Harper."

Seeing her name pop up on the screen sent a chill up her spine. He was watching her. It was the only possible way he could know her identity. Panicked, her eyes scanned the room for cameras. Nothing.

"I'm afraid you've got the wrong person."

"Do you see the silver pen resting on the far left corner of the desk?"

Harper shifted her eyes in the direction he indicated. It was tucked in neatly among a few stray textbooks.

"Yes.'"

"Pick it up."

Harper did as she was told. A cursory scan of the pen revealed nothing unusual.

"Good girl. I can see you much better now."

Harper was certain there was no lens on the pen. She unscrewed the bottom to take a closer look. A quick burst of aerosolized fentanyl sprayed her directly in the face. Her head dropped to the desk within moments.

•••

Moscow, Russia - Ararat Park Hyatt

Fletcher and Gordon approached the front desk in the spacious lobby of the Ararat Park Hyatt. The Ararat was the perfect blend of modern and traditional with dark leather sofas, armchairs, shining marble flooring and rich red wood walls.

Though Fletcher hadn't spoken of it last night, Gordon could sense Melanie's sudden disappearance had rattled him. The two men had waited at the table for twenty minutes, in the event that she had popped off to use the powder room, but she never returned. They sat and nursed their drinks in silence. Fletcher's gut told him it wasn't because she needed an early night and he allowed himself to question her motives. She had seemed overly enthusiastic, but then again, he did have that effect on women. *Stupid mistake.*

Fletcher eyed the attendants at the front desk and quickly chose a pretty young woman to work his charm on. Eager to learn from the master, Gordon observed from his side.

"Hello there, love." Those three simple words, combined with the disarming smile and gravelly British accent, had opened many doors.

"Good evening, sir. How may I help you?" The cheery smile was a good sign.

"One of your guests, a Ms. Melanie Johnson, left her scarf in my room last night and I was wondering if you could tell me what room she's staying in?" Fletcher cocked a right eyebrow and flashed a cheeky grin. He could write a textbook on this stuff.

"Let me check for you," she replied with a knowing smile. She typed Melanie's name on the computer, discreetly tucked into the desk. She perused the results with a puzzled expression on her face.

"I'm afraid we don't have any guests checked in under the name Melanie Johnson. Are you sure she's staying here?"

"Did she perhaps check out late last night?"

"Well, I'm not supposed to give out that kind of information...but I can tell you if you leave the scarf here at the desk, I will have no way of getting it back to Ms. Johnson."

Fletcher reached across the desk, gently holding her hand in his. "You've been very helpful. Thanks, love."

She appeared to melt under his touch. Gordon wondered if he should be taking notes. Clearly he was in the presence of The Woman Whisperer. No wonder he had had so little success with women. He had been doing it wrong all along.

The two men left the desk and headed toward the exit.

"Thanks, love," Gordon mimicked in his best English accent.

"Well, look at that. There's that sense of humor again. You know what your problem is?"

Gordon shrugged his shoulders. He was pretty sure he didn't want to know.

"You interact with women like they're computers. It's all about the first five seconds. You need to make them smile...and save your jokes. They don't make sense."

"I don't have an accent."

"Don't worry about the bloody accent. You just need to find one special thing. She may weigh more than a Mini, but that doesn't stop her from having beautiful eyes or a nice smile. Just like war. Disarm them first, ask questions later."

"Are you married?"

The question caught Fletcher off guard. "Yes...no...was."

Gordon instantly regretted asking him. It was the first time he had seen Fletcher speechless. The two men walked in silence as they descended into the subway station and boarded the train bound for Konstantin's home.

"My wife was a scientist too." Fletcher looked out the subway car window, lost.

•••

Moscow, Russia - Chekhov Residence

The lifeless eyes staring down upon Gordon made him feel about as comfortable as an ant under a magnifying glass at high noon. His nervous knee-bounce kicked in as he settled into a chair opposite Konstantin, at the ancient mahogany desk that looked like it had stories of its own to tell.

"Thanks for inviting me here," Gordon offered as an icebreaker.

"I assure you, it wasn't a selfless gesture."

Konstantin's desk was cluttered with papers, books, rocks and a few forgotten coffee mugs. Gordon fought back an urge to tidy it. He had no idea how anyone could work under such conditions.

Then, he saw it.

Peeking out from behind one of the mugs was the blackest thing he had ever laid his eyes upon. Its very presence seemed to darken the room.

"May I touch it?" Gordon inquired, his covetous gaze focused on the pyramid.

Konstantin pushed the object toward him.

Gordon turned it over and over in his hands; its unexpected weightiness and color seemed its only extraordinary characteristics. He had hoped to feel something...anything, but all that came of the exchange was a nasty scratch on his palm. As he set the pyramid back down on the desk, the small wound began to bleed.

Konstantin pulled a handkerchief from his pocket and handed it to Gordon. Gordon reluctantly accepted, taking just a little too long inspecting its cleanliness.

"It's freshly laundered," Konstantin reassured him.

"Sorry -- germophobe." Gordon applied the handkerchief to his wound and watched the blood seep up through the thin white cotton material.

"Indeed." Konstantin pushed a notebook toward Gordon. "My studies."

Gordon skimmed through the notes. Though predominantly written in Russian, and thus unintelligible to Gordon, it was nonetheless an impressive lifelong accounting of a single object.

"I thought your friend would be joining us?"

"He's...waiting outside," Gordon replied, opting for truth over fiction.

"I see. So tell me why this pyramid means so much to you, Dr. Gray? Did it play a role in your death?"

Gordon mustered a weak smile. *Perhaps Fletcher was right. Scientists just aren't funny.*

"Have you heard anything about the anthrax attack in West Virginia, by chance?"

"I saw the video on the news. Curious incident."

"Well, the anthrax story was a cover. Twenty-two people disappeared into thin air. No trace of their existence remains. One kid survived, but he's blind and has little to offer as a witness. The man outside your front door found a pyramid exactly like yours on site. I was working with the U.S. Army, but due to a rather complicated chain of events, I am no longer in contact, nor assisting them. And that's why I'm here."

The revelation excited Konstantin. He had always known something was special about the object the moment his grandfather handed it to him. *Tunguska. Perhaps the rumors were true?*

"What is your opinion of the pyramid's relation to the disappearance?"

"I believe it's either a window or targeting device for some sort of directed high-energy weapon."

"Are you aware of the rumors surrounding the Tunguska event?"

"Yes. Black holes, anti-matter, meteorites…aliens." Though young, Gordon was a scientist through and through. Science offered answers based on fact. There was little room for blind faith in his world. Based on logic alone, if one were to ask him if he believed there was a possibility that intelligent extraterrestrial life could exist elsewhere in the universe, he would have to answer, "Yes." Statistically, one would be foolish not to allow for the possibility. However, the discussion of intelligent alien life in academic and scientific circles usually led to odd looks, whispers and bad jokes. Gordon felt silly even mentioning it to Konstantin.

"The first two are simply ridiculous from a scientific point of view. Would you agree?"

"Yes." The black hole theory had been batted around in the early '70s by two physicists from the University of Texas who proposed that the Tunguska event was caused by a small black hole passing through the Earth. Their hypothesis was considered flawed, as there was no so-called exit event--a second explosion occurring as the black hole, having tunneled through the Earth, shot out the other side on its way back into space. Based on the direction of impact, the exit event would have occurred in the North Atlantic, close to the seismic recording stations that collected much of the evidence of the initial event. No such readings were recorded. The black hole and antimatter theories also failed to account for evidence that cosmic material was deposited by the extraterrestrial body, including dust trails in the atmosphere and the distribution of magnetic spherules around the impact area.

"Leaving only a meteorite or the little green men."

"So it would seem," Gordon concurred, shifting uncomfortably in his chair.

"My grandfather Gregor found this pyramid along with hundreds more in the heart of the impact zone in Tunguska. He was instructed to leave the pyramids at the site, but he chose to keep one. Not a single pyramid was scratched, burned or scarred in any way. More than 800 square miles of trees were flattened. I have visited many impact craters and seen many things, but nothing like this." Konstantin held up the pyramid in admiration.

"Did he ever mention the coordinates of the site?"

"I'm afraid not."

A prolonged silence passed between the men. They both knew where the conversation was heading.

Gordon dropped his gaze. "Did your grandfather find any signs of alien life at the site?" There was no avoiding the awkward nature of the subject. Two scientists talking about aliens. It was like creationists discussing the Big Bang.

"There was a second expedition team that reached the site at the same time as my grandfather. They erected a large geodesic dome over a portion of the site. It was heavily guarded and he saw no more than three or four men enter or exit it at any time. The skies around the dome glowed a bright blue, even in the dead of night. My grandfather and his team all suffered intense nausea and migraines during their short expedition. He died from an extremely rare disease called sporadic fatal insomnia. There are only a handful of diagnosed cases on record. Doctors still do not know what caused it, but his autopsy revealed a large inoperable glial cyst on his pineal gland."

Gordon looked at Konstantin with a quizzical expression. "Biology isn't one of my strengths."

"Some call the pineal gland the 'third eye.' It's an endocrine gland in the brain. It produces the hormone melatonin, which controls wake and sleep patterns. After returning from Tunguska my grandfather would go without sleep for two or three days and then sleep for an hour or two at most. The disease progressed and by the end he was lucky to sleep ten minutes a month. He hung on for years and years, far longer than any of the other documented cases. My grandmother remained by his side but it destroyed their marriage. Have you ever observed someone who hasn't slept for four days?"

Gordon shook his head.

"It is like living inside your worst nightmare – one you can not discern from reality. He suffered hallucinations. He'd see moving shadows. Ultimately it caused dementia and paranoia. He spent the last ten years of his life in the Kashchenko Psychiatric Hospital."

"I'm sorry. That must have been rough."

"I was just a boy when he died."

"Did he ever mention what he thought might have been inside the dome?"

"No. Through the years, he spoke on and off about the expedition, but he was not a man of conjecture. He handed me the pyramid two hours before his last breath and in a rare moment of clarity, he said 'It's there.'"

Konstantin took a moment to gather himself. He had never discussed his grandfather's passing nor the cryptic pyramid with anyone before, and here he was talking to a complete stranger...an American, at that. The odd thing was that it felt completely natural, as if he was in the right place at the right time, speaking to the right man.

"I'm sorry for your loss. I have already taken too much of your time, but I have just one last question. Do you have any idea where the remainder of the pyramids were sent?"

"No, I'm afraid I don't. I was hoping you might be able to answer that for me," Konstantin replied. "Please take this. It is of no use to me anymore. Perhaps it will offer you some guidance." Konstantin handed his notebook to Gordon. He had not intended to do so, but the hands of fate were moving.

•••

Somewhere Over The North Pacific

Harper awoke to the deafening sound of helicopter blades cutting through the thin glacial air. Her head felt as though it was on the verge of rupture, and the pain was so intense, she welcomed the idea. She had suffered through her share of blistering hangovers, but nothing ever like this. She could barely lift her head from the cold metal floor it rested upon.

Everything was black. Pitch black. She struggled against the blindfold that covered her eyes and the straps that bound both her hands and feet, only for a moment. Pain coursed through her veins and each movement only made matters worse. Her thin black hoodie offered little protection from the cold winds above the North Pacific. She balled up, calling out in agony and frustration. Her scream was no match for the roar of the chopper.

The Kamov Ka-60, painted black against the deep blue midnight skies, floated on, like a lone bird over a sea of possibility.

•••

Moscow, Russia - Subway

Fletcher had always been able to sense impending danger, a power he cultivated growing up on the rough-and-tumble streets of South London's Brixton. He knew something was amiss the moment he and Gordon entered the subway car. A drunk vagrant sprawled across the bench and a twenty-something goth girl draped over her cello, performing Elgar's sorrowful "Cello Concerto in E minor," were the only other occupants. Neither traveler bothered Fletcher. It was the 6'4" steel-jawed ironman who thrust his arm between the closing doors of the departing train that worried him. Responding to his brute force, the doors sprung open with little resistance.

The adrenaline surge was instantaneous. Fletcher's heart rate escalated. Vision sharpened. Hearing became unusually acute. He could feel the pulse of the hulking man through the thickening air. Time slowed to a near-standstill as Fletcher watched him pull a Makarov pistol from his waistband. *Gordon.* Fletcher spun around to find Gordon with his back to the assailant walking toward the bench opposite the goth-girl cellist. He was too far away. Fletcher spun back around. He had only one option. As the man raised his gun Fletcher dove through the air, placing his body in the line of fire. It was just enough to throw off the aim of the startled assailant. When the bullet grazed Fletcher's shoulder, he felt nothing but a flash of heat. His impact with the bench was another story altogether. Fletcher heard the cartilage in his shoulder tear as it dislocated, but there was no time for pain. From his prone position on the floor, Fletcher swept the assailant's leg with a powerful roundhouse kick, sending him crashing to the floor. The pistol flew from his hand.

The assailant landed just inches away, face to face with Fletcher. The two men shared a fraction of a second's eye contact.

The intimacy of the moment was not lost on Fletcher. War had introduced him to the absurdity of it all. Killing another human, a complete stranger. *And for what? At the orders of another, who's taking orders from another and so on. Who's at the top of the heap? Or is it just a sick circle?*

The assailant was the first to move. He looked in the direction of the gun. It was just out of reach of both men. He turned back toward Fletcher and wrapped his gargantuan hands around Fletcher's throat, pinning him to the floor. With only one operable arm, there was little Fletcher could do to ward off the attack. He struggled for oxygen as he tried to free himself from the two hundred and eighty pounds of solid muscle bearing down on him.

Everything happened so quickly that Gordon had barely turned around by the time the two men had hit the floor. He froze the moment he saw Fletcher struggling beneath the behemoth of a man. He had allowed himself the luxury of relaxation the moment he had come under Fletcher's watch, but he too felt the effects of the adrenaline surge almost immediately. The metallic taste in his mouth had become far too familiar. Gordon's mind seemed to separate from its own logic core; his hearing dulled and his limbs felt as if they were under the control of someone else. He looked down at the gun on the subway floor. It seemed a universe away.

The goth-girl cellist shouted something in Russian at Gordon in a vain attempt to pull him out of his stupor. She could see his friend was hanging onto life by a gossamer thread. She dropped her beloved cello to the floor, rose to her feet and kicked the gun toward Fletcher. The assailant was so focused on Fletcher's neck, he didn't even notice the girl's movement. As fortune would have it, the gun slid directly next to Fletcher's good arm. In one fluid motion, he snatched the weapon, held it to the assailant's temple and fired the kill shot. Blood and brain matter painted the entire side of the subway car and the full weight of the assassin landed squarely on top of him. He gasped for air as he shoved the dead body to the side. He brought his hand up to his throat; he was lucky his trachea hadn't been completely crushed.

The sound of the second gunshot brought Gordon straight back to the present. He ran to Fletcher's side and helped him to his feet. He felt ashamed. If the girl had not interceded, his friend Fletcher would be dead right now.

"I froze."

"Time to thaw. Put one hand here and here."

As directed, Gordon grabbed Fletcher's lifeless arm at his wrist and just above his elbow. The goth-girl retrieved her cello, regarding the scene before her with a befuddled expression that conveyed both atrocity and admiration.

"Now flex my elbow at a ninety-degree angle, hold my wrist firmly and rotate my lower arm in towards my chest." Fletcher gritted his teeth as Gordon obeyed his instructions exactly. Thankfully, his pain was masked by the adrenal cortex hormones coursing through his veins.

"Alright, mate, this is the bad bit. Rotate my arm out to the side...slowly." Fletcher closed his eye in anticipation of the pain. It wasn't his first dislocated joint reduction, so he knew the most painful part of the procedure was about to begin. Gordon hesitantly rotated out Fletcher's arm, until it was just past ninety degrees to his chest. They both heard a loud pop as it slid back into the pocket. The relief was immediate. Fletcher couldn't help but smile.

"Right as rain."

"You're bleeding." Gordon pointed to Fletcher's shoulder wound from the first gunshot.

Fletcher looked down at his bloodied shoulder. "Nothing. 'Tis but a flesh wound." Fletcher walked over to the homeless drunk sprawled out across the opposite bench. "Don't mind if I do." He grabbed the bottle of cheap vodka that dangled precariously from the man's relaxed grip, took a hearty swig and set the bottle back down next to the inert form.

"He's a sound sleeper, that one." Fletcher shifted his gaze to the goth-girl cellist, who had essentially saved his life. Gordon could see she was already well under his spell. *Even covered in brain matter.*

"And you, love, I thank you from the bottom of my heart." Fletcher got down on one knee, lifted her outstretched hand to his lips and gently kissed it. She didn't understand a word of English, but understood Fletcher just fine. Her blackened eyes sparkled under his direct gaze. She handed Fletcher a few bunched up tissues from her jacket pocket. As the train slowed to a stop, he wiped the assailant's blood from his face.

"I believe this is our stop."

The subway doors opened and the two men exited the subway car.

Fletcher scanned the station, expecting to find the dead assailant's partners, but instead found an elderly couple and a few drunk young men returning home from an evening out. He didn't let Gordon see it, but he was relieved. He wasn't sure how much more he could take at the moment. His adrenaline was waning and all he really wanted was a hot shower and a bed.

"Stoi!" shouted the goth girl. She rose from her seat, picked up Konstantin's journal from the floor and rushed toward the closing door. Gordon hurried to meet her, but barely grasped the corner of the splayed open journal which sat suspended between the closed doors. He ran alongside the now moving train and tugged on the corner of the journal as hard as he could, only managing to tear away a single page.

"Dammit." Everything was going wrong all at once. He was beginning to feel the unfamiliar, crushing weight of failure. But then Gordon looked down at the paper, and the numbers popped off the page as if they were inhabiting a dimension of their own. He had felt this eureka moment before, and it had won him a Nobel Prize.

"Forget about it. I know her type well," Fletcher said, recalling his equally ballsy daughter. "The journal is safe with her. We need to get out of Moscow, stat."

"A map," Gordon responded cryptically with a wide grin on his face.

"You okay, mate?"

"A map. I need a map."

Fletcher pulled a small tablet device from the pocket of his parka. "Where to?"

"Latitude 61 degrees 52 minutes, longitude 94 degrees 10 minutes. Where is it?" Gordon held the paper for Fletcher to see. Konstantin had recorded the weight of the pyramid as 0.61529410 kg. Konstantin had probably stared at the numbers hundreds of times in his life and to him, all they represented were a basic measurement. Gordon didn't even need to hear Fletcher's response; he already knew the answer. He felt as if he was speeding down a one-way street at the speed of light. *At one with the universe.*

"Tunguska. Well done, mate." Fletcher patted him on the back, cringing as an arrow of pain shot up his bloodied shoulder.

•••

Dimock, PA - State Rt. 2023

Bathed in moonlight, a man emerged from the backseat of a black Lincoln Town Car. He glanced down at his phone and

double-checked the coordinates: Latitude: 41.7324281°
Longitude:-75.9570169°. He stole a quick glance at his
surroundings. The uninterrupted countryside seemed to extend to
the edge of forever. In a different life, it was the kind of place he
could see himself retiring: fishing, hunting, breathing. It made no
sense. *Why here?* A question that would remain internalized.
Questions get people killed.

Resigned to the task at hand, he grabbed the combo-
locked, titanium Zero Halliburton briefcase from the backseat. He
entered 6-1-6 and snapped open the two bolt latches.
Unceremoniously, he pulled the black pyramid from its foam-fitted
encasement and tossed it into the heavy bramble that lined the
rural route.

He stepped back into the idling car and never looked back.

CHAPTER EIGHTEEN

Convergence

Rysevo, Russia - Farmhouse

THE MORNING SUNLIGHT colored the inside of her eyelids a bright rusty orange, gently rousing her from her deadened slumber. Disoriented, Harper awoke to find herself in a small bed in an unadorned bedroom. She looked down at her wrists and ankles, where bruises marked the location of her former restraints. The crippling head pain from the chopper had lessened considerably, but her mind still wasn't clocking in at its usual speed. She looked around the room. Bed, side table, window.

A plastic jug and an empty paper cup sat atop her bedside table. Dehydration had already established a foothold; her tongue was practically glued to the roof of her mouth. She eagerly poured herself a cup of water and guzzled it down, allowing the overflow to dribble down the front of her dirtied t-shirt.

She arose from the bed and walked to the door that she felt certain would be locked. The old brass doorknob rattled under her hand, but held firm. Next, she approached the large window, from where she appraised her surroundings. Her bedroom was perched at the top of an old blue farmhouse. A blanket of snow extended for miles around the house and beyond that, an immense forest. The nearest sign of life was a gray plume of chimney smoke floating up above the trees, miles away.

She examined the aged wooden-framed sash window. Its lock was welded in place. Not insurmountable, but from this height a broken ankle or leg was almost guaranteed, with the distinct possibility of incurring a far greater injury.

She ran down her options. Yelling for help was pointless, and besides, she felt oddly at ease considering her current predicament. She knew she was the bait at the end of the hook and that her father and Gordon were the intended catch of the day. Without her, her captors would have nothing.

A mechanical sound drew her attention away from her escape plans. She looked around the spartan room. From the opposite upper corner, a small white security camera panned with her movements as she traversed the room. She hated the feeling of being watched, especially by strangers. She waved at the camera, smiled and flipped it the bird.

Moments later a slender, fine-featured man dressed smartly in a patterned wool sweater and flat-front corduroys entered the room. Fifty-something, with a close-cropped haircut and black framed modernist eyeglasses, he looked more like an architect than a would-be kidnapper.

"Peter," the man said, touching his chest as if to confirm his curt introduction. "Are you in any pain?"

"I have a headache. And I'm hungry."

"Yes. The fentanyl will do that. I will see that your pain and hunger are both resolved immediately. I presume you know why you are here?"

Harper nodded her head.

"I'm sure you've considered escape," Peter said, gesturing toward the window. "Please be assured that a jump from this height will render you incapable of walking. And crawling through a foot of snow in minus ten degrees Fahrenheit - dressed as you are - will

give you a life expectancy of approximately thirty-seven minutes."
As if to accentuate Peter's point, a gust of wind whistled through a
small crack in the frame.

"Why are you doing this?"

"We simply want to speak to your father and Dr. Gray.
We have similar interests."

"Who are you? And how did you know I would be in
Gordon's office?"

"I'm afraid I can't answer the first, and the second...well,
let's just say, great minds think alike." He smiled warmly. Oddly,
she felt unthreatened ... almost safe.

"And when you're done with me and my father?"

"Assuming no one makes any rash decisions, I see no
reason why we can't all coexist. It's a very big world."

The words offered Harper little comfort. If one were to
look up the word "rash" in the dictionary, a picture of her father
would surely accompany it.

"Enough chit-chat for now. After you've eaten, we can
resume our discussion." Peter turned and walked toward the door.

"I need to use the bathroom."

"Certainly." He opened the door and spoke quietly in
Russian to someone in the hallway. He re-entered the room
accompanied by a woman who could surely bench-press their
combined weight.

Where Peter was warm, the woman was ice cold. Her
colorless eyes and toneless face revealed no emotion whatsoever.
She was certainly the bad cop to Peter's good. "This is Nika. She
will escort you to the toilet. Should you require anything further,
simply knock on your door and she will assist you."

As Peter left the room, Nika reached for Harper's upper arm, taking a firm grip as she steered her out the door and down the hallway toward the bathroom.

The hallway had a completely different feel. With its rustic decor and worn furnishings, it was a true Russian farmhouse. Nika's perch, a simple wooden chair, sat directly outside the bedroom door.

Any sense of comfort Harper had felt in Peter's presence evaporated under Nika's cold grasp. Their silent walk felt more like a death row processional than a walk to the bathroom. When they reached the door at the end of the hall, Nika entered directly behind Harper. Harper turned to her, offering a weak smile, as if to suggest she would be fine on her own for a minute. Nika answered with a frosty stare. Clearly she had no intention of leaving her side. Harper looked around the bathroom. Bath, shower, medicine cabinet, small window, toilet, sink - definitely not kiddie-proofed. *Possibilities.* Resigned to the fact that Nika wasn't going anywhere, Harper unbuttoned her jeans.

"Can you at least turn around?" Harper asked.

Nika was a woman of few words. She maintained her rigid stance.

Harper shrugged her shoulders. She would have an audience. She pulled down her jeans and sat on the cold porcelain. She hadn't urinated in over twenty-four hours, but even her dehydration and stage fright couldn't stop the flow. The situation was so uncomfortable, Harper instinctively began to hum nonsensically in order to cover the sound of her urination.

Wiping was the most humiliating aspect of it all. She felt like a two-year-old. She flushed the toilet, washed her hands and hung her head in shame as Nika escorted her back to the room.

She missed her dad.

Dimock, PA - Louden Residence

The dryer buzzer startled Nancy Louden. She had just closed her eyes in anticipation of grabbing a much needed quick catnap, and the jarring sound nearly brought her to tears. She hadn't fully realized the important role sleep played in maintaining her mental well-being, until the birth of her seven-week-old baby girl, Skye. She and her husband George had been operating on only three to four hours a night. They lovingly referred to it as boot camp, and resented friends whose babies managed to sleep for six or seven hours right from the get-go.

"Darn it," she whispered under her breath as she ran to silence the machine. She held her breath for a moment in anticipation of the inevitable wail.

"Waaaaaahhhh." Sure enough. Tears would do no good. She put on a smile on and went to retrieve her little bundle of joy. Perhaps she could coax her back to sleep with a little rocking and a lullaby?

Skye calmed immediately once she was in her mother's arms. Nancy touched her nose to the top of the baby's head. No other scent compared...well, except for maybe the smell of the freshly baked blueberry muffins that drifted in from the kitchen. She had been strict with her dieting since giving birth, but every once in a while she just needed a freshly baked treat. She chuckled to herself, realizing the buzzer for the oven was just about to go off as well. For whatever reason, she and Skye were not meant to sleep this morning.

As the last thirty seconds ticked down on the oven timer, Nancy walked with Skye over to the photo-covered refrigerator door, from where she removed a picture of her husband. She held up the photo in front of Skye. She swore it brought a smile to her little angel's face, but at this early age that expression was more likely due to the passing of gas.

As the last five seconds ticked down on the oven timer, a brilliant blue pulsing light washed over the room. It was mesmerizing. A fraction of a second later, the entire two-bedroom house shook to its very foundation. And then nothing. The light and sound vanished as quickly as they had arrived. The room appeared untouched, but both Nancy and Skye were gone. The photo of George lay on the ground next to where they had been standing.

The oven timer beeped, echoing through the vacant house.

One hundred and twenty-eight men, women and children - the entire population of Dimock, Pennsylvania - disappeared into thin air.

•••

Moscow, Russia - Irkutsk International Airport

Fletcher and Gordon's uneventful journey aboard a small four-seater Cessna, began on a private airstrip just outside of Moscow and ended at Irkutsk International Airport, a two-and-a-half-hour drive from Tunguska.

Fletcher had made arrangements to have a four-wheel drive vehicle available for their use upon landing. Gordon smiled when he saw the maker -- it was a brand new matte finish army green Lada Niva, with all the bells and whistles one could hope for in an off-road vehicle. Certainly, it was a world away from the old Lada he had passed on to Dr. Batkin. He wondered how Dr. Batkin and the missus were making out with his father's old beater. *His father.* He quickly turned down a different corridor in his busy mind. *No time to be distracted.* After the subway incident, Gordon resolved to stay strong, focused and present. He owed it to Fletcher and to himself.

Though worlds apart, the two men had become close - Fletcher was even mulling over the idea of introducing Harper to Gordon after their return to the States. It was a first for him -- he had never considered another man worthy of his beloved Harper. She had introduced her father to many potential suitors over the years, but he had always managed to find dozens of flaws with each of them. Though fiercely independent, Harper valued her father's opinion above all else and whether she knew it or not, that played a role in the demise of each failed relationship.

Gordon offered to drive. He had slept through the entire six-hour flight from Moscow to Irkutsk. Sleep had not come as easily for Fletcher, however. He knew their odds of survival were decreasing by the minute. They had barely escaped Moscow alive and he was certainly not capable of another major physical altercation. The ligaments in his dislocated shoulder would take weeks to heal and the bullet wound in his other shoulder was far more than a graze. He had cleaned and bandaged it himself, and followed that with a strong series of self-prescribed antibiotics, but it would certainly require medical attention at some point not too far in the future.

"Sleep. I've got this. Really." Gordon grabbed the keys from Fletcher and took the driver's seat. Fletcher reluctantly walked around the side of the SUV, spitting out a spent sunflower seed shell, before entering through the passenger door.

"Don't over-think the subway," Fletcher offered, setting aside his normal wisecracking self. "There's plenty of muscle to replace me, but without you, the ship sinks. Keep the head clear - I know what you've been through." He caught Gordon's eye for a moment before Gordon turned away, embarrassed.

Gordon started the car and proceeded toward the airport exit. A light snow was falling, just enough to leave behind a dusting on the road. The temperature hovered around seventeen degrees Fahrenheit. The crunching sound of the snow under the Lada's off-road tires resonated all the way up through the gas pedal. His weather-beaten saddle shoes had been replaced by a pair of Sorel hiking boots at Fletcher's insistence - a vast improvement. He had also acquired a new weatherproof parka and gloves. Underneath it all, he still wore the uniform - Scottish-made Taransay Harris Tweed jacket, gray flannel trousers, white shirt and maroon tie. *His uniform.* It was his last connection to the life he dearly missed.

Fletcher leaned forward and tuned in the satellite radio to a soft-rock classics station. It was barely audible, but just what he needed to settle his thoughts.

"Rock-a-bye baby, on the treetop," Gordon jokingly sang.

"You're learning, mate."

Fletcher reclined in his seat and allowed his weary eyes to close. He needed the sleep, but he also hoped Gordon saw it as a sign of his trust.

•••

Rysevo, Russia - Farmhouse

Harper sat cross-legged on the bed, staring out the window. The flurries were just sporadic enough that she could almost count the individual flakes as they drifted past.

As a child, she often tried to send telepathic messages to her father - concentrating with such a ferocity that it physically caused tension headaches. He would play along and try to read her mind, occasionally guessing somewhere in the ballpark - just close enough to instill a sense of belief in his daughter. To this day Harper still sent out a message to him every now and then. She was silently calling out to him as Peter entered the room.

"I trust you are feeling better?" Peter inquired with a tone of genuine concern.

Harper shrugged languidly as she held her gaze on the window.

"It's time to contact your father," Peter said, handing her a satellite phone.

Harper held the phone in her hand. It was almost identical to her father's. He travelled everywhere with it. She shut her eyes - one last message. *You are in trouble.*

Harper opened her eyes, looked directly at Peter and threw the phone against the far wall. It shattered on impact.

"Well, that is disappointing." Peter walked over to the phone and picked up the jagged pieces, which were certainly more than sharp enough to inflict bodily harm. Harper had responded precisely as Peter had anticipated.

"Nika."

Within moments, Nika entered the room.

"Take this and bring me the syringe." Peter handed her the shattered phone remnants. Nika left immediately, threw the phone fragments in the bathroom trash and returned with a needle in her hand.

"What is that?"

"Scopolamine. It will simply make you more agreeable." Peter nodded his head in Harper's direction and Nika obediently charged forward. Harper's primal kicks and screams were no match for Nika's strength. After a brief struggle, Harper conceded. If she was going to win this battle it would be through the power of her mind, not her body.

Nika gently depressed the end of the needle until a bead of liquid appeared on the needle's tip, before thrusting it in the side of Harper's neck.

The immediate effects were obvious. Harper's eyes glazed over and her head fell back to the bed.

Peter approached and stood over her.

"That's better. Now, Harper, I simply need your father's sat phone number. We just want to let him know we have you here and that you are safe and sound," he proposed gently.

"011 - 8816 - 000 - 5552. Tell him I feel so dizzy. Gordon's not dead."

"I know, Harper. Close your eyes. Sweet dreams."

Scopolamine had long been used by intelligence agencies around the world as an interrogation tool. In most people it loosened lips and inhibitions and caused short-term memory loss, drowsiness, nausea and light-headedness. Colombian criminals had more recently taken to using scopolamine or burundanga for robbing tourists. They slipped it in the victim's drink at the bar, robbed them of everything on their person, and then drove the victim to an ATM where they "willingly" withdrew their daily cash limit. The tourist would awake the following day remembering nothing after the drink at the bar.

When the effects of the drug wore off, Harper would recall nothing.

•••

Washington, DC - White House

Over the years, Chief of Staff Harold Corbin had learned to gauge the president's frustration level by the volume of the tennis ball's steady *thwonk* against the backboard. The president's strong flat forehand allowed him to unleash his full wrath upon the ball when his mood called for it. On a scale of one to ten, this morning sounded like an eleven.

Corbin walked straight out onto the court, paying no mind to the "White Soled Shoes Only" sign posted on the gate. Theodore Roosevelt had been the first president to install the court on the south side of the West Wing and President Jack Wakefield had been the first to install a backboard. He had tried yoga, but it just didn't provide him with the same level of stress relief as hitting inanimate objects.

"Grab a racquet," the president said as he pounded one last shot into backboard before turning to face his Chief of Staff.

It wasn't an unusual request. Corbin occasionally wandered out during the president's daily sessions to deliver pressing news and would sometimes pick up a racquet and knock a few shots back and forth dressed in full business attire. The president loved the fact that he was a much better player than Corbin, and Corbin liked the fact that, on the court, he had the president's undivided attention.

"Not today."

"Oh?" the president asked with an apprehensive edge to his voice that had become all too familiar since the disappearances.

Corbin directed the President's attention to the moon, fully visible in the clear early morning sky.

"Is this someone's idea of a joke?" the president asked incredulously.

"I wish it was."

As if on queue, six Secret Service Special Agents appeared to materialize from thin air as they surrounded the President and whisked him away from the court.

●●●

Fort Huachuca, AZ - Huachuca Mountains

Mile six was always the toughest. Wilkinson's muscles cramped and his mind wandered. He had been a sprinter by nature, but the Army had a way of taking one's nature and dropping it on its head.

"Official leave" was killing him. He didn't know what to do with himself. Without the routine and order the Army had provided him with for the last forty years of his life, he felt purposeless. Running kept him sane and out of his wife's hair.

He ran along a dirt trail at the foot of the Huachuca Mountains. He could hear the coyotes running parallel in the tall grass that lined the path. They followed him every day, just waiting for him to weaken and collapse. A not-so-subtle reminder of the fragility of it all.

The distant sound of a motorcycle engine caught his ear; its increasing volume indicated that it was heading straight for him. *Odd.* Occasionally, he would run into hikers, but never vehicles of any sort. It was a simple footpath, after all. He stopped and turned to look back. A rising cloud of dust marked the path of the rapidly approaching motorcycle.

In a soldier's reflex, the muscles in his abdomen and jaw tightened. He stepped off the trail into the tall grass. The coyotes scurried off in search of less imposing prey.

The motorcycle slowed to a stop beside him. He recognized the driver, Pvt. Keith DeWitt from his office.

"Sorry to bother you, Lieutenant General, but this call couldn't wait. It's the White House." The NCO pulled a satellite phone from his motorcycle side-satchel, pressed a few keys and brought it up to his ear. "Ma'am, I have the Lieutenant General standing by...Yes, Ma'am. Thank you."

Pvt. DeWitt handed the phone to Wilkinson.

"Wilkinson here."

Wilkinson continued walking down the trail with the phone pressed to his ear as the president brought him up to speed on the looming situation.

It was difficult for Pvt. DeWitt to make much of the conversation, try as he might. A lot of "yes sirs" and "I understand, sirs." Standard military subordinate speak. Wilkinson clearly wasn't the one steering this conversation.

Wilkinson terminated the call and handed the sat phone back to the private, shaking his head in disbelief as he gazed up at the moon.

"Damn curious, ain't it, sir?" Pvt. DeWitt asked with his eyes cast skyward.

"More like, damn ominous. I'm going to need a lift back to base, Private."

"Not a problem, sir," Pvt. DeWitt responded as he handed Wilkinson a helmet. "Your skull outranks mine."

Lieutenant General John Wilkinson fastened the helmet and mounted the bike behind Pvt. DeWitt. A cloud of dust swirled up around them as DeWitt started the engine and sped off in the direction of Fort Huachuca Army Base. The full moon loomed overhead. A projected image of a digital clock covered its entire surface. The countdown had begun. 7:36:59. 7:36:58. 7:36:57.

CHAPTER NINETEEN

Tunguska

Tunguska, Russia - Lada Niva

THE RINGING SAT PHONE woke Fletcher from his much-needed deep slumber. He bolted upright and reached for his duffel bag in one fluid motion. He had the uncanny ability to open his eyes and fully engage within moments of waking. He had years of SAS training to thank for it.

"Fletcher here." Sharp as a tack.

"Mr. Crisp. I'll keep this brief. Can you see the moon?"

"The what?"

"The moon. Luna, lune, orb of night -- shall I continue?"

Fletcher wiped away the condensation on his passenger window and squinted to better penetrate the overcast skies. "What the bloody--?" Fletcher's voice trailed off as his jaw slackened. 6:32:22. 6:32:21. 6:32:20. The countdown continued.

"You have until the clock reads exactly one hour to come retrieve your daughter alive. It will be a simple exchange. Harper for Dr. Gray," Peter said in a cool, even tone.

"Who the hell are you and how do you know my daughter's name?" Fletcher had been trained to maintain clarity and temperament under pressure, but hearing Harper's name mentioned in a threatening manner struck his Achilles. He wanted to reach through the phone and strangle the man on the other side, but was forced to settle for punching the dash of the car.

Gordon hadn't seen this side of Fletcher; it was all a little intimidating. He observed his passenger to get a better read on the situation, but Fletcher was consumed by rage. Untouchable.

"My name is Peter, but I hardly think that matters, does it? You're asking the wrong questions, Mr. Crisp." Peter had struck the exact nerve he'd aimed for.

Fletcher's blood boiled and the pulsing of his jugular revealed his rapidly escalating heart rate. Rage affected him in a funny way. A myriad thoughts raced through his mind, but his tongue lay dormant like a leaden paperweight.

Peter continued, "What you should be asking is, 'Where are you?' The clock's down to six hours and thirty-one minutes now."

"Put her on the phone." His tone was sharp enough to slit Peter's throat.

"I'm afraid that's not possible at the moment."

"If you so much as lay a hand on her head, I will not stop until I find you and erase every trace of you from this godforsaken Earth. You will regret this day." Fletcher did not so much say those words as spit the words into the phone.

"Rysevo. We're in Rysevo. The old blue farmhouse. I have no doubt you will find it. I look forward to meeting you." Peter hung up.

"Hello?" No response. Fletcher smashed his fist down on the dash. He checked the time. Three p.m., so LA would be eleven hours behind. Four a.m. He dialed Harper's cell phone and got her outgoing message. He tried the house. Same thing. *Maybe she's working late.* He called her office at Caltech. After a few rings, her voicemail picked up, "Hi, you've reached Harper Crisp. Please leave your number and I will get back to you as soon as I can. Have a nice day." Tears welled in his eyes.

"What happened?" Gordon's voice cracked as he broke the uneasy silence.

"They have Harper...my daughter." Fletcher hadn't discussed Harper with Gordon. It was his way of distancing her from the mess.

"What do they want?"

"You." Fletcher turned to look at Gordon as he addressed him. It wasn't difficult to see the conflicted desperation behind his eyes.

"Well, then, I guess you better deliver the package." It was the only choice. He owed Fletcher. "Where to?"

"Tunguska." Fletcher set the timer on his watch. "We're going to Tunguska."

Gordon pulled the utility vehicle over to the side of the road.

"You know as well as I do. We're chasing whispers. I don't know what we're doing here. We've got nothing."

Fletcher took a deep breath. *Focus.* "Wrong. We've got you and we're thirty minutes from Tunguska." Fletcher looked up at the moon and then down at his wrist as he synchronized his watch. "We've got hours to figure this thing out and we're going to bloody well do it."

"Tunguska is just a guess. I'm a physicist, not Sherlock Holmes."

"One hundred and twenty-eight people disappeared into thin air yesterday and today the bleeding moon's been transformed into a doomsday clock. This thing ain't going away, and by my thinking, if everyone's after you, then I'm with the right bloke."

"Doomsday clock?" Gordon leaned in across Fletcher to gain a better view. "Impossible."

"Impossibly real mate."

"It's just that the power and size of a projector needed to create a lunar image of this magnitude is astronomical and you would need a satellite the size of the Earth. Companies have been batting around the concept of moonvertising for years, but we're just not there – technically speaking."

"Well someone is and we're gonna find out who. Let's go."

Gordon pulled back onto the road. It was an odd feeling -- someone counting on you to save the world. He glanced at Fletcher. He was a completely different man then he had been moments ago. Clear, composed and resolute.

"We'll get her," Gordon offered. "I know it."

Fletcher nodded his head as they continued down the snow covered one lane road leading into the heart of nowhere.

•••

Tunguska, Russia - Latitude 61 degrees 52 minutes, longitude 94 degrees 10 minutes

"In the space of a second, eighty million trees were snapped in two, like twigs underfoot," their guide, Ollie Kerr, said as they dismounted their snowmobiles. "Short walk from here. You know we're nowhere near the impact zone. Miles in the wrong direction."

"So you've said," Fletcher responded impatiently. Storm clouds had rolled in, shrouding the moon in a thick wintery blanket, but his ticking watch served as a constant reminder. Time had become yet another enemy.

Ollie shrugged his shoulders and continued on foot to the coordinates Gordon had discovered in Gregor Chekhov's journal.

Ollie looked like he knew his poisonous berries from his non-poisonous. A U.S. expat living full-time in Russia, he had led upwards of thirty Tunguska expeditions from countries all over the world. Russia had been generous with permitting international scientists to study the Tunguska region. It was, after all, the largest impact event of the past few centuries, and there was still much to learn from studying the site.

Felled trees still covered the region. Gordon could almost picture what it might have looked like when Chekov's grandfather had first arrived. The scorched earth and fallen forests, framing a perfect post-apocalyptic postcard. Today was a little different, however; a thick blanket of snow covered the ground for as far as the eye could see.

Fletcher was not quite as receptive to the experience. His mind was elsewhere. He was running on autopilot -- *Protect Gordon, save the world, get Harper.*

"Over there," Ollie said, as he pointed toward the exact location.

The area was thick with barbed brush, overgrown vegetation and felled trees -- a natural barrier of sorts.

"Funny, isn't it? Almost as if someone doesn't want us to get in there. You're with the right guy though. Follow me," he said cockily, pulling a machete from his backpack.

Ollie carved a path through the bramble and overgrown vegetation to the exact coordinates Gordon had given him.

"See? Nothing."

He was right. Gordon and Fletcher took a good look around them. The heavy brush seemed to continue forever.

Gordon's heart sank. He was so sure of the coordinates. "You sure this is the right place?"

Ollie tipped the screen of his handheld GPS navigator toward Gordon. "Latitude 61 degrees 52 minutes, longitude 94 degrees 10 minutes."

"Go a bit further," Fletcher demanded.

"You're the boss." Ollie continued hacking away at the bramble. It seemed an exercise in futility.

Gordon turned his back to Ollie and Fletcher and started walking back toward their snowmobiles.

"Where are you going?" Fletcher asked.

"Gotta take a leak." Gordon hung his head and continued walking. He did in fact have to relieve himself, but he also needed a moment alone to wallow in disappointment. *What kind of scientist allows himself to naively place his trust in instinct and the voice of destiny?*

Gordon retraced his steps, then stopped to urinate. He watched the yellowing snow patch slowly expand and melt at his feet. After a lightning quick shake in the sub-zero air, he zipped up and walked back toward Fletcher and Ollie. He resolved to stay strong for Fletcher; he owed him that, at least.

On his approach, something caught his eye. About fifty feet to the west of Fletcher and Ollie's position, a fine wisp of steam rose up from the bramble. He rubbed his eyes, not quite believing them. A second look confirmed the first.

He called out to Fletcher, "Fifty yards to your left."

Fletcher quickly turned his head. It was tough to see from his angle, as the filmy wisp blended almost perfectly with the overcast skies. But it was definitely there. His pulse quickened.

"Well, I'll be damned," Ollie chimed in, not quite trusting his eyes, either. He raised his machete and immediately started cutting a path to Gordon's curious discovery.

"Good eye, mate." Fletcher looked down at his watch. Two hours had passed since the call. "Why don't you give that to me?" Fletcher said as he grabbed the machete from Ollie's hands. He cut twice as wide a path in half the time. *Time waits for no one.*

The men reached the destination in just minutes.

"A vent." Fletcher revealed the source as he removed his glove and held his hand over it. The steam condensed on his hands, tiny water droplets forming. "Exhaust."

He bent down to take a closer look. It was approximately 18" x 36" – plenty wide for entry. Fletcher pulled out an elaborate multi-tool from his backpack and went to work prying open the hardened plastic seal around the vent's edge. It popped out with minimal effort.

"And we're in," Fletcher said, proudly holding the vent cover in the air. As he rose to his feet he experienced that all-too-familiar feeling of cold steel against the back of his head.

"You. Get back or he dies," Ollie shouted at Gordon, as he held the gun to Fletcher's head. It had happened so quickly, Gordon hadn't even seen Ollie pull the weapon from his waistband.

Ollie's voice had taken on a crazed tone, as if they had just struck gold and only one of them was going to stake the claim. "Did you honestly think you were the only ones looking for this? There's a reason why I've spent the last fifteen years of my life living in this godforsaken swamp."

Fletcher looked at Gordon, confused. *Fifteen years?*

"Easy, mate," Fletcher replied, "I think we may be looking for two different things. Just lower the gun. We can work this out."

"Don't 'mate' me." Ollie's left eye began to twitch uncontrollably. "Aliens. Underground."

Even with a gun held to the back of his head, Fletcher managed a smile. *Aliens.* There were many Veritas members who held onto strong beliefs in alien civilizations, but Fletcher wasn't one of them. He would believe it when he saw them with his own two eyes.

Gordon hungrily eyed the machete lying on the ground, less than two feet away. Fletcher caught his attention and shook his head "no." Fletcher knew Ollie had already waited too long to be able to pull the trigger. What could have been a quick reflexive execution had now evolved into one requiring thought and intention. The guy didn't have it in him, and Fletcher knew it.

"No aliens, mate. But there is a weapon down there that's capable of making entire populations disappear in mere seconds," Fletcher calmly explained. "We're here to stop that."

Gordon could see the maniacal look in Ollie's eyes soften slightly. Fletcher was simply talking him down off the ledge.

"Did you see the video from Dust, West Virginia? With the blue light?"

"The UFO video." Ollie lowered the gun slightly. The talk was already working.

"No. That was this weapon, in use. Twenty-two people disappeared into thin air that night. Same thing happened in Pennsylvania last night. Except they took one hundred and twenty-eight this time. *And* they used it in China. And in Mexico."

"Abduction."

"No, sadly, this was the work of human beings. You can shoot me and you can shoot Gordon, but you better have a helluva lot more bullets to take care of the evil empire down below too. Just drop the gun and we can laugh about this over a pint later. Whataya say?"

Fletcher sensed Ollie's softening constitution and turned his head to make eye contact. The move startled Ollie. He rammed the gun into Fletcher's forehead and repositioned his nervous finger on the trigger.

Fletcher had no choice. He grabbed Ollie's arms and knocked the gun from his hands just as it went off, sending a bullet into the distance. As Fletcher jumped to his feet, he extended his leg and swept Ollie's legs out from under him. Ollie grabbed Fletcher's jacket collar as he was falling, dragging them both to the ground. Ollie had a good six inches and forty pounds on Fletcher and managed to overpower him quickly. This time, Gordon reacted immediately. He picked up the pistol and pointed it at Ollie's head.

"Ollie," Gordon called out.

Ollie shifted his weight for just a moment to look in Gordon's direction and Fletcher seized the opportunity. He pulled his right arm from Ollie's grasp and blindsided him with a blazing right hook to the jaw. For a brief moment, Ollie stared ahead with a dazed look on his face, before passing out cold and crumbling atop Fletcher. Fletcher pushed him off and grabbed his own aching fist and right shoulder. Gordon offered him a hand, pulling him back up to his feet.

The two men stared down at the inanimate figure.

"What now?" Gordon asked, uncomfortable with the prospect of killing an unarmed, unconscious man.

"Can't bloody well kill the fool like this, can I? Thanks for that. You're not as cute as the cellist, but you'll do."

Gordon smiled. It was Fletcher's true gift; beyond all the tough guy training and bravado, he just made people smile.

"Won't he remember what happened when he awakens? And the coordinates?"

Ollie stirred on the ground, moaning.

"Back to sleep," Fletcher commanded as he drop-kicked Ollie's head, sending him back to unconsciousness. "Might not even remember his name after that one."

Fletcher pulled the bag of sunflower seeds from his parka pocket and offered it to Gordon. "Calms the nerves."

"No thanks. I'd kill for a Yoo-hoo right now, though." Gordon smiled.

Fletcher looked at his watch. Four and a half hours to reach Harper. He ran the numbers in his head. They would have to leave now or she was as good as dead. He didn't like the plan, but he knew what had to be done.

"Crunch time, mate. If we leave together, we don't make it back in time. We're juggling two ticking time bombs here. Save Harper...save the world. Sophie's choice."

"Hmmm?" Gordon asked.

"The novel. Nazis capture Sophie. They tell her they will spare one of her children if she chooses which one to send to the gas chamber. She chooses her daughter over her son, becomes a depressed alcoholic and then commits suicide."

"Spoiler alert." Gordon quipped. Both men's forced smiles evaporated into a taut silence. The kind of silence where thoughts screamed louder than any spoken word ever could. "Listen, you don't need me here anymore. I'm a useless wingman. They want me, so that's what they'll get." Gordon averted Fletcher's piercing gaze. "You'll see her again. You have my word."

The two men stared off into the middle distance, both held captive by their respective fears. It went against Fletcher's every ounce of being, not chasing after Harper, but someone or something else was making his decisions now. He was a mere dot in a connect-the-dots puzzle, with the bigger picture yet to be revealed.

"Guess I should be going," Gordon said. "Remember, if all else fails, press the big red emergency button."

Fletcher mustered a smile. *The kid really was trying.* "Here, take this," Fletcher said as he handed Gordon his satellite phone and huge wad of cash. "Just in case they call again. Blue farmhouse --"

"Rysevo. I got it."

"And this," Fletcher commanded, as he handed Ollie's gun to Gordon. "It's loaded. Point the end bit at your target and pull the trigger. Don't over-think it, mate."

Gordon smiled and tucked the gun into his waistband. The cold steel sent a shiver through him.

"Careful not to shoot your bollocks off," chuckled Fletcher. "Take the snowmobile back to the Jeep. From there, it's about a three-hour drive. Hang on." Fletcher pushed Ollie's unresponsive body on its side and pulled the GPS device from his parka pocket. He quickly entered in both destinations and handed it to Gordon. As Gordon took the device from him, Fletcher pulled him in for an embrace. "You're a good man, Dr. Gordon B. Gray. Tell Harper I love her."

Gordon broke free of Fletcher's tight embrace. "You'll be able to tell her that yourself." Gordon turned away quickly and started walking back toward the snowmobiles. Any further delays would result in second-guessing and damp eyes. No time for that.

He didn't look back.

•••

Rysevo, Russia - Farmhouse

Harper sat upright in the bed. The headache had returned. Her thoughts were jumbled and her eyes were slow to focus. The last thing she remembered was Nika standing over her with the needle in hand. Everything after that was gone.

The residual effects of the drug clouded her system, chipping away at her resolve. She wanted nothing more than to collapse in the arms of her father.

The surveillance camera buzzed to life as she stirred on the bed. She glanced up at it, with her middle finger fully extended.

The calling wind whistled to her outside the window. She made her decision.

She would jump.

•••

Tunguska, Russia - Latitude 61 degrees 52 minutes, longitude 94 degrees 10 minutes

The snow continued to fall and despite the thick cloud cover, Gordon couldn't resist glancing up in the direction of the moon. Nothing felt real anymore.

He shook off the eerie feeling and donned Ollie's snow goggles and helmet. It would be his first time driving a snowmobile. The past eleven days had been full of firsts. He felt as if he had crammed an entire second lifetime into the span of a week and a half. Exhaustion nipped at his heels.

The snowmobile was easier to manage than he expected. If he hadn't been under such extreme duress, he would have enjoyed the freedom of riding through the uncharted wilderness. He carefully followed the fading snowmobile tracks back in the direction of base camp.

Ollie's goggles were a poor fit and steamed up within minutes. Gordon pulled to a stop, removed the goggles and wiped the condensation away with his gloves.

A gunshot rang out.

It came from the direction where he had left Fletcher and Ollie. He was sure of it.

His instincts told him to drive as fast as he could back to base camp, just as Fletcher had instructed him. *Fletcher*. There was no way he was going to leave him behind. In just a few days he had grown very fond of him. They still might have time to save Harper together, the world could wait.

That's when the idea occurred to him. He could save both.

He pulled Fletcher's sat phone from his pocket and dialed Wilkinson's number.

With each unanswered ring of the phone, Gordon's heart sank. Finally, Wilkinson picked up. The distinct sound of helicopter blades chopping through the air distorted the sound coming through the small phone speaker.

"Hello?" Wilkinson shouted over the din.

"John, it's Gordon. Please listen carefully -- I only have seconds. They have me in a blue farmhouse in Rysevo, Russia. They are planning to kill me when the moon countdown reaches one hour. I know about the weapon."

"Gordon, thank God, tell me--"

Gordon terminated the call and removed the phone's battery, tucking it away safely in his jacket pocket.

•••

Prince George's County, MD – Joint Base Andrews

Wilkinson stepped down from UH-60 Black Hawk onto the tarmac at Joint Base Andrews, the home of two Boeing VC-25A aircraft that fly under the distinguished call sign Air Force One.

Four Secret Service special agents seemed to materialize from thin air, surrounding Wilkinson as they guided him toward the idling Air Force One. Nods sufficed as introductions. The departing Black Hawk's thunderous roar would allow for no more.

With each step, Wilkinson retreated further within his own swirling thoughts. Would he see his wife again? Gordon? Unexpectedly, an image of Caden Crimm surfaced. He wondered how the kid was managing his newfound identity, restored vision and adopted family? Not many people get a chance at a fresh start. It was difficult not to envy the kid.

"Lieutenant General John Wilkinson. Follow me please," the voice of the president's bodyman, Demarius Johnson, brought Wilkinson straight back to the present. A former Pro Bowl tight end and Harvard poli-sci PHD, Demarius was the perfect marriage of brains and brawn; a man who could break you in two whilst discussing post-genocide Cambodia. Demarius led Wilkinson to the conference room at the center of the aircraft, stopping just short of the door. "They're expecting you, sir," Demarius said as he opened the door for Wilkinson.

The president sat at the head of a rectangular mahogany table that occupied the majority of the real estate in the room. Even seated, it wasn't difficult to see why the election had been a landslide. Measuring in at a statuesque 6'3", with Kennedy-esque looks and unyielding charisma, he was a dream candidate. The less winsome Vice President Flynn sat at his right side. It was a first. The two men had never flown on the same aircraft together. It was a testament to the grave complexity of the situation. The Joint Chiefs of Staff and the president's closest advisors flanked them. If this plane were to go down, America would go with it.

The president looked up from the situational intelligence briefing resting on the table before him. "John, have a seat," he said gesturing toward the last empty chair at the table. "Harold, please bring John up to speed."

"Certainly," Chief of Staff Harold Corbin replied. "We're still working on Dr. Gray's phone, but we have the Rysevo farmhouse. There's only one blue house within a 50 mile radius of Rysevo and recent activity we pulled up on the sat indicates it's the one. Seal Team Six is enroute from Mongolia."

Wilkinson glanced up at the state of the art monitor on the far wall. A grainy live aerial view of the Rysevo house consumed most of the screen, while a static shot of the ticking moon occupied the lower right corner.

"And the moon?" Wilkinson inquired.

"Well, we now know that the image isn't projected," Corbin replied.

"I'm lost," Wilkinson said, puzzled.

"It's not being projected from a satellite, because it's coming from within the moon." Corbin almost sounded embarrassed to utter the latter half of the sentence.

"I'm still lost. The moon is hollow?"

"We have our top people at JPL and NASA working on the answer to that very question."

The phone resting on the table in front of the president buzzed to life.

"Mr. President, I have CIA Director Mitchell and Lieutenant Commander Chip Harrow, Seal Team Six, sir," the voice of the president's secretary silenced the room.

"Put them through please Margaret," the president said as he straightened his tie. A loud click from the phone indicated that the call had transferred. The president cleared his throat. "Director Mitchell, Commanding Officer Harrow, this is President Wakefield. Operation Golden Boy is a go. I repeat, Operation Golden Boy is a go. Godspeed."

CHAPTER TWENTY

Blue Light

Tunguska, Russia - Latitude 61 degrees 52 minutes, longitude 94 degrees 10 minutes

A NEWFOUND OPTIMISM warmed Gordon. He felt confident that John had taken the bait. The U.S. Army would be forced to save Harper in his stead.

He threw down the worthless goggles, revved the snowmobile engine and raced back toward Fletcher.

As he sped along, a pestering thought hung in the back of his mind. If his plan failed, he could lose both of them. He pushed the pointless distraction from his head and focused on the trail ahead. The snowfall had picked up, allowing him only a few feet of visibility. He tucked his chin to his chest in an attempt to shield his unprotected eyes. The momentary lapse in focus was all it took. A bone-crunching *thud* was the last sound Gordon remembered hearing before waking up, face-down in the snow, at the foot of a large oak tree.

He couldn't be sure how long he had been unconscious, but the tingling numbness of his ice crusted face told him it was more than just a moment. A cursory examination of his extremities confirmed everything was in working order. His neck was tender, but the helmet had surely saved him from far greater damage.

The snowmobile had not fared so well. It lay on its side a few feet past the large dark object Gordon had struck. *What is that?*

He wiped the remaining snow and ice crystals from his face and in the process, tore away the two large Band-Aids from his cheek. His wound re-awakened with exposure to the elements, but the searing pain brought him focus.

"Dammit." He pulled the sticky bandages off his glove and tossed them to the ground. Standing proved more difficult than he had anticipated. His legs felt alien beneath him. Dizziness overcame him as he brushed the snow from his body. He leaned back against the tree trunk for support, as he pulled the GPS from his pocket. He was less than a hundred yards from where he had left Fletcher. He removed the heavy, open-face helmet and inhaled a few sharp breaths. His mother's voice echoed in his mind, "One thing at a time, Gordon."

He pushed himself upright from the tree trunk and took a moment to steady himself. His equilibrium slowly returned. He took one tentative step away from the tree and then another. His eyes narrowed in an attempt to bring the large black object into focus.

His heart sank.

It was a body. *Fletcher's navy parka.* He ran toward the lifeless form, almost choking on the growing lump in his throat. Tears welled in his wind-burned eyes. *No, no, no.*

He stumbled and fell to his knees, as his strength evaporated like a mist in the Sahara. Every emotion he had failed to acknowledge over the last eleven days poured forth. He wept freely.

"Get it...together...Gordon," he stammered through flowing tears, which had already begun to freeze on his cheeks. He wiped them away on his sleeve, and pushed himself upright. He walked the remaining five yards with leaden feet.

Gordon stood above the body, lying prone and half buried in the freshly fallen snow, contorted at an unnatural angle. He knelt down and gently tugged on the shoulder. The body had already begun to stiffen. He closed his eyes for a moment in anticipation of the dreaded unveiling.

"C'mon, Gordon."

He lowered his shoulder and threw his full weight into the motion. The body awkwardly dislodged from its snowy grave. The vacant eyes of Ollie Kerr, tour guide, stared back. A huge smile blossomed on Gordon's face as he broke out in nervous laughter. *Was it wrong to find joy in a moment like this?* Perhaps, but it did nothing to eclipse his complete elation.

He gently lay the tour guide's body down, careful to place the parka's hood beneath his head. Blood and brain matter colored the snow behind him, damage only a high-powered rifle could inflict. The scene was all too familiar. One bullet, straight through the temple. The similarity between Ollie's and his father's death were obvious. A chill ran up his spine.

Based on the contorted angle of the body and the blood splatter, Gordon deduced the shooter had been situated on a wooded crest about two hundred yards north of where he had left Fletcher.

He jumped to his feet. The adrenaline surge had all but wiped out the effects of his probable concussion. With a bent steering column and a green viscous fluid leak, he quickly determined the snowmobile would be of no further use. Wasting no time, he ran toward the location on the crest.

No plan. No fear.

•••

Rysevo, Russia - Farmhouse

Harper had a plan. It was not her finest, and it involved far more unknowns than she would have liked, but given her current predicament, it would have to do.

As the last remnants of daylight lingered above the distant horizon, her room slowly slipped into darkness. It was time to act.

She turned toward the surveillance camera, waving to gain the attention of her watchers. With a pained expression, she clutched her stomach, doubling over in imaginary pain. No response. She repeated the motion. Still nothing. She walked across the room and stood directly beneath the camera. *Impossible.* The camera remained fixed upon the center of the room. In disbelief, she walked to the opposite corner. Same result. *Seriously? No night vision?* Her father had always said the Russians couldn't organize a one-car funeral and the proof lay before her.

She approached the door.

"I'm sick. Need the restroom," she barked as she pounded her clenched fist on the old oak door.

The familiar sound of Nika's heavy footsteps answered.

Harper's adrenaline surged, as her racing heart pounded in her ears.

The sound of the skeleton key clattering around in the keyhole seemed ten times louder than before. Her heightened senses tingled as time slowed.

After an agonizing pause, Nika stomped into the room, immediately reaching to the right of the door to flick the light switch on. The room remained in darkness. Harper laughed. Apparently her captors hadn't bothered to check the only light bulb in the room either. *One-car funeral.*

"Chush' sobach'ya," Nika cursed under her breath, flicking the switch on and off in vain.

"I'm sick," Harper whimpered as she bent over, clutching her stomach.

As Nika's feet entered her line of vision, Harper shoved her middle finger down her throat, forcing herself to vomit. Her bodily fluids splattered all over Nika's pants and shoes.

"Bitch!" Nika exclaimed in her heavy Russian accent as she looked down at the mess in disgust.

Harper stomped down on Nika's left foot with her full weight. In her heightened state, she swore she could hear the tiny bones crack beneath her heel.

Nika reflexively bent down to grab her foot. Harper seized the moment, placing her hands atop Nika's head as she yanked it down to meet her rapidly approaching knee. Nika tumbled to the ground clutching both her broken foot and bloodied nose. Harper drew her leg back as far as she could and issued the coup de grâce, a knockout kick to the head. Nika's neck snapped back unnaturally as it slammed into the unforgiving floor.

"And don't call me bitch."

The room fell into silence, splintered only by the whistling wind from the storm brewing outside her window.

Harper froze. Had anyone heard the scuffle? She held her breath in anticipation of discovery, but no one came. She glanced down at Nika, who was clearly out cold. Harper patted her down hastily, finding only empty pockets.

She walked over to the door and peeked out into the dimly lit corridor. A sudden burst of boisterous laughter drifted up the stairs, freezing her in her tracks. Judging by the sound, there were at least five or six men, clearly far too consumed by their own enjoyment to notice the disturbance above their heads.

The bathroom light at the end of the hallway beckoned. Harper exited the room, silently skating down the hall as if she were crossing a lake topped by paper-thin ice.

The laughter and merrymaking continued as she entered the bathroom and hurriedly rummaged through the medicine cabinet above the sink. She found two syringes of the scopolamine she had been dosed with earlier. They were both destined for Nika's thick neck.

The cabinet beneath the sink harbored an ancient hair dryer, a few rolls of toilet paper, a filthy plunger, and a screwdriver. She instinctively reached for the screwdriver. She momentarily considered what it might feel like to plunge it into Nika's neck.

She pushed the macabre thought from the forefront of her mind as she retraced her steps down the hallway to her room. She was no murderer.

Nika lay motionless on the floor, with the vulnerability of a sleeping giant. Harper administered both syringes of scopolamine, taking particular pleasure in jabbing Nika's pulsing jugular.

She glanced over at the bed. It would require almost Herculean strength to lift Nika's dead weight up onto the bed frame. First, she yanked the thin mattress from her bed and dragged it over to the window. *Anything to cushion the fall.*

A burst of wind rattled the pane. She gazed out at the dark stormy skies. Staying alive would require far more clothing than the cotton tee, hoodie, jeans and Chuck Taylors she was wearing. After some struggle, she managed to remove Nika's wool sweater, trousers and boots. Everything was four sizes too big, perfect for layering.

She placed her hands under Nika's sweaty armpits and dragged her bulging half-naked body to the bed.

Here we go. Harper stepped on top of the bare bedsprings, balancing deftly, as she threw her entire strength into lifting Nika. She managed to get Nika's shoulders atop the frame, but quickly ran out of leverage room. Rather than allowing Nika to slide back down to the floor, Harper sat squarely on Nika's face, leaning forward to grab her right leg. It was awkward, but Harper managed to lift the entire right side of Nika's body up onto the bed. She hopped down, squatted at the bed's side and pushed the remainder up onto the frame. She turned Nika's body to face away from the camera and covered her in the thin quilt. *Hardly a perfect body double.*

Nika's clothing easily slid on over her own. She even managed to wedge her shoes inside Nika's gargantuan boots.

She withdrew the screwdriver from her pocket, walked over to the window and went to work on the welded lock, her last remaining obstacle. Her palm blistered after just a few forceful jabs. The weld was going nowhere. However, she noticed the base of the lock had begun to loosen from the frame itself. She chipped away at the wood and eventually made a gap large enough to wedge the screwdriver into. She forced it in as far as it would go and torqued down on the makeshift lever with all her might. The lock splintered away from the old frame.

Do or die.

Harper slid open the window frame, allowing an arctic blast of air to rush past her as she popped her head out for one last look.

Snow. It was everywhere...on the ground, swirling through the air and covering the treetops for as far as she could see. Even with the added clothing, she could feel the cold's tireless pursuit, like a bloodhound on a rabbit trail. It wasn't a question of "how," but "when."

She lifted the thin cot mattress from the floor, folded it in two and slid it out the window. It would serve as both a cushion and a target.

Harper straddled the window frame and looked down. The mattress seemed so far away. She held onto the frame with a vise-like grip and swung her other leg out. As her anxiety peaked, the metallic taste of fear filled her mouth. Her hips easily slid off the frame, jarring her shoulder as she caught herself and dangled from the ledge by her fingertips. *Now or never.*

She plummeted to the ground below and instead of slowing, time seemed to accelerate. With her legs fully extended beneath her, she landed feet first. The pain was sharp and the accompanying sound unwelcome...a distinct *crack.*

Overwhelmed, her mind fell into a dizzy stupor. As she looked skyward, she thought she could make out what appeared to be a digital clock on the surface of the moon. It read 01:43:22 and was counting down with each second. *Crazy.* The world seemed to melt around her as her eyes closed.

•••

Tunguska, Russia - The Facility

Fletcher plummeted sixty feet down the exhaust ductwork, attempting to slow himself by leveraging his weight against the walls of the ducting as he fell. The impact acceleration was still enough to partially tear the peroneal tendon in his right ankle.

"Sodding hell," Fletcher murmured to himself as he crouched down in the cramped space to massage his already throbbing injury. Between the ankle, the dislocated shoulder and the bullet wound, he was in sad shape for a battle.

That's when he heard the gunshot. He gazed skyward. The tiny window of light above his head looked a universe away. He was well past the point of no return.

From his cramped crouch, he considered his limited options. The ductwork split off in three different directions from his location. An old children's counting rhyme his grandmother had taught him, randomly popped into his head. *Hickery pickery, pease scon. Where will this young man gang? He'll go east, he'll go west, he'll go to the crow's nest. Hickery pickery, hickery pickery.*

"West, to the crow's nest," he thought aloud, glancing down at the digital compass on his watch. The display on his Timex Expedition rapidly shifted through a multitude of readings. He tapped the face a few times before pressing the reset button on the side of the watch. No change.

"Bloody Bermuda Triangle down here," Fletcher mumbled as he committed to a direction. "Left it is."

The ductwork offered just enough space to allow Fletcher to crawl on all fours. Thankfully, he had never been one to fear tight spaces. As he left behind his point of entry, the light dipped down dramatically. He pulled a small tactical flashlight from his parka pocket, illuminating his destined path.

Fletcher's thoughts jumped wildly back and forth between his current predicament, and thoughts of Harper and Gordon. The odds were certainly against them all. He was not a religious man, but moments like this created believers. He prayed to a God he wasn't sure existed.

With each movement, his ankle throbbed and his shoulder ached. "Way too old for this," Fletcher grumbled as he crawled along. Finally, as he rounded a bend in the seemingly never-ending ductwork, a sliver of light beckoned.

Far too exhausted to feel anything but relief at the thought of exiting the human hamster tunnel, he eagerly approached the small exhaust fan. A familiar sound welcomed him. *Running water.* He beamed at the thought of finding himself directly above the women's locker room showers. A teenage fantasy, about to come true. His catlike crawl quickened at the mere thought.

"You in here, Williams?" an American voice barked, shattering Fletcher's fantasy.

"Showers," Williams responded, in a heavy British accent.

Fletcher looked directly down through the whirring exhaust fan, which fragmented the scene below into discrete frames, like watching an old super 8mm film.

"Fifty says it's D.C."

"My very hefty paycheck is on New York. Shame they can't target gents only," Williams responded. "Consoling lonely women is one of my specialities."

"I prefer to make them cry," the American retorted.

"I miss women. Real women, not the beakers down here. And sunlight. And Theakston's Old Peculier. Kill for a pint right now."

"Twenty-eight days and counting until we surface. Just in time for the Superbowl," the American replied.

"My, my. You Americans truly are a naive lot. You really think when you get back up there everything will be just as you left it? Sports, recliners, super-sized soft drinks, cheerleaders? After today, the world's going to be a different place, mate. Governments in chaos, anarchy, fear...war."

"Maybe, but if things get too bad, I can always commit suicide by jumping off my wallet," the American said, laughing as he rinsed his hair.

"This disappearing act does pay well," Williams chuckled. "As long as we don't end up on the Tetris wall of death, I'll be a happy man."

The American took pause, "You don't think...nah...they wouldn't."

"We don't even know who 'they' are and clearly ethics don't factor into their thinking. Haven't you noticed you can't get any higher than level three with your access card?"

The two men exited the showers and migrated to the dressing area, escaping Fletcher's field of vision. He pulled his trusty multi-tool from his pocket and began to loosen the exhaust fan, listening as he worked.

"Well, Dmitry seems nice enough," the American said as he pulled on his crisp white lab uniform.

"He's a shadow of his former self. I saw him speak at Oxford years ago. A vibrant, passionate man...nothing like the soulless automaton he's become."

"You're making me a little nervous, Williams."

"You should be. I am." Williams glanced up at the large digital clock that rested above the locker room entrance. "Time to punch in."

The two men departed the locker room.

Fletcher removed the final screw from the exhaust fan and glanced down at the floor below, weighing his options. The narrow opening would barely accommodate his shoulders and then he'd be left with a twelve-foot drop to the ground. Pain was inevitable. He took a deep breath, dropped his legs down through the opening, hanging onto the edge as he forced his shoulders through. He dangled for a moment, dreading the landing. *One, two, three.*

An intense bolt of pain shot up from his already bruised and swelling ankle. Fletcher grimaced. "Stupid git." He hobbled out of the shower area into the main dressing room. A quick glance revealed nothing out of the norm -- a few rows of lockers, benches, a stack of clean towels and an overflowing laundry cart.

Fletcher grabbed his multi-tool and jimmied open the fixed combo lock on the locker directly in front of him. Empty. He tried another five lockers from different rows, to no avail.

He eyed the laundry cart. *It will have to do.* He rummaged through it in search of a pair of white pants, a shirt and a lab coat in his size. He disrobed and changed, throwing his things in an empty locker, taking only the necessities with him. Gun. Sunflower seeds. He had hoped to acquire the access card the two men had spoken of, but would just have to make do.

The clock was ticking.

•••

Tunguska, Russia - The Facility

A spent shell, footprints and a fresh snowmobile track confirmed Gordon's instinct. The sniper had stood in this exact position.

Following the snowmobile track was easy; the difficult part was not knowing where or to whom it would lead. As he walked forward briskly, he re-played his call with Wilkinson over and over in his head, analyzing each nuance of their brief conversation. *Had he taken the bait?* Panic fluttered through him as he considered the weight of his decision. He would not be able to live with himself if something happened to Harper. And Fletcher...it would kill him.

A blast of icy air assaulted the bare wound on his face, jarring him back to the present. He paused for a moment to gather his bearings. As he watched the last glimmer of sunlight disappear behind the distant mountains, the temperature plummeted. Without shelter, he'd be dead by morning.

The oversized moon cast a breathtaking blue glow on the snow-blanketed world before him. The clock ticked.

The assassin's trail continued on toward the base of the imposing mountain that rose up before Gordon. Recognizing the time for caution had long since passed, he quickened his pace. The icy touch of the steel pistol against his taut stomach was a constant reminder of what was to come. He thought of his father lying dead in the snow with the back of his head blown off. It was the only fuel he needed.

Gordon neared the base of the mountain. The path didn't end at the mountain...it appeared to go right through it.

The door's facade was seamless. Even under Gordon's intense scrutiny, the only clue to its existence was the terminated set of snowmobile tracks. He scanned the immediate area, desperate to find a way in.

A sound interrupted his search, quiet at first, but gradually increasing in volume. Though muffled, it was a sound that Gordon had come to associate with death. The snowmobile.

He ran to a small outcropping of rocks at the base of the mountain, and ducked behind them for cover. He stole a glance as a twenty-foot section of the mountain opened as effortlessly as a suburban garage door. The snowmobile slowly emerged from the opening, pausing as its driver pulled on his gloves.

Even in the glow of the moonlight, Gordon recognized his father's killer. His blood ran colder than the snow at his feet. A wave of nausea hit him. He spat out the acidic bile that welled up in his tightened throat and pulled the gun from his waistband. Stepping out from behind the rock, he had the gun pointed at his target. Whether it was the sound of his retching or that of the snow beneath his boots, it was enough to attract the attention of the driver, whose look of surprise was immediately followed by one of recognition. The assassin reached for his gun, just as Gordon's went off.

The two men shared an intimate moment, holding each other's gaze for what felt like decades. Gordon imagined he could see the bullet sailing just wide of its target. He felt certain he would soon meet the same fate as his father, at the hand of the same man. *Surely it was destined.*

The shared moment came to an abrupt halt as the assassin raised his handgun and swung it in Gordon's direction, but before his trigger finger completed the all-too-familiar motion, a racking cough broke his momentum. A peculiar expression blossomed on the assassin's face. He coughed again, this time splattering blood over the pristine white canvas before him. A third cough sent him falling to the ground.

An emotional stew of joy, regret, sorrow, fear, dread and hope, washed over Gordon, almost bringing him to his knees. He had always considered himself to be the unemotional type, immune to fleeting feelings that seemed to govern others' lives, but this was different. A man's life had ended at his hand and although his actions were justifiable, he feared that he was now no different from the assassin -- a weight he was sure to carry to his grave.

He approached the body, which lay sprawled out at the base of the snowmobile. The assassin's head was pushed awkwardly to one side; his vacant eyes fixed on the middle distance, aglow in the light of the full moon. Gordon had seen far too many corpses in the last ten days, each illuminating Dmitry's theory of Dusha in its own unique way. The haste with which energy departed the body was indeed intriguing. *Surely it went somewhere?*

He crouched down to pick up the assassin's silenced pistol and noticed a security badge peeking out from the snow. He lifted it, brushing away the icy crystals, to reveal the assassin's austere gaze. The name under the photo read Tatar Zakhaev; it was both an introduction and a farewell of sorts.

He felt hollow inside.

•••

Tunguska, Russia - The Facility

Fletcher exited the locker room with his head hung low, stealing brief glances as he shuffled down the stark white hallway under the glare of the overhead fluorescents. The mechanical sound of a tracking surveillance camera followed his every movement. It was unnerving.

Notably absent, were doors...and people. He hadn't passed a single one of either since he'd exited the locker room. The hallway terminated about a hundred yards in front of him, with only one door leading in or out of the cavernous room that flanked him.

Everything about the environs made him uncomfortable. His right hand reflexively reached for the gun in his waistband. As his fingers brushed against the warm steel his jangled nerves immediately settled. A pacifier of sorts.

A loud buzzer broke the spell. The door at the end of the hallway opened, releasing two men into the corridor. Seemingly lost in conversation, they took no notice of Fletcher, who continued his approach. As they neared, Fletcher picked up the muted strains of a song he had long since banished from his memory.

"The final countdown, do-do do do, do-do do do do," the older of the two sang, atonally.

"I hate you...really," the other replied. "That virulent melody will likely infect my dreams tonight."

"You're welcome."

As Fletcher passed the two men in the hallway, he brushed shoulders with the tone-deaf singer.

"Hey, watch where you're going," the man scolded as he spun around to catch a rear view of Fletcher receding down the corridor.

Not breaking stride, Fletcher raised his arm in apology, smiling to himself as he looked down at the security badge he had artfully pulled from the man's lab coat pocket.

The smile faded as he gazed through the window of the door before him. "Bloody hell."

•••

Rysevo, Russia - Farmhouse

Operation Golden Boy caught the occupants of the farmhouse by surprise. The MH-X, Stealth Black Hawk's whisper of a sonic footprint, was easily buried by the stormy winds, while its silver infrared suppressant finish and thermal masking allowed the MH-X to cross over into Russian airspace undetected. A ghost in the night.

Inside the aircraft were twelve Navy Seals from the Naval Special Warfare Development Group, commonly referred to as Seal Team Six, two pilots from the 160th Special Operations Aviation Regiment, and one Russian-American translator. Wearing full winter camo, each Seal carried a silenced Heckler & Koch MP7, silenced Sig Sauer P226 pistol, extra ammo, infrared goggles and a laminated photo of Gordon, codename Tesla. Their orders were simple. Bring Tesla back alive at all costs.

The MH-X hovered forty feet above the ground just fifty feet behind the blue farmhouse. Eight Seals fast-roped to the snowy ground below. The MH-X pulled up and flew into position above the farmhouse. The remaining four fast-roped down to their rooftop infiltration point.

Within twelve minutes of their arrival, Team Six killed five armed men, discovered one deceased female and captured an unarmed Swiss national by the name of Peter Grumman.

"Where is he?" Lieutenant Commander Chip Harrow shouted as he held a silenced Sig Sauer P226 pistol to Peter's temple.

"He?" replied Peter. "I'm afraid I'm the only 'he' left. Surely you mean 'she?'" Peter calmly replied, his pulse barely elevated.

"The woman upstairs is dead," Harrow barked. "You have ten seconds before you join her."

"Women. There should be two women upstairs," Peter replied with a bit more urgency. A smile slowly crept across Peter's face. "She did it. She jumped."

The Seals found Harper face down in the snow...she was ice cold to the touch and her right leg had rotated one hundred and eighty degrees so that her foot was now pointing skyward.

Navy Seal Lieutenant Michael Collins plucked her ID from her back pocket. "What the hell? US citizen. She's from LA. Crisp. Harper Crisp." He bent down to feel her pulse. "Barely."

"Get her and Swiss Miss to the bird, stat," Harrow directed, "and put her in a hypo-wrap." He looked down at his watch. Running time on the mission was Twenty-two minutes and thirty-seven seconds. Time to deliver the bad news to Washington.

•••

Tunguska, Russia - The Facility

Fletcher held the hijacked badge up to the door's security panel, triggering its green glow of approval. As the door buzzed open, he entered the tubular ballistic glass-walled capsule, which offered an expansive view of the achromatic chamber before him.

He had never seen anything like it.

The brilliant bleached light pouring from the room assaulted his tired eyes, beating them into a submissive squint. He blinked in disbelief, as if the simple gesture would somehow either validate or invalidate the inconceivable sight before him. The surreal shifting wall contained what appeared to be hundreds of bodies, harnessed in haloed head braces. *The kid's right. They're harvesting the energy of the soul.*

Fletcher checked his watch. With less than an hour remaining before the depopulation of a major American city, he exited the capsule and stepped into the sepulchral chamber.

With their attention fully dedicated to their handheld computers, not a single one of the six other men in the room looked up when the door opened. *Scientists. Odd bunch. Able to spend their lives buried in microscopic particles, but blind to the life-size humans around them.*

He spotted Dmitry immediately. The others buzzed around him like worker bees to the queen. Fletcher continued his approach, still formulating his nebulous plan with each step.

It was Dmitry who noticed Fletcher's presence first. *A fly in the ointment.* The moment their eyes met, Fletcher knew the ruse was over. He ripped the Sig Sauer Sig P226 from his waistband and pointed it directly at Dmitry's head.

"Drop 'em," Fletcher shouted. The five scientists surrounding Dmitry complied immediately, allowing their devices to fall to the floor.

"Now get on the ground, face down. All of you except for him," Fletcher barked as he held aim on the center of Dmitry's forehead.

Dmitry defiantly continued to type away on his device. "Drop it now or die, Dmitry."

"And you would be?" Dmitry asked as he glanced up.

"The guy who's going to end your little science experiment." Fletcher motioned the gun toward the device Dmitry still held in his hands. "Now."

"I wouldn't recommend that," Dmitry remarked, pointing to the gun.

"And why's that?" Fletcher asked, stepping over a scientist, as he approached Dmitry.

"Just one bullet will set off a chain of events which may alter the very course of mankind," Dmitry calmly stated as he entered one last code into the device, before throwing it to the ground, where it shattered into a dozen pieces.

A red light on the upper corner of the wall of death began to blink rapidly and a large LED clock next to it began the countdown.

"Event initiated. 90, 89, 88... " A computerized female voice spoke calmly from an overhead speaker.

The jarring reminder of his abbreviated operational timeline was the only excuse Fletcher needed. He had come too far and given up too much to fail. As he thought of Harper, the side of his pistol slammed against Dmitry's pronounced cheekbone, sending a spray of blood across the floor.

Unfazed, Dmitry slowly turned his head back to meet Fletcher's fiery gaze. Blood flowed freely from his gaping laceration. "Are you finished?" Dmitry's eyes were empty. No fear, anger, pain, joy, regret. It was the look of a man who was unreachable and Fletcher knew it.

"Stop the countdown...now." The edgy tone in Fletcher's voice slowly transmuted to one tinged with anxiety.

"Mine seems to have broken," Dmitry replied as he gestured toward the shattered device lying at his feet.

"77, 76..." the voice announced from the speaker, immune to the unfolding drama.

"Why are you doing this? Money? Power? What did they promise you?"

"As you might have guessed, they promised me the world," Dmitry chuckled. "But that's not the reason I do it. I do it simply because I can."

"What would Sarah think of you now?" Fletcher challenged.

"Sarah is, now...nothing but a figment of my imagination," Dmitry retorted, coldly. "That card has already been played and I lost."

"61, 60, 59..."

Fletcher thought he caught a slight shift in Dmitry's resolute stare. He had opened a window that had long been closed.

"I lost my wife too." Fletcher's voice cracked slightly as the words spilled from his mouth. "Buried her at the bottom of a whiskey bottle."

"How poetic. Is this the moment where we share our histories and forge a friendship based on common ground?"

"No, I can see the only common ground we share is resting beneath our feet. This is the moment where we lose our footing. Stop the countdown or I will shoot us all into oblivion."

Dmitry stood as still as the stars above.

"38, 37, 36..."

Fletcher looked down at the five scientists. "Is there an override?"

An older male scientist lifted his head off the ground as he addressed Fletcher, "Yes, but he's the only one who can initiate it. He's not lying about the gun."

"Is that a safe room?" Fletcher asked as he gestured toward the tubular capsule.

"In theory, yes, but --"

The question would remain half-answered. All of the scientists' heads fell to the ground at the same moment. The remote-triggered cyanide release killed them within seconds.

Dmitry grinned as he looked up from the bulky watch he wore on his wrist. "Did they really believe the RFID implants were for solely for identification purposes? Money-drunk fools."

Fletcher threw a booming right hook, sending Dmitry plummeting to the ground.

"They're no better than me," Dmitry remarked, as he pushed himself back up to his knees.

"Perhaps not, but they're entitled to a trial by peers, not by a psychotic boffin."

"15, 14, 13..."

"And me?"

"You? Well, you would be the exception. I'm afraid I'm your judge and jury. Any closing arguments?" Fletcher asked as he slowly began walking backwards toward the safe room.

"They'll get what they want, one way or another."

"8, 7, 6..."

"But they won't get you," Fletcher responded as the flexor tendons in his trigger finger tightened.

•••

Tunguska, Russia - The Facility

The explosion of blue light impregnated the night sky, illuminating the remote wilderness for hundreds of miles, followed, moments later, by a deafening sonic aftershock which rattled Gordon's bones to their very core. Concussed, he stumbled back, tripping over the assassin's corpse that lay at the base of the snowmobile. He landed awkwardly, face to face with the man he had killed. The assassin's skin had begun to take on a ghostly blue tint and his eyes were frozen open, staring right through Gordon.

Horrified, he shoved the man's body, which rolled stiffly to the side.

Fletcher.

Gordon scrambled to his feet, staggering toward the mountainside entrance with a primal determination. His vision was blurred and a high-pitched tone rang in his ears. The blue light lingered in the upper atmosphere, painting the evening skies with an eerie otherworldly glow. The countdown on the moon had ceased.

He entered the stone-walled alcove cut into the mountainside, which housed a handful of snowmobiles and ATVs, as well as a high-tech surveillance hub.

A security booth lined with a wall of LCD screens rotated through a series of live shots from both inside and outside the facility.

Gordon's eyes darted rapidly back and forth between the shifting screens, looking for any sign of Fletcher. For that matter, any sign of life at all. The endless corridors on each level were empty, the locker rooms were empty, the dormitory was empty, the bizarre looking cavernous white room was empty...not a soul anywhere.

Gordon took off down the corridor, double-checking each of the four levels in the facility.

It was an empty gesture, but one he felt obliged to make.

They were all gone.

He approached the door at the end of the very last hallway and turned the doorknob. It was locked. He pulled the assassin's ID card from his pocket and held it up to the door's security panel. The buzzer startled him and he practically leapt into the tubular capsule. The thick glass walls were now sheathed in undulating tendrils of violet light. The effect reminded him of the treasured plasma globe that had entertained his younger self for hours at a time. He held his hand to the glass, half expecting the tendrils to converge upon it.

He pushed open the heavy steel door and entered the main chamber. It was unlike anything he had ever seen.

A sci-fi morgue. Death hung in the air like a sickly sweet perfume.

He did it. Dmitry really did it.

The realization spun his thoughts in a million different directions. Was it proof of an afterlife? If the soul existed as an energy beyond the life of its host, it certainly became a possibility.

A blood stain on the otherwise pristine white floor caught Gordon's eye. He crouched down and ran his finger through it. Still wet. Next to the stain lay one final clue.

A sunflower seed. His heart sank.

A piercing red light flashed above his head, followed by an announcement over the intercom.

"Code red initiated. 30, 29, 28...," a computerized female voice announced.

Gordon's eyes scanned the room. He picked up one of the scientist's handheld computer devices and randomly pushed a few buttons. The screen remained unlit. Nothing. He tried another. Same. He tucked the device in his waistband and ran from the room.

As he sprinted down the long corridor, the countdown continued. "25, 24, 23..."

The four flights of stairs passed by in a moment. Staggering from exhaustion, he stumbled back into the alcove.

"12, 11, 10..."

Gordon jumped on the snowmobile closest to the exit. The keys were in the ignition. It turned over. He throttled out of the cave, as the countdown continued in his head — five, four, three, two, one. A massive fireball, followed by yet another ear-shattering boom, blasted out from the opening, singeing his back as he sped away.

With the mountain behind him and the wide open tundra ahead, he felt the immensity of the universe and his small place in it.

•••

One Month Later - Pasadena, CA- Pasadena General Hospital

The last month had passed by like the countryside through a bullet train window. It was all a blur to him.

With Wilkinson at his side, Gordon had undergone a taxing series of debriefings and formal inquiries. It felt like every three-letter US government agency wanted a piece of him, yet none of them asked the right questions. They all seemed captivated by the minutiae of the moment and blind to the bigger picture. The *what*, *where* and *when* of it all was far too obvious for Gordon's booming intellect; it was the *who* and the *why* that demanded his attention. And sure, it was easy to pinpoint Dmitry as the mastermind, but he certainly wasn't the grand architect.

And the moon? The moon was the elephant in the room. Government lips were sealed. What had begun as whispers about a hollow moon had turned to exclamations, but the public's interest in the subject lasted only as long as the headlines. The few who persisted were quickly labelled and discarded as conspiracy theorists. It astonished Gordon, how easily the public psyche could be manipulated. *His psyche* was a different story altogether. An unanswered question was a challenge, one that would not go unheeded. He picked up bits and pieces of information here and there, but it was apparent that he was a mere cog in a gargantuan machine.

The last conversation he shared with his father echoed in his mind:

"Can I trust John?"

"John is a pawn who thinks he's a king. He's stuck in the middle of a much bigger battle that he knows nothing about."

"Is that a 'no'?"

"It's a 'don't trust pawns'...or kings, for that matter."

Trust no one. It was a tough principle to live by.

Flowers in hand, Gordon walked down a busy hallway in the Pasadena General Hospital.

He hated hospitals.

At the tender age of seven, he'd fallen ill with a sky-high fever and severe abdominal pain. A visit to the Fort Huachuca base hospital ensued. After a quick once-over, Gordon's family doctor requested a urine sample. *A urine sample?* Gordon's limbs froze as the doctor offered him a clear plastic cup. He had never heard such a preposterous thing in his life and was absolutely appalled at the thought of having to carry out the repulsive request. He imagined himself slowly walking back from the bathroom with urine sloshing over the cup's sides, and nurses, doctors and patients laughing in his wake. He responded with a firm, yet teary refusal. His mother and the doctor both looked on with amusement at the early display of his unwavering constitution. He had never cared much for hospitals, doctors, or urinating on command since that day.

Room 213. Gordon checked the number twice. The moment had played out in his mind an embarrassing number of times. His heart fluttered and stomach quivered with anticipation. He stole a quick glance through the window. She was awake and sitting up in bed. He knocked lightly before entering.

Her eyes. They were so like her father's.

Gordon opened his mouth, but no words issued forth. On the bedside table sat an open bag of jumbo salted sunflower seeds.

No, it can't be.

"Are those yours?" Gordon uttered impulsively as he pointed to the bag.

Harper's knowing smile said it all.

"You must be Gordon."

THE BEGINNING.

WITHOUT WHOM DEPARTMENT:

Wilder & Stephen. My boys. My heart. My inspiration.
My awesome family.
Family, friends and strangers who have offered assistance and
support during Stephen's battle with cancer. I will *always* be
grateful. Thank you.
The good people at UCLA, Camp Kesem, Disney Oncology
Rehab and WeSpark.
Steven Spielberg. Just because.

"A BIG THANKS" INDIEGOGO CONTRIBUTORS:

Balfour-Lynn Family, Barchie Family, Benn Carr, Neville &
Cindy Johnson, Alan Moulder, Tony Rancich, Stewart Family,
Teggart Family, Matt & Marthe Vasquez and Patrick Woodroffe.

BOOK CREDITS:

Editor/Proofreader: Jill Bailin
Cover design by iamthinker.com
Cover font *Vertigon* by Andrew Bertram
Interior font *Moonflower* by Denise Bentulan

ABOUT THE AUTHOR

Darcy Fray is a multifaceted American artist born and bred in the Endless Mountains of Northeastern Pennsylvania. After graduating from high school with salutatorian honors, Darcy went on to earn a bachelor of music from the University of Miami, FL. She currently resides in Los Angeles, where she is the Director of Creativity at iamthinker.com, a multi-disciplinary visual boutique specializing in photography, film & graphic design. *The Officially Unofficial Files of Dr. Gordon B. Gray* is her first novel.